SOUTHERN SOUTH AMERICA:

Puerto Montt
to
Cape Horn

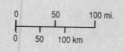

```
0        50      100 mi.
0    50    100 km
```

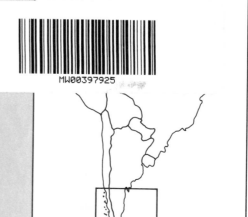

A T L A N T I C

O C E A N

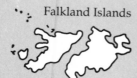

Falkland Islands

• • • Shipping lanes

See inside back cover for Tierra del Fuego and the Strait of Magellan.

WHO WILL REMEMBER THE PEOPLE...

A NOVEL BY
JEAN RASPAIL

translated by
Jeremy Leggatt

Mercury House, Incorporated
San Francisco

English translation copyright © 1988 by Mercury House, Incorporated. All rights reserved under International and Pan-American Copyright Conventions. Originally published in France under the title *Qui Se Souvient des Hommes . . .*, © Editions Robert Laffont, S.A., Paris, 1986.

Published in the United States by
Mercury House
San Francisco, California

Distributed to the trade by
Kampmann & Company, Inc.
New York, New York

Manufactured in the United States of America

Library of Congress Cataloging-in-Publication Data

Raspail, Jean.
  [Qui se souvient des hommes. English]
  Who will remember the people— : a novel / by Jean Raspail : translated by Jeremy Leggatt.
    p. cm.
  Translation of: Qui se souvient des hommes.
  ISBN 0–916515–42–7 : $18.95
  1. Ona Indians— Fiction. 2. Indians of South America— Tierra del Fuego (Argentina and Chile)— Fiction. 3. Tierra del Fuego (Argentina and Chile)— History— Fiction. I. Title.
PQ2635.A379Q513   1988
843'.914— dc19   88–10016
                                                            CIP

In memory of ethnologist José Emperaire,
who knew everything we shall ever know
about the Alacalufs,
who loved and respected them,
and who vanished on December 12, 1958,
in a cave in the Strait of Magellan,
where, from remains dating back a hundred centuries,
he was attempting to reconstruct the history of this rejected people.
In memory of Annette Laming-Emperaire,
his wife, who continued her husband's work,
and died in 1977.

CONTENTS

A WORD TO
MY READERS

This book is a novel.

I based it on historical accounts, on personal research, and on a number of different hypotheses. It was the complete lack of modern understanding in all those (but particularly Darwin) who encountered the Alacalufs over a period of five centuries, their inability to put themselves in the "other's" place, that dictated my choice of the novel form. Only through the heart and the imagination could I hope to do justice to this people whose voice no one had ever listened to before.

No one except José Emperaire. This scientist from Paris's Musée de l'Homme devoted his whole life to the Alacalufs. He died at the task, to be forgotten almost as completely as the people whose secret he had penetrated. His book *Les Nomades de la Mer* (The Sea Nomads), published in France by Gallimard in 1955, has never been reprinted, not even in paperback. To me this absence is as cruel as the disappearance of the works of Margaret Mead, of Claude Lévi-Strauss, or of Alexandra David-Neel would be.

I must also stress one event: As I sailed through the Strait of Magellan in 1951 during a visit to Tierra del Fuego, I had an hour-long encounter in snow and wind with one of the last Alacaluf canoes (see the maps reproduced on the endpapers of this book). I shall never forget it. It was the very same picture as that painted by other travelers, Byron, Bougainville, Dumont d'Urville, Admiral Barthes, and José Emperaire himself. It haunted me, particularly in the writing of *The King's Game,* and through two of my other books. This time I am exorcising it once and for all, by giving it what I hope is its true dimension — commensurate with the eternity in whose bosom this people now sleeps. That encounter at the crossroads of time is the foundation of this book: a few embers in the center of the canoe for rekindling the fire; two women in rags; a sad child; three oarsmen with eyes from beyond the grave. Gauging the abyss that separated me from these wretched people was what drew me closer to them.

In the course of their long history, the Alacalufs have borne many names; but until José Emperaire no one knew what name they gave themselves: *Kaweskar,* the People. It was once believed that they had no true language but expressed themselves through onomatopoeic grunts. In reality they possessed a very rich language, lacking only — and tragically — the words to express happiness and beauty. To avoid boring the reader, I have made only minimal use of their vocabulary as established by José Emperaire. There is no need for a glossary. Through the few words I have borrowed from them I have sought merely to recreate the music of a soul that has now vanished forever.

Catholic readers may be shocked by the chapter on the Salesian Mission on Dawson Island. I can only reply that (however painful it may be) there was a dual and complete incompatibility there — Alacaluf incompatibility both with civilization *and* with evangelical revelation. The Catholic mission on Dawson remains one of the prime factors in the disappearance of the Alacalufs. They did not believe in a good and merciful god, and that god made them pay for their disbelief. I have found it difficult to accept this, so I have inserted another element into the story: God Himself is a character in this novel.

J.R.

CHAPTER ONE

A MAN AND
A CANOE

God, watching the island from on high, knew it was almost time. His gaze cut down through the upper cloud layers, through black, angry clouds whirled along by storm winds, through the thick veils of snow and hail that blanket all this corner of the earth. It was three in the afternoon. It would soon be night. A small canoe crept between the vertical, ice-coated walls of an endless channel. Aboard was a lone man, nearly naked, face streaming salt spray, bent double over his rowing bench, fists gripping his oars. There was not another living soul for scores of leagues around.

For a small handful of centuries the island has been called Santa Inés. It is covered with glaciers that break off and tumble into the sea with apocalyptic roars. Great spongy masses of seaweed bar its approaches. Its outlines are ill-defined. It is sliced and segmented by channels that writhe through its mountainous mass like octopus tentacles. Its forests are a soggy morass where huge decomposing beeches surge up like monstrous moss plants the color of death. God knew: Death, not life, regulated all existence on this island. The man in the canoe knew too. For thousands of years the island has borne another name in the

1

language of his people, its true name: *Katwel,* the Killer. The strangers never ventured here. What could they possibly find to satisfy their greed? The last of the whales swam past far out to sea, and even the big furred sea lions avoided Katwel and the razor-sharp rocks sown like so many deadly traps along its waterways. The white men's ships lost here were never seen again. Katwel held on to its shipwrecked men and slowly digested their bodies. But every now and then the island has been known to welcome other canoes and other men, who came here to hide when the strangers arrived bearing misfortune.

Kaweskar: The People.

Before the time of the strangers, who called them Alacalufs or Pécherais, they had known themselves by no other name. For thousands of years they had lived in isolation in the bosom of this liquid labyrinth, never dreaming that their own kind might exist beyond the islands and their endless succession of channels. At sunrise, at noon, at sunset, three furious tides. Overhead, a low, eternally black sky and a witches' dance of cruel winds. It was the only world they knew of. All dry land beyond sling-range was unpropitious, the preserve of malevolent spirits. The mountains terrified them. Water alone was their element. They traveled from island to island, from beach to beach, religiously confining themselves, whenever their feet touched land, to the narrow strip of shore above the waterline. A canoe to carry them, embers to keep the fire alive, sealskins to cover their wigwams — that was all.

Big canoes carried ten people, a family and one or two solitaries to make up the numbers. The father was the leader, and above the father there was no other leader. They were not a nation. Not even a people. At best, clans, meaning enough arms to handle the canoe. How many canoes in the old days? Who had ever known? Perhaps a hundred. Sometimes they met by chance, rounding some headland. They called to one another with smoke from their fires. Occasionally several canoes might come together at once in one of the more sheltered channels that served as meeting places, or at whale feasts whenever one of these monsters stranded itself. For a day or for a moon, their isolation was shattered. Staring at one another and at the people from the other canoes, speaking to one another in the language of the People, they felt for once less alone. They exchanged news, filled up the gaps in crews caused by deaths or births; males chose females; and then they went their separate ways again. They manhandled their canoes back into the waves and the small flotilla dispersed. It was their fate. They could never stay in one place; they had to get back on the move, to flee the most inviting spots; for Ayayema was watching and waiting.

Ayayema, the spirit of evil. Potent spirit, malevolent spirit. Tireless persecutor, whose curse had hounded the Kaweskar since the time of first time, without any benevolent divinity arising in the interminable night to throw a protective mantle over this forsaken people. There had never been a place in the memory of the People for a benevolent god. Not a single benign or even compassionate spirit. No hope in the beyond. No hand reaching down in blessing and forgiveness through the clouds. God had so ordained it, but this the Kaweskar did not know. They knew nothing of their mission on this earth. Lost, forsaken, condemned to wander the world's most desolate reaches, utterly unchanged from millennium to millennium since the remote beginnings of the Stone Age, forgotten at the bottom of the imaginary ladder up which all peoples have struggled to reach their different rungs, they were the chosen people. God had never chosen any other.

And God, watching the last Kaweskar in the last canoe battle the elements to reach his night's resting place on a narrow strip of pebbled shore, had already assigned him his place — the first — in what we call paradise.

The first place. Before all others. Before thousands of thousands, before all the people of this earth. Time's course would soon be run . . .

★   ★   ★

Four rowers with four oars could have wrestled a canoe of this size and weight to the shore despite the sudden rise of the williwaw, which whistled furiously as it bounced from wall to wall of the channel. Their hands would have been bleeding and their lungs near to bursting as they sucked in the icy air, but at least they would have been drawing nearer, foot by painful foot, to the shore of salvation. There had been four of them once; not so long ago they had been eight . . .

Lashed by snow and spray, pierced to the marrow by hail and wind, the man in the canoe kept his gaze fixed on the shore. Measuring his distance from it, he summoned his last strength. The game was still even, so long as Ayayema did not interfere. Unless he turned back and started all over again, there was only one strip of shore accessible through the morass of dead vegetation blocking the approaches to the island, barely visible in the gloom between two foaming rocky headlands: Santa Inés's only smile. Katwel's last offer of hope. If he was swept beyond that shore, the man was doomed. The williwaw had only to tug him to the point where the current veered and he would be carried out into the night beyond the Western Furies, murderous rocks planted like knife blades at the gates of the Southern Ocean; and Ayayema would be lurking there too.

The man heaved desperately at the oars. There had been four of them, they had been eight . . . He made a song of it, and chanted in time to the bite of the oars. Other, unneeded oars lay at the bottom of the canoe. The man was alone.

Taw had left him ten years ago. Taw was his father, a muscular old man who never yielded an inch to a williwaw. Nor did Taw beg, preferring to barter for what he needed from the big ships that still came by a little farther north, near the mouth of the Barbara Channel, as they headed for the great Strait. Taw and Lafko and a handful of others had fled in a single canoe from the military post at Puerto Eden in the Messier Channel, where the last of their brothers, festooned with sores, coughing blood, eyes glassy, were dying of disease and boredom. Taw died standing upright, in a storm, after giving one wild yell. His body toppled overboard and Ayayema carried it off. Lafko was left in command. Lafko was the name of the lone man. *Lafk,* or *Lafko,* meant "Day" in the language of the Kaweskar. Ayayema did not like the day. Night was Ayayema's accomplice. Lafko was a good name to bear against Ayayema. Taw's father was called Lafko, and his father's father before him. Before that, Lafko did not know. He had simply been told that it had always been so. The first of the Kaweskar to set off at dawn, thousands of years ago, fleeing from Ayayema, was also called Lafko, and his firstborn son was Taw.

Yerfa was his mother. She had lived through many winters. Her black hair had turned gray, setting the mark of death on her. But she did not die. With her wrinkled hands and paralyzed fingers, she pushed on the oars like a man. Until the very last day of her life she dived down among the rocks to harvest the clusters of cholgas with her clawlike hands. The shells she brought up were always bigger and tastier than anyone else's because she swam down twenty feet and could hold her breath longer than the other women in the canoe. Ayayema had waited for her on the seabed. They set aside her oar, now useless. They burned her sealskin cape. It had happened eight years ago. But she still prowled through Lafko's dreams.

For Lafko's dreams were populated. At night his own moaning woke him whenever Wauda came to haunt him. Wauda did not fish well, she was sickly, and he had beaten her often, but she had borne him two children. Her even face had the softness of the moon. The only way he could sleep was by laying his hand on her womb. One morning, as he rounded the bend in a channel south of Clarence Island, which the Kaweskar call *Kariar,* the Island of Pain, Lafko's canoe was chased by three boatloads of *loberos,*★ bearded men who shouted that they wanted a woman. The channel rang with their cruel yells and the throb of their engines reverberating off the cliffs. Through binoculars as dark and threatening as gun muzzles, one of them kept his eyes fixed on the canoe, and Wauda covered her breast with the hem of her cape. Then the man shouted, "I'll buy that one!" and like a dying bird Wauda flattened herself in the bows of the canoe. Yannoek, and Kyewa, and Lafko's two sons, not yet ten years old, leaned on the oars with all their strength. The chase was brief. The bearded men had only to lean down and pluck the struggling Wauda like

---

★ Seal-hunters from Chiloé.

a package from the bows. Her cape was ripped. They hoisted her out naked and dumped her into the bottom of their boat. They tossed cigarettes into the canoe, a box of tea, a bottle, a box of rusty nails — the going price on the *lobero* boats for an Alacaluf woman. It had happened five years ago. Wauda had never returned. In Lafko's dreams her lips were painted red and her face was covered with white powder. Her skin gave off the smell of death, the smell of white men. He had no wish to bring her back from where Ayayema had taken her, but the dream returned every night.

Yannoek was as puny as his sister Wauda. But he was brave and his spirit was resolute. On stormy days he pulled his scrawny carcass upright in the canoe to gain stronger purchase on the long oar. He hunted otters with his dog, killing them with a single blow of his club, never missing. He knew the old songs, the song of the rat, of the spider, of the seal barking on the rocks, or of Palpal the parrot. Then one day he gave up. He suddenly stopped singing. The warm, bright light in his eyes went out, and Kyewa, who was his wife, never heard him speak another word. Lafko had taken the canoe to a sheltered beach in the Charles Islands, at midpoint in the Strait of Magellan between the two oceans. The Chileans called the Strait *Carrera,* and the Kaweskar called it *Tchas,* or Exchange, for there the waters of two monstrous seas met and mingled. And there they waited for two months. When the gray ship came in sight, flying the Chilean flag, they pushed out to sea and brought the canoe across her bows. The compassionate ship slowed and hove to. Sailors with white berets unrolled a rope ladder. From the gangway a friendly voice called down: "Tell us what you need and we will try to give it to you."

"Puerto Eden?" Lafko shouted.

"We're headed there," answered the man, who wore a cap with gold braid.

There was no joy in the officer's voice. The last debris of the Alacaluf clans were dying in Puerto Eden. Not of hunger — the Chilean government, however ham-fisted it might otherwise be, saw to that. One after another, in the long night of their memory, they were dying of despair. The dead were not replaced. They no longer bore children, for they knew they were doomed, they knew there was no place for them in the world of the living. Going back to these dying people meant giving up the struggle.

"How many this time?" the officer sadly asked.

"Three," answered the sailor dangling at the bottom of the ladder.

He helped Yannoek across the watery frontier between the canoe and the bottom rung of the ladder. Kyewa jumped too. She clutched to her breast a silent baby, attached to her lean nipple.

The wind had died; now it blew up again, driving heavy, ice-cold rain squalls across the water. Lafko looked at his two sons Taw and Tonko. "Go," he said. Taw said no. Tonko stood up, and without looking back took the sailor's outstretched hand and swung across an abyss of one hundred centuries. The canoe moved away, quickly fading from sight in the rain, while the ship slowly got under way. Numb with cold, drenched to the skin, with desolation in his heart, the officer continued to stand there, lost in contemplation of the gray sea where the last canoe of the Alacaluf nomads had disappeared in its stubborn retreat back to the beginning of time.

There were four of them, they had been eight . . . Now they were only two. This had happened a year ago.

Lafko did not dream of his son Tonko, now forgotten. Nor of Yannoek, nor of Kyewa. Taw did not dream either, and six months went by. Rarely speaking to one another, never smiling, they wandered from beach to beach in the Cockburn Channel and the Melville Channel and the long Barbara Channel where the williwaws were born. The endless day came, followed by the long night. Now and then Taw asked if they would ever see the great Strait again. Perhaps he regretted not boarding the gray ship, but Lafko would point south, and south they would go, threading their way among thousands of islands, until the day when the wall of waves of the great icy ocean forced them to turn back. They returned to the shelter of their old campsites, to the ashes of their dead fires, to the curved canelo* ribs of their

---

* Fuegian hardwood.

wigwams, which they draped with seal pelts to shelter them, and to the empty shells of the cholgas on which they had fed. Like ghosts, they walked in their own footsteps. Those who had been there before offered them no hope, left them no news, gave them no sign of life, for they were none other than themselves.

One day, drawn by a powerful smell, they came across the carcass of a stranded whale calf. They made a fire and roasted fat slices of blubber and red meat marbled with black. The fat ran down their chins and trickled over their naked bodies. Their bellies swelled up and their stomachs rumbled. Once, ten or twenty canoes would have rowed in, lured by the smoke and the smell. They would have sung and made merry. They would have hacked the animal to pieces and heaped the canoes high with bloody chunks of rotting meat. A beached whale meant a six-month lease on life for the Alacaluf clans. Gorged, Taw and Lafko exchanged sorrowful looks. How could they eat this mountain, now that the Kaweskar could be counted on two fingers of one hand? For whom should they bury these precious meat reserves in the sand? They fell into a heavy sleep, and the dreams returned. Next morning they talked. Lafko had seen Yannoek stealing around the outside of the wigwam, and had heard Kyewa calling him in her cracked voice above the silent baby's cries. Taw had seen his brother rekindling the embers of the fire. The dreams of the Alacaluf never lied. Tonko, Yannoek, Kyewa, and the baby were dead. Or if not dead, they were doomed. A day, a month, a year made no difference to fate. Ayayema had marked them down. In the language of the Kaweskar, even if they still lived, *they were already dead*.

They pushed their canoe out into the water, but the dreams pursued them, growing clearer with each passing night. There was Wauda, Yerfa with her claw hands, and old Taw, always yelling the same wild yell that had taken his life away, and dozens of other faces Lafko had never known, recruited by Ayayema from the remotest depths of the past to attack the wigwam in the dreams of Taw and Lafko — all the leaders of the big canoes, Tchakwal, Tsefayok, Tereskat, Yuras, Kyewaytçaloes and Tçak-wol, Petayem, and Kanstay, the whole ancestry of the Kaweskar, processions of men and women whose cries and moans woke Taw and Lafko before dawn as the rain and wind ballooned the sealskin flaps of the wigwam and breathed Ayayema's icy breath on the sleepers. They sat bolt upright, ears cocked, each of them reflecting the fear he saw in the other's eyes. These nights peopled with ghosts left them more alone than ever in the morning.

One night it was Taw, Lafko's son, who appeared to Lafko in a dream. Then Lafko understood that of the last two Kaweskar, Ayayema would take the boy first. Ayayema would make an end by eliminating whatever last hope this young life represented. When Lafko awoke, the child's skin was waxlike. He looked like an old man. Lafko took his hand, and when he released it the hand dropped limply back. His chest rose and fell painfully, his eyes were still open in the dawn light bathing the inside of the wigwam, but Taw was *already dead*.

Calling on his memories, and on the memories of his memories, Lafko went into mourning. One after another he recalled the rites of passage from life into death. He carved three wooden stakes. From a small seal-gut bag containing the sacred treasures of the nomad he took a ball of red mud mixed with fat. He colored the stakes red and embedded them in the ground in the form of a pyramid, fastened at the top with a harpoon line tied above the dying boy's head. Then he combed the beach for an albatross skull. He tied the skull with white rags to the inner apex of the wigwam and stuck two axes, handles in the ground, blades turned outward, at the two entrances facing each other across the wigwam. Finally he made a great fire in the middle of the wigwam, confident that Ayayema would be scared off by all these defenses, at least as long as daylight lasted, and would leave the dying boy in peace. He squatted and began to wait.

Now and then Taw whimpered. Sweat rolled off his forehead, plastering it with the gray ash floating down from the flames. Lafko watched him in horror, but made not the slightest attempt to comfort his son, not even trying to wipe the ash from his forehead. Taw was *already dead*. He no longer needed help. His role among the living was over.

The waiting lasted two days. Lafko neither drank nor ate. Through the long night he made the fire crackle and roar. Ayayema feared light. In the old days, the Kaweskar had kept this same vigil in every wigwam. Shot with glowing red cinders, the smoke rising from their wigwams had formed a protective screen amid the rocks, the blue glaciers, and the twisted trees, and the dark green, wind-threshed sea had glowed frighteningly whenever the moon appeared between rifts of clouds heavy with sleet. Tonight the smoke of only one fire rose heavenward. Leaning over the balcony of the clouds, God watched it with a smile.

Taw became a corpse three hours before the second night. In the past the old women had drawn together and sung the praises of the departed. Who would do it now? What was there to say? What had he to add? The Kaweskar were nothing but silence now. Lafko put up ribs for a small wigwam at the far end of the beach. He took the colored sticks, the desiccated bird head, the white rags, and Taw's harpoons and oar. He picked up the body, which weighed little. He folded its knees and arms and set it down like an infant on the point of birth in the middle of the funeral hut. Next to it he lit a small fire and prepared shellfish. He covered the hardwood ribs with seal hides. He had to act quickly now, for Taw was no longer Taw, simply Ayayema's thing. He gathered stones. He threw them at the hut, saying, "Now leave me in peace!" The ritual phrase was "leave *us* in peace," but Lafko now spoke for himself alone. The other voices were silent. He burned Taw's cape and his soaked sealskin bed, which gave off black smoke; then, taking advantage of the tide, he pushed the canoe out into the water and fled as fast as he could.

He would not return to the beach. No one could camp there again. The departed's ghost would haunt it forever. In the old days the Alacalufs' dogs had known this. Every canoe had its dog, which howled whenever the Alacalufs strayed close to these forbidden beaches. Even if the wind had torn the funeral wigwam to pieces and scattered it, even if the heavy soil of the shoreline had digested the corpse, the dogs still howled. Then the People sought more welcoming shelter elsewhere, straining in terror at their oars. *Kana kyeratlâlat!* Cursed! This place is cursed for eternity . . . There were hundreds of these places, kept alive for hundreds of years in the memory of the Alacalufs. But their universe was vast: From the Messier Channel to Tierra del Fuego it numbered so many channels, it was so empty, that every Kaweskar since the birth of his race could have died a thousand times in a thousand different places, and the living would still have found room to sleep in this boundless graveyard. In terror, Lafko rowed. This taboo was the last. It concerned him alone. This had happened one month ago.

Lafko had a choice: He could go back up the Barbara Channel and wait for the gray ship to reappear at the confluence of the two oceans and there throw himself on the white men's mercy; or else he could push boldly into Santa Inés's icy, forbidding mists. He chose Katwel. He did not even hesitate. At first the wind helped him. "There were four; they had been eight . . ." He rowed in time to his song. When he found a spot he liked he stayed there for days at a time, astonished that Ayayema no longer pursued him into his dreams.

Lafko no longer dreamed. His nights were peaceful. He no longer feared the wind and the rain rattling on the wigwam. Cholgas were becoming plentiful, as well as a dozen other varieties of mussel he roasted and swallowed burning hot with a hollow click of his tongue. He harpooned a seal he found sleeping on a beach. Every night he ate his fill and slept dreamlessly. Three times he even saw the sun shine all day long, unheard of at this time of year. Happiness was a word that did not exist in the language of the Alacalufs, nor any other word approaching it. You were hungry or you were full, sick or well, cold or warm; you huddled together under the sealskins in the wigwams, and from this carnal, animal warmth you drew a kind of appeasement of the soul that you wordlessly shared. But happiness? You laughed sometimes, you sang, but since this never lasted long, and always cost you dear later on, the Alacalufs had never put a word to it. On the other hand, they had a hundred words for expressing distress. Distress in the face of hunger, of night, of storms, of sickness, of the williwaws, of gales, of death and life, of solitude; and above all distress in the face of

being so few and of seeing your numbers dwindle from year to
year . . . That was why Lafko remained mute before this quite
new sense of peace. At night he questioned the stars. He studied
the path of the moon. How could he understand that after
thousands of years he was entering the peace of God?

Then the weather changed again, but not Lafko's good spirits.
Yet it was appalling weather, an unleashing of hostility of such
sustained malevolence that he could not recall experiencing its
like. First snow, then sleet like grains of sand that stung with the
sharpness of thousands of needles, and finally rain, icy, drum-
ming, endless, all day and all night. A deluge. Along the coast and
on the islands, the outlines of the mountains seemed to melt in a
gray liquid haze. The forests ran water, waterfalls thundered
down from the clouds, glaciers breaking through the mist
seemed to float in the heavens. The channels were swept by
foaming white races that tore free of the surface and reared
themselves skyward like geysers on the march. And all to the
accompaniment of a din like that of Judgment Day. The winds
blustered down the channel canyons, butting head-on into each
other and booming like burst organ pipes. The waves rushed to
their destruction on the rocks and the land trembled at the shock
of the blows. From the forest came thousands of explosions, the
sound of upper branches cracking and big trees crashing down.
But mightiest of all—what the Kaweskar call the voice of
Ayeyema—was the distant hellish thunder of the raging ocean as
its breakers pounded the coastline lying defiantly in their path.
Lafko no longer feared this voice. He smiled.

And yet his condition was precarious. His life was in danger.
The beach where he was camped had vanished beneath the rising
storm tide. The impenetrable forest offered no retreat. He folded
the sealskins of the wigwam, collected a few embers from the
fire, and hauled himself into his canoe, which bucketed and
twisted like a mad dog as it banged against the rocks. He shoved
clear with his oar. Instantly snatched away by the current, the
canoe was beyond his control. Several times he noticed that
instead of shattering against half-concealed rocks, his canoe was
whisked clear of them by unexpected shifts in the wind.

Amazed, he realized that the williwaws had saved him. For an hour he raced out of control. Soon night would fall. He felt no fear. And yet the whole length of the Barbara Channel between Santa Inés and Clarence Island, between the Killer and the Island of Pain, was a monstrous bubbling cauldron gashed with foaming crests. Huddling in the bottom of his canoe, he baled with a cholga shell and scanned the shore. He knew that his fate was slipping from Ayayema's clutches, and he sought a sign.

There it was: a narrow channel. A kind of fracture in Santa Inés's blank cliff face. There lay salvation. He set his oars. Almost wrenching his arms from their sockets as he thrust with the long blades, he began his last struggle. To struggle more comfortably, he threw off his short sealskin cape. He was naked. Hail lashed his face, but he kept his eyes wide open. A powerful current thrust out toward him from the mouth of the channel: Foot by foot, the wind across his bows, he fought it. He sang: "There were four; they had been eight . . ." He was alone but he had the strength of eight. Suddenly the wind died. Lafko sensed it high above his head, sealing off the sheer walls of the channel as if with a lid. Now all he had to fight was the current: He fought it without panic, without distress, without losing his timing. His whole body hurt. His muscles stabbed him. Blood ran from his palms. He was in pain, but he smiled. The unknown channel had just taken a sharp turn; around the bend, sheltered and defended by two rock pinnacles, he saw a narrow sand-and-pebble beach lapped by water as smooth and calm as a lake's. It was the only beach at the foot of the sheer canyon walls.

It was dusk as Lafko glided in. His prow stuck in the sand with a soft crunch. At once he saw the spring, the dead trees that would provide wood for the fire, the bunches of mussels and shellfish visible in the pellucid water, the animal burrows, the wild celery, even the mushrooms. He could no longer hear the rain. The fury of the storm came to him only as muffled sounds. There was no trace of a hearth on this beach, none of the heaps of empty shells that spoke of the passage of men.

On a flat stretch of ground at the edge of the forest he found some canelos and cut a score of straight branches to fashion the ribs of the wigwam. He selected strong ones. He knew he would never build another shelter. He tied the sealskins to them with sturdy knots. He would never untie them.

Next he kindled a big fire in the center of the wigwam and one by one heated the hardwood branches he had cut from the beeches fringing the shore to carpet the wigwam. On them he laid all he possessed: a few otter pelts, a big broken knife, gull wings, a piece of candle, an iron axe head, an assortment of rusty nails, a whole array of bone harpoons, a sturdy club, a net fashioned from strips of sealskin, cholga shells sharpened and tempered like knives, a bundle of rags, empty food cans, a small roll of wire, and that was all, except for a few remains of sea lion meat; scraping off the rotten parts, he held them to the fire, for he was hungry.

Before stretching out to sleep he hung the little seal-gut bag containing the sacred treasures from one of the hoops above his head. As he did every night, he carefully ascertained that nothing was missing from it: the white and red mud balls, the bird-skin headband still covered with white down, a necklace of pearly shells, and a carved stone spearhead from the time when the Kaweskar hunted on foot across the great plains far to the north, where there were no whales whose bones could be worked to make tools.

Lafko had not known those times. Taw, his father, had not known them. Nor had Lafko, his father's father. Nor any Alacaluf, as far back as memory had been handed down. One evening shortly before his death, after Ayayema had visited him in a dream, old Taw had opened the bag and taken from it the stone object no bigger than his palm. With his finger he showed Lafko the lines carved on it. They made a kind of drawing. There was a dot, then a long straight line, with two more lines radiating from it at top and bottom.

"The head," said old Taw. "The body. The legs. The arms. That is Lafko. My father told me, his father told him, so did all the others before him: 'When I die, do not destroy this stone. Keep it for your son. It protected us in the past. If it is warm when you touch it, that is good: Ayayema is moving away. It has always been cold to my touch, and to my father's touch, and to all the others. Perhaps you will be luckier . . .'"

Just above the little man's head were another four dots, arranged in diamond pattern, but of this Taw's memory knew nothing. Lafko took the stone in his hands. His sons were dead. He was alone. But the little carved man was as warm as a living being.

Lafko's journey was over. Night fell.

In the language of the white men, this winter moon had a name: the month of August. The year: one of the last in a century in which so many millions of men from the highest and most progressive civilizations had slaughtered one another.

It had been more than 5,000 years since Lafko lit the first fire and raised the first wigwam on the rim of this forsaken world, and another 10,000 since Lafko began his march from the opposite rim, where the northern sun shone, to escape from those who came behind . . .

CHAPTER TWO

THE NIGHT
OF TIME

Lafko was born with the day, thousands of years behind his memory.

When the red disk of the sun appeared on the rim of the great plain, bathing the snow with its light, his mother cut the umbilical cord herself and buried it far from the hut. Then she returned, drew water into her mouth, rinsed it around to warm it, and sprinkled it on the newborn baby. She did this several times, then washed herself by sprinkling her thighs and sex. Then Lafko's father came in.

He was a small man with short legs and long muscular arms. His black hair was long and thick. His skin was a dark yellow-brown. The eyes beneath his sloping forehead were brown and slanted. The fleshy, everted lips beneath the short flat nose curved downward in a sad line that determined the set of his features and was the mark of his destiny. His son would resemble him. The son was alive. The son was crying. Ayayema had spared him. The little man went and dug up the cord and braided it into a ring, which he hung from his neck. As long as the child could not walk and remained this small, threatened, pitiful thing, his father would wear the ring against his skin to deceive Ayayema

16

and deflect against his own person the anger Ayayema felt at each new life. It was an act of great courage, but no Kaweskar had failed in it since the dawn of time.

Lafko was not yet Lafko. Naked against his mother's naked body under the thick fur of her cloak, he did not yet have a name. He was not even a Kaweskar, a Man. If he died like so many newborn babies, Ayayema would be cheated: All that Ayayema's talons would carry off into the night would be a small obliterated trail leaving neither memory nor regrets.

In their wigwams not long afterward, many Kaweskar dreamed. Blood was flowing. Men were falling. Hunters returning from a deerstalk announced that they had seen numberless footprints in the snow, and on the edge of a forest dozens of tall pointed wigwams topped with buffalo skulls; they expressed the numbers by opening and closing both hands and saying, "*Akwal,*" many. They had heard harsh voices speaking an unknown tongue. Crossing a valley on their way back, they had encountered strangers wearing antlers on their heads and bearing terrible weapons: They were led by a gigantic chieftain brandishing an enormous lance. It was hung with black hair still sticky with fresh blood — and they understood why five of their number had not returned to camp the day before. They had returned at a run to give the alarm: *Pektchévés!* Strangers! These were not the same strangers they had been forced to flee so many many moons before. Those too had been brown-skinned, and the clans had kept a memory of them, but these newcomers seemed more numerous and above all more hostile, with fierce eyes. They killed.

In every wigwam the father said, "*Arka!* Up! Walk!"

The skin coverings for the wigwams were quickly rolled up and the embers of the fire packed into little bags hung from their necks. The strongest among them bore quarters of meat on their shoulders like bloody ponchos, cutting holes in them to pass their heads through so as to leave their hands free. They traveled lighter than the strangers. The only fur they carried was what protected their naked skins from the cold, and their meat stores would not keep them alive more than ten days without hunting.

Their light stone weapons were laughable compared to the heavy polished stone axes of those who came behind. But they walked faster, and by nightfall were beyond pursuit. So it was for the Kaweskar, endlessly fleeing, scurrying along on their short legs, marching across the great plain, following streams and valleys in the direction of the sun when it is at its highest point in the heavens: *Oykyemma,* sun above, the south. The south was empty of men, while behind them came the threatening footfalls of unknown peoples driven onward by Ayayema, not one of whom ever made a peaceful gesture to the Kaweskar.

Yet they were not cowards. In the past they had often stood and fought. In the evenings, under the wigwams, the elders who held it from the elders who held it in their turn from other elders told the story.

After long periods of respite had rebuilt their strength, they stood their ground when strangers appeared. It always began in the same way. The wind blowing in their backs, from the north they had left moons and moons ago, would carry strong smells which were not those of buffalo, of deer, or of the great tusked elephant, but an acrid stench that was both the strangers and the animal skins they wore. The sky would be thronged with screaming birds. The earth would tremble beneath the hooves of stampeding buffalo. The respite was over. In every wigwam the young warriors armed themselves, painting their bodies red, the color of war, the color of attack, then left to hide in wait for those who came. When they caught one, they smashed his head and tore out his eyes so that they would no longer have to meet that haughty gaze, filled with violence and contempt, that frightened them even in death. They killed ten, or twice ten, and then the plain was covered with warriors uttering hideous cries. Few of the young Kaweskar returned from these uneven battles. They had to flee and flee again. Those who delayed were exterminated, their wigwams burned down, their women disemboweled, their children hacked to pieces alive and their limbs hurled to the four corners of the sky to mark the refusal of those coming to tolerate other men than themselves on this earth. Ayayema's determination to annihilate all hope . . . At nightfall, the Kaweskar

counted their numbers. Half of them were dead: *akwal,*
many . . . Twice the fingers of two hands was enough to number the wigwams where the survivors cowered.

At this point in the story the elders fell silent. In the wigwams
the women's voices rose through the smoke and the flames
flickering on despairing faces. The voices wailed in mourning.
Slow and modulated, words rose from their throats like a cry of
pain at the cruelty of life. It was their great song of lamentation,
the same dirge the Spanish captain Juan Ladrillero first heard
thousands of years later on the shores of Madre de Dios Island, at
the western end of the Strait of Magellan, after a brief and
lopsided scuffle that had left three savages dead . . . The Alacaluf
had a name for this dirge: *akwal aswal yerfalay,* the song of the
world. Many suns and many moons, everything—past, present,
and future mixed up together—that the sun and the moon had
ever illuminated, that was what they called the world in which
their tragic destiny was spun . . .

★   ★   ★

They walked.

They walked and they fled, for nothing could stop those
coming behind, roaring as they lapped at the Alacalufs' heels like
the waves of the ocean. Even if they could have overcome one
wave, the next would have broken them, to be followed in its turn
by still others, all the way back to the first and most distant,
powerful and faceless, which they vaguely believed to be at the
origin of all these migrations, in Ayayema's eye.

They were not aware of it, but they had already been walking
for hundreds of years. They were the farthest-flung spray of a
storm that had blown up ages earlier in Asia, washing wave after
wave of tribes—the Alacaluf knew only those closest to them—
across the land bridge into empty America. Sometimes the
migrations marked time for five or ten generations. But when
the stranger appeared again, with his odor, his strength, his
superiority, his cruelty, his contempt for these forlorn, backward,
weak, ugly little people, they pushed on south again and their

memory set off with them, telling them through the voices of
their elders that their flight would never cease until the death of
the last of them. *Arka!* Up! Walk!

Lafko walked behind his father. He was very proud. A small
bag packed with embers from the fire swung around his neck.
He was now three years old. With a club fashioned to his small
stature, he had killed his first otter and skinned it himself.
Lahaltel, the otter, would be his totem animal. Later, when he was
head of his family, his clan and his wigwam would bear the same
name. Remembering that he had been born with the day, which
is called *Lafk* in the language of the People, his father had named
him Lafko. It was a good start in life, for with the new day,
Ayayema's grip relaxes and he flees. Children born on moonless
nights, at the darkest hour, under the noses of malevolent spirits,
did not survive. They could not be allowed to survive, for it
would have brought bad luck on the whole clan. If they were
stubborn they were smothered at dawn, and the clan immediately packed up and left. It was the price they had to pay to keep
the small flickering flame called hope alive.

The strongest clans walked in the van, for they were faster than
the others. Lafko's father's clan was one of these. They walked
silently, not speaking, not dislodging the stones in the rapids or
snapping dry twigs in the undergrowth. If a flight of birds
suddenly rose ahead and scattered in the sky with frightened
cries, they trembled and cowered low, for the birds might have
given their presence away. They never doubled back on their
tracks, not even to help another clan in difficulty, unless certain
that they were at a safe distance from the strangers. At camp in
the evenings, they counted their numbers. Some would not be
joining them; they would never be heard of again, whole clans
lost. That was also the price they had to pay.

They were thin and exhausted, for they rarely stopped to hunt,
and then only for small animals whose carcasses they buried as
carefully as they covered the remains of their fires. They crossed
mountain ranges and forests, plodded along beside countless
frozen riverbanks, marched over endless plains. Many died,
others were born, and the sun grew hotter.

At last they stumbled on a hidden valley teeming with game and watered by a small lake whose ice was beginning to thaw. Lafko's father said, "Here." Twenty wigwams were put up by the clans arriving behind them. The elders met in council, and they too said, "Here." There were deer in the mountains, buffalo in the adjoining plain, big fat birds roosting on the lake, and not the slightest trace of the passage of men. Nobody had been here before them. Solitude was their world, and here they had finally found it again, while scores of years to the north the feared strangers had also halted their long march.

The Kaweskar did not know it, but they were still only halfway to the other end of the earth, where their fate would finally be sealed . . .

★   ★   ★

Lafko was twenty.

Around the lake, in the peace and isolation of the valley, the number of wigwams had doubled. *Akwal,* many children had been born. However far the young hunters wandered, no matter how many days' march, they encountered neither smoke nor fires. The stranger was forgotten. Only the elders, lying down to sleep, listened in the silence of the night for the blood-voices of those who came behind. The winters were milder, and there were deep caves in the mountainsides where you could shelter and keep warm. The men carved stone knives, spearheads, axes, and scrapers, repeating, without the slightest variation, techniques they had learned from their fathers who held them from their fathers and from their fathers before them. The women cured pelts, cut wood, and tended the fire. They never lacked for meat. The great *ai,*★ the height of a man, was child's play to stalk. Plunging your knife into its throat was easy. With flaming torches they herded deer and buffalo to clifftops where they plunged to their deaths, terrified by their pursuers. Every night they slept with full stomachs. Men and women came together before

---

★ Large forest-dwelling sloth.

falling into a heavy sleep. The Kaweskar asked nothing more. They were alive.

Then Lafko's father died, and when the hyenas and buzzards had done with his body, which had been carried far from the camp to conjure evil spirits, Lafko fastened the skin of a fresh-killed otter to the top of his wigwam. He was the head of his clan. He decided what they would do and where they would go. He was the equal of the other chiefs and no one else dictated his conduct. The women served him, Wauda the younger and Kyewa, who was his dead brother's wife. Taw, his son, would soon be five. There were other children in the hut, who squabbled like a wolf-cub litter, as well as strong young men drawn by the light in Lafko's eyes. And Lafko was lucky. He scented game before the others, he could anticipate the anger of the heavens, and could heal bone pains with nettle poultices. Wauda, his wife, never wept, nor did Kyewa. All the children they brought into the world lived. And Lafko knew the words that kept Ayayema and evil spirits at a distance. But Lafko was no more able to express happiness in words than his remote descendants of the southern archipelago and of Tierra del Fuego would be. He could not give thanks to any god in this life or in the beyond. The Almighty who watched over him and stretched out His hand over him kept him in his ignorance, reserving for other men the pride of believing in His mercy.

Lafko was often thoughtful. In the evening, braving the cold and the terrors of the night, he squatted outside the wigwam entrance. Down the sky from *Oykyemma,* the sun above, four stars in diamond formation peeped over the horizon. He watched them for a long time before going to lie down in the wigwam, his heart at peace. He had no idea why. He did not try to understand. He lacked the power of invention. He knew only Ayayema and his two other incarnations, Kawtcho and Mwono. Kawtcho was a giant who burrowed under the earth during the day and emerged at night, spreading a powerful stench of putrefaction. Mwono haunted the mountains where he moved with great crashing sounds, overturning everything in his path.

An evil trinity. Lafko had nothing to add to it. And yet he fell asleep at peace these evenings.

One morning inspiration seized him. The men of his wigwam were chipping flints. Tapping sharply and repeatedly with a hammer of hard stone, they detached flakes of various sizes from lumps of flint. Many splintered. But axes, knives, spearheads, or javelin points would be fashioned from the other flakes, depending on their size, by the same persistent chipping. They were not beautiful objects. Visual pleasure did not matter to them. All they wanted was to produce a good cutting edge. For that matter, the Kaweskar had no idea of beauty and no word to express it. What Lafko was about to do had no precedent, and no one in all his long posterity would ever repeat it. The men of his wigwam watched him blankly, and the women, squatting by the river bank tanning hides, did not even raise their heads.

Selecting a spearhead with one face flatter than the other, Lafko gouged a straight line on it with a sharp piece of flint. The scratch was barely visible. It took him a lot of gouging and a lot of flint to make a clear groove. Then the legs. Then the arms. Then the head. Finally the four stars above the drawing. Several days of stubborn, painstaking, relentless scraping. He broke off only to eat or to sit thinking, his eyes closed, because he did not understand the purpose of what he was doing although he was working as hard as if his life depended on it. At night he pushed Wauda away and repulsed Kyewa when she came to lie beside him. He nearly killed Yannoek, who had made the spearhead and wanted it back so that he could fit it onto a shaft. He had not spoken a word since beginning the work. His clan began to gaze at him with fear. In the other wigwams they whispered that Ayayema had driven him mad.

But at last he was finished. He looked at his handiwork and said simply, "Lafko!" striking himself on the chest. Wauda the younger repeated, "Lafko!" His son Taw also said, "Lafko!" He had to explain everything to the others—the legs, the arms, the head, and the four dots arranged in diamond pattern that Lafko said was the south. By tomorrow they would have forgotten. Today they were relieved. Lafko shut the object away in a small

skin bag and never spoke of it again. He asked for food. He ate
heartily. He laughed. In the wigwams that night, they heard
Wauda's small piercing screams and Kyewa's hoarse moans once
again. And on certain nights, when the Southern Cross was
barely visible above the horizon and Lafko squatted for long
periods at his wigwam entrance, squeezing the stone object in
his hand and turning over and over in his head something he
could not express but that might be called hope — and is also
called "elsewhere" — nobody would notice.

The Promised Land . . .

If we pause to consider this strange event, experienced thousands of years ago by Lafko and Lafko alone, it suddenly reminds
us of something. God created man in His image — but Lafko did
not know that, and after him no Kaweskar, no free Alacaluf,
would ever know it, right down to the last of the last of them who
still had not learned it, down there on his lonely beach on Santa
Inés Island. And yet, when he engraved his own likeness on the
spearhead, Lafko was engraving God's likeness, even though he
was unable to decode the message, and still less the will that had
inspired him. God had so willed it — while during these same
uncertain times He showered other peoples with words and with
signs, made bushes burn, rained down manna, and thundered
upon Mount Sinai wreathed in smoke and flames.

Down where the four stars of the Southern Cross are born,
the Promised Land was only just emerging from the ice, but the
movement was gathering speed and momentum. The cap was
beginning to melt and lay bare hundreds of islands, and as the ice
pack cracked open it liberated the channels one after another
from their millions of years of slumber. The snow shrank back
from the shore, giving way to forests and dripping rocks. From all
the mountaintops, the glaciers began to march . . .

★   ★   ★

Lafko was old. His otter's-tail totem still hung from the roof of
his wigwam, but his son Taw now had his own wigwam, topped
with a fox skull, and obeyed only his own voice. *Akwal,* many

wigwams stood on the lakeshore. Despite deaths and battles with the great tusked elephants, despite the many carried off by Ayayema because that was the law of life, the Kaweskar now mustered many hunters, as well as vigorous young women who gave birth to strong children. In the bosom of this secluded valley they had forgotten that for them nothing on this earth lasted forever. It was their undoing. And it was Lafko who gave the warning.

He called the elders and the clan heads to the lakeshore. He spoke. That night he had wakened with a start, as if someone had stolen into the wigwam. There was no one there, apart from himself and his clan. Everyone was asleep. Yet he felt a presence. It was not Ayayema, for he was not afraid. But something was stirring. The little bag suspended above his head was twisting and turning on the end of its thong. He opened the bag. He grasped the carved stone, which was warmer than his own hand, and it seemed to him that its four stars were shining. It had lasted only a moment, but it was a sign, he told the Kaweskar. They had to flee at once toward the south, never stopping, for those who came behind had resumed their march and were as numerous as the trees of the forest. *Arka!* Up! Walk!

Yuras asked, "Who sends this sign?" Lafko did not know. Another said that it was a trap set for them by Ayayema, and that he would not leave this valley where he had lived in peace. Tçakwol, just back from hunting three days' journey north, had seen no smoke as far as his eye could see from the peak of a high mountain. He too would stay. Tsefayok, Tereskat, Petayem and Kanstay, Tchakwal and Kyewaytçaloes would also stay. The old fool did not know what he was saying. He wanted to walk? Then let him walk, if he still had the strength! Taw, his son, said he would follow him. And Yannoek his nephew, leader of the clan of the rat. Five other wigwams as well, but Lafko reflected sadly that both his hands, once, were sufficient to count the clans that were leaving.

Lafko hurried through the preparations for departure. They even left the wigwams behind in order to walk faster. They

took only their furs, their hunting weapons, meat, and fire.
Arka! Walk!

Next day, just before nightfall, Yerfa the younger, daughter of
Tchakwal, told them the story. She had found them by a miracle.
She alone had escaped. She had run all day to catch up with
them. Her naked body was lacerated by the forest branches. The
strangers had been so many that there was not even a fight. They
had spared no one. The water's edge was red with blood, and they
dipped their hands in this blood and smeared it on their faces.
Then their chieftain gave a loud shout and raised his arms to
heaven, and they all prostrated themselves before him. Tchakwal
was still alive, and Kostora, his youngest wife. They had tied them
both to a pole embedded in the ground. One of the strangers
came forward, a tall man clothed in white furs and wearing white
feathers on his head and carrying a long knife in his hand. The
man raised his weapon to the sun, then drove it into Tchakwal's
breast, cutting and hacking until he tore the heart out with both
hands. Kostora died the same way, then the strangers raised great
shouts that still rang in Yerfa's ears. She was shuddering. She was
exhausted. Lafko said, *"Arka!"* Walk! Tears flowed down Yerfa's
cheeks. She was not strong enough to follow them, and they
could not wait for her. *"Arka!"* Lafko said again, looking anxiously at a flight of black birds in the sky. Yerfa was young. It
would be only a few moons before her belly was ready to receive
a child. Yannoek looked at Yerfa. Taw also looked at Yerfa. Barely
fifty of them had escaped the valley. They had never been so few.
They would need Yerfa's belly. Yannoek carried her. Slinging her
across his shoulder like a deer carcass, he plunged southward
into the forest in the footsteps of old Lafko, leading the way with
a long staff in his hand.

Only God knew how many times this same scene had been
played out over the centuries, how many times they had been
near perishing down to the last of their number, from how many
peoples they had been forced to resume their flight after believing they had found sanctuary — peoples who were always
stronger and more numerous, peoples served by powerful
deities, strangers who despised them and showed them no

mercy because they found them small, ugly, useless, less worthy of life than animals. And only God knew how many times and after how many slaughters the great song of lamentation had risen from their thinning ranks, that dirge rising to deaf ears because no god existed to hear it; that dirge that wove a web of sorrow from heart to heart in the wigwams, the one common voice shared by this forsaken people. *Akwal aswal yerfalay,* the song of the world . . .

★   ★   ★

Lafko found enduring respite hundreds and hundreds of years later on the shore of a gray and hostile sea where the clans made a halt. Today this desolate place, just as empty now as the day Lafko discovered it, is called the Gulf of Penas. They had come to the outer confines of a world of which they knew nothing, for they had been walking so long that their closest pursuers had been left infinitely far behind in the furthermost recesses of their memory. No one followed them here because this country was vast enough for them to hide in, and because no other people was gifted enough to endure the anguish that floats over this ultimate outpost of the earth like a permanent fog. Once again they were alone: the Kaweskar, the People. When the four stars of the Southern Cross broke through the clouds, they burned almost directly overhead. The days were evenly divided under the cold, grudging sun. Winter nights were very long. They would become longer and longer the deeper they went into the world of the archipelagoes that began at the Messier Channel, south of the Gulf of Penas.

For that was what they decided, Lafko, Yannoek, and the others: They would leave dry land, which had brought them only calamity and blood, behind them forever. It became an instinct for them, a kind of unconscious synthesis of all they had endured through their endless wandering. Perhaps it took them a hundred years, possibly a thousand, to arrive at their decision. Far to the north, out of their knowledge, out of their hearing, empires had emerged, civilizations had been born, others had faded.

There were kings covered in gold, cities with carved gates, white-clad high priests served by countless virgins of flawless beauty. But they, the Kaweskar, were as small and ugly as ever.

And most of all, they were slow. They still shaped their stone axes the way Lafko had shaped them. Their wigwams merely became a little rounder, the better to withstand the wind. Their life did not change. Thus they truly needed at least a thousand years of painful trial and error to develop a seagoing canoe able to carry all the members of a clan and withstand the storms that sweep the archipelagoes. A thousand years to take the measure of a watery world and learn to wrest from it what was needed for life. A thousand years to transform themselves from nomads of the land to nomads of the sea, to reconnoiter all the waterways and recognize all the winds booming down them, to name the numberless islands, to anticipate the chaotic impulses of the tides and to sniff out the murderous williwaws the way they once sniffed out the strangers and the animals of the forest. A thousand years to learn the ways of the sea lions and to recognize beaches where whales died, to invent the bow and the sling, to turn spears into harpoons, to substitute whalebone and seashells honed to razor sharpness for chipped stone, to go from wolf's pelts to sealskins and from relative warmth to the bitterest cold . . .

A thousand years . . .

A thousand years, but no new gods, no compassionate spirits, no goodness, no hope, no salvation. Still the same malevolent trinity that had dogged them, step by step, along the unchanging migration of their soul: Ayayema on the seabed or crouching in the swamps, Mwono barring the way to the mountains, Kawtcho prowling along the shoreline and marking with his invisible presence a land frontier the Kaweskar never dared cross.

The engraved spearhead stayed cold. Lafko did not think of it again until it was time for him to die, when he handed it on to Taw, who would hand it on to Lafko. The Kaweskar had no more need of signs.

They were home.

They had time.

CHAPTER THREE

THE YEARS OF STANDING STILL

Let the reader too pause to take the measure of this world, of the infinite disproportion between these southern vastnesses and the tragically small number of humans peopling them. In hard figures: From the Gulf of Penas to Cape Horn, nine degrees of latitude, the forty-seventh to the fifty-sixth parallels, that is, 540 nautical miles or 620 land miles as the crow flies from north to south, although the network of inner channels winding in and out of the archipelagoes — the canoe-dweller's world — doubled this distance. Yet in their best years of good fortune, Lafko and his people never numbered more than a thousand. Imagine France or Texas inhabited by just 1,000 people, wandering the streams and rivers in tiny, isolated nomad groups — that was how it was! A sidereal solitude. With none of the relative comforts our own Stone Age ancestors derived from a temperate climate.

First, the Cordillera. Dominating the archipelagoes from their northernmost point all the way south to Mount Sarmiento on the southern tip of Tierra del Fuego, they face the rising sun in a continuous wall of snow and ice. When they break through the clouds they shut out the whole horizon. When covered, their presence lingers, impenetrable, frightening, mysterious. Heavy rainclouds from the west break on this rampart at least ten months out of twelve, tipping the world's most relentless rainfall down on the archipelagoes, an icy rain that quickly turns to snow or hail.

Facing the Cordillera, and parallel to it, a second and equally unbreachable wall marks the western marches of this universe: a cold, gray liquid front of enormous waves and storms rolling in across thousands of miles of raging, empty ocean. Discovering it at a moment of rare calm, in one of those tricks Nature delights in to mask her hostility, Magellan called it the *Pacific*.

And all was deception and trickery in this last place on earth. Beyond six or seven feet above high-water mark, the forest began, a vast snare, a tangle of living corpses feeding on their own decomposition. Live trees would suddenly topple, eaten through, dragging down in their fall huge lianas as tangled and intertwined as nets. Nothing was solid. Everything was counterfeit or dangerous. Away from the narrow strips of accessible beach, land vegetation merged seamlessly into a world of submarine weed, and from this monstrous marriage deadly morasses were spawned. Higher up, blanketing the ground, fallen trunks decomposed in a spreading gelatinous magma. A fearsome populace of secondary vegetation rose to assail all the big trees, smothering them in an alien foliage nurtured on an alien sap. Feeding on an absolute humidity that was at once its womb and its death sentence, the Magellanic forest teetered permanently between life and death, with the odds slightly in favor of life. Thirteen or fourteen hundred feet higher up, everything stopped. Mosses and lichens, emerald green, black, sticky, tentacular, vegetable octopuses clinging to rocks and slopes, died out at the foot of black granite cliffs where glaciers formed thousands of years ago slowly advanced.

Lafko and his people turned their backs on this forest, tossed down into the last place on earth. They entered it only when it was vitally necessary, fearfully, like thieves, afraid of everything, heads and souls bowed under Ayayema's threats, just long enough to uproot and hurry back to the beach with the straight trunk of a coigué* for building a canoe, or the flexible branches of a canelo for the ribs of a wigwam. Rats too, and foxes, sometimes stole down out of this forest, amid a silence occasionally broken by the *hued-hued,* a black-backed, red-headed woodpecker, which sometimes ventured as far as the shore, tapping on dry tree trunks, or at night by the owl's scream, which froze the Kaweskar's blood: the only sounds of life. Otter ruled the swamps and peat bogs. And sometimes, very rarely, the great *huemul,* the elk, would appear on a clifftop, inaccessible except when the terrible winter drove it down from its peaks to the sand strips by the shore. Dry land too was slow death, the gradual erosion of all your energies, unless, like Lafko and the other clan heads, you kept changing camps. Later, those arriving from the east in their great canoes, strangers with white skins, would learn this at terrible cost.

And Lafko realized it. He became a man of the water. He hunted the cormorant, and the albatross when it strayed in from the open sea and lost its way in the maze of channels, and seal on the rocky outcrops where they lay digesting their food, and the dolphin when it lazed through the shallows where fish were most plentiful. Lafko had his pick of the thousands of eggs that penguins, terns, and gulls laid on the rocks every spring. He wrung the necks of ducks, clubbed newborn sea lions and ate their tender meat raw, scented a stranded whale from twenty leagues' distance. He knew all the varieties of mussel that clustered in bunches on the seabed, particularly the enormous cholgas; the women of the clan dived naked for them, and the Kaweskar gorged themselves. Out of respect for the sea, they never threw back the empty shells; there were heaps as tall as wigwams on every beach from the great Strait all the way to the Messier Channel, for they had been doing it for five thousand years.

Lafko knew that the wiro, a giant seaweed rooted in the depths, marked off dangerous coastlines and indicated the direction and strength of the currents. He knew changes in the

---

* Fuegian beech.

weather, the calms that preceded the hurricane, the deceitfulness of certain warm winds that could change with hideous swiftness and freeze to death those it caught out in the open. He knew that in a northwest wind you had to pull the canoe high and dry even in the teeth of Ayayema; that in certain channels at certain times of day the tides converged and smashed headlong into one another in enormous waves. All that he knew, for it had been happening for five thousand years.

Body and soul, he survived through thousands of nights, those long nights in the channels, pitch-dark nights drowned by torrential rain, submerged by the mournful thunder of the storm against which his only defense, his only hope of warding off panic and the constant assault on his life, was the shuddering ribs of his wigwam and the fire smouldering beside him. Every morning for the past five thousand years, without the help of anyone here below or in the beyond, Lafko had summoned up anew the courage to live. He knew no other fate at the end of the sun's daily course than another such night, and yet, alone or almost alone, this courage never failed him. He did not measure the years beyond a limited span of moons and seasons. He was home. He had time.

He had time . . .

Five thousand years had gone by and he had done nothing with them. It was God's will. He was Lafko, son of Taw, son of Lafko. With him in the same canoe and the same wigwam were Wauda, his wife, and Yannoek, Yerfa, and little Tonko, Tsefayok, and Kostora, and a few others . . . Squatting on their haunches, they scraped away at whalebone to make the same harpoons, hollowed out the same coigué trunks to make the same canoes, and sang the same songs on the same continuous note, the songs of life, of the rat, of the spider, of the seal barking on the rocks or of Palpal the parrot, and the song of death as well: *Akwal aswal yerfalay,* the song of the world . . . Nothing had changed . . .

Lafko, son of Taw, son of Lafko . . . But lost time now counted against him. He did not suspect the existence of other men. He could not conceive that beyond the rising sun, on the far side of a liquid, gray, and tumultuous desert that held no meaning for him, a stranger kept vigil in a tower overlooking the waves of the same ocean — a stranger who had realized that the frontiers of the world did not end with the setting sun.

He stood with a finger on the unrolled parchment, crisscrossed with mysterious lines traced by his monks — lines constituting the very first intelligible representation of the earth. He stood surrounded by Moorish captains; by Jewish scholars; by German geographers; by "Poor Knights of Christ" — Portuguese Templars in disguise, possessors of the nautical secrets of their ancient Order; by illiterate Portuguese, Breton, Catalan, and Majorcan shipmen. Don Enrique, called The Navigator, son of King João I of Portugal, had just discovered Tierra del Fuego and the *paso* thrusting into it toward the West. It was not a land, but a sudden blinding intuition. From the top of his lighthouse tower at Sagres near Cape St. Vincent in the Algarve, where he watched the movements of the heavens and listened to the reports from his secret agents in every port of Europe, Don Enrique projected his new thought so far that the geography of the world was at once gathered into his hand.

Don Enrique *saw*. He saw everything, understood everything. Obeying his prophetic injunctions, the copyists in his workshops drew unknown continents and unknown archipelagoes that he saw with total precision. For his captains he drew up instructions closed with his seal and not to be opened until out of sight of land. From his shipyards came sturdy vessels that scudded toward the south and the setting sun.

For Lafko the time of the strangers was once more at hand.

Lafko did not yet know it.

He waited. Without knowing that he waited . . .

CHAPTER FOUR

THE SECRETS OF NUREMBURG

At this turning point of two centuries, when Lafko would finally be run to earth, all the great captains of the day, Portuguese, Spanish, Dutch; all the ocean-eaters, sailors of the high seas and of uncertain horizons; geographers hugging their secrets; half pilots, half wizards pointing the first astrolabes at the stars beneath the frightened gaze of their ragged crews; every venture-mad shipowner ready on the slightest hint picked up in a dockside tavern to engage his vessels on the fabled gold and spice routes; every shipbuilder who could read — the way you read the lines of a hand — the fatigue of timbers and the distortion of the rigging in ships miraculously returned to port from beyond the realm of certainties with their shiploads of dying men; all the princes of port cities and all the advisers of those princes, lavishly maintaining spies in a Europe where the elaboration of a perfectly round globe was in its final phases; every crow's nest lookout who had glimpsed birds of an unknown species far to the west, telling of the nearness of land that obstinately remained hidden; all of them, literate and illiterate, humble and mighty, ready at a moment's notice to reembark for the hells they had barely left and where the truth they sensed was hidden; all of them were the spiritual sons of Don Enrique the Navigator. He had died forty years earlier, in 1460, but from the spume-blown tower where he built his tomb he held them all in his hand, hurling them into the assault on a world he had wholly divined.

Don Enrique's secrets were no longer altogether secret. Those who shared them with him in his tower at Sagres had scattered after his death, taking back to their ports of origin visions of islands and continents they hastened to transpose, working from memory, onto fabulous portolans — the outlines of unknown shores, the coasts of the two Americas, of Africa with its cape separating two oceans, of India, China, Japan, and even the distant mythic Moluccas, so christened long before they were discovered. They were the great initiates of the day. The fee for joining their brotherhood and sharing in their secrets was . . . more secrets. Prevailing winds, ocean currents, indistinct lands glimpsed through fog by terrified whale catchers, accounts by lost captains of floating tree trunks still covered with green leaves thousands of leagues from known shores, Celtic or Norse legends, seagoing sagas unearthed in the libraries of northern monasteries, stolen ships' logs, loose talk from sailors plied with drink in the stews of Lisbon, of St.-Malo, of Antwerp, and later found in the gutter, a dagger buried between their shoulderblades, their lips forever sealed — such was the currency that bought the keys to a world the initiates were dividing up among themselves. From port to port, as the first great seagoing expeditions got under way, they hated, envied, and spied on one another. They sent out killers against each other, spell-casters, soul-buyers, but in the long run their passion proved stronger than their rivalries. Even as they killed they could not avoid helping one another. This was their greatness and their abiding fascination, for no single one among them possessed complete mastery of the puzzle. There was always a piece missing here or there to explain the unexplainable, the telling detail that gave intelligibility to the madness of the portolan.

And by now they had progressed from the portolan to the terrestrial globe. It was the last great shaft of light in the waning years of the century. The thunderclap that ballooned the sails of the ponderous caravels lying low at remote wharfsides far from prying eyes, marked out for mad destinations only their captains knew.

The methodical visionary of our round, perfected globe, its illuminated begetter, was a converted German Jew, a bookworm ablaze with intuition: Martin Behaïm.

★   ★   ★

Far from seas or oceans, on imperial German soil, Nuremberg was the Rome of geographers, a pilgrimage every ambitious captain had to undertake before the great departure, the way physicians went to Montpelier, mathematicians to Salerno, philosophers to Heidelberg. The possessor of the secrets of Sagres, passed on to him by the Jewish scholars who had surrounded Don Enrique, Martin Behaïm was now the master, the beacon of geography. Getting to him was no easy matter. First you had to negotiate a whole network of intermediaries whose task was to filter visitors. When a captain was finally admitted into his presence the master asked, "What have you to tell me?" In the world of Martin Behaïm, this was the price for sharing in the great secret. A Fleming had run the white whale in close under unknown cliffs, a Saint-Malouin had traded for amber with plumed savages far to the west, a Portuguese had run along the coast of Brazil without realizing he had discovered a continent, a Dutchman running south before a gale that had blown for a full month had seen a snowy cape loom ahead over a powerful current that seemed to come from the land . . . Twenty years before Magellan, that Dutchman had unwittingly approached Lafko's watery kingdom.

Sitting in a straight-backed armchair, dressed in black, a bonnet with earflaps pulled down over his skull, Behaïm listened in silence. His eyes (he strove to curb their intensity) never left the speaker; they masked his innermost thoughts as he sifted the real from the imaginary, all too often confused by these God-fearing shipmen nourished on legends and as superstitious as old women. The dead weight of the Christian faith fettered science, still in the crawling stage, and terrorized the most enlightened minds of the day a hundred years before the birth of Galileo, who would be condemned by the Inquisition, and ten years before the birth of Copernicus, who delayed publication of his theories until a few days before his death for fear of pontifical wrath and physical danger. But Behaïm, a converted Jew, was no longer a Jew and no more of a Christian. The weight of the Scriptures could not hold him back. The only law he acknowledged was the rigor of his own intelligence. An extraordinary and a dangerous attitude. That was why he was so scrupulous to protect access to his house, revealing himself only rarely, and gradually, to those he agreed to receive, and then only in proportion to their willingness to cooperate and their scientific usefulness.

He listened. His secretary's quill scratched audibly as it set down the conversation, word by word. Then Behaïm read the transcript aloud, and nodded. "Clarify," he commanded. "How many days at sea? How stood the winds? What changes of course? Estimated position? Estimated rate of knots? Estimated sea temperature? Estimated air temperature? What manner of fish and fowl encountered? Can the captain draw? No? The scribe will draw to his direction. Let us resume. This abandoned canoe, half-waterlogged, resembling nothing known . . .?"

The captain's reply: "I dared not approach to examine it. The crew threatened to mutiny if I gave the order to draw near and touch the cursed canoe. They saw it as an augur of death. We had been lost three months. We could no longer find our way back under this sky of unknown stars. The Pole Star had disappeared . . . All I saw of this canoe was planks, seemingly stitched together, with what appeared to be a spade-shaped oar affixed . . . To tell the truth, I had no wish to see more. A wave had carried two men overboard, and they sank like stones between my ship and the canoe."

Behaïm shrugged. This captain was a dullard, a little man, unequal to his discovery, unable to interpret its meaning. He questioned him about the stars, but without letting him guess under what skies this canoe, the advance guard of a new world, had been drifting. The shelves of his library were packed with fat

books bound with silver clasps, with rolled parchments, with
dossiers stuffed into leather cases stamped with Latin names. He
threw one of these names to the scribe climbing the ladder
propped against the shelves. The dossier was brought to him.
Everything fit. He knew these stars. He knew the position of this
cape, looming over what seemed to be a broad estuary. And this
was the second time he had heard of this canoe with its stitched
planks. He even possessed a sketch, executed a few years earlier
by a Portuguese, and the accompanying description: The canoe
was intact and floating. At the bottom of the craft, in a crude clay
container, were the remains of a fire . . . The captain he was
questioning confirmed it. "Yes, it was a canoe of this kind." He
had nothing more to offer. Behaïm sent him packing, armed
with a few crumbs from his own store of knowledge, to the
whale-runs off the Azores, a gold mine for this dull seafarer who
could see no farther than barrels of stinking oil heaped in the
belly of his vessel.

Thus did Lafko suddenly emerge from the obscurity where
God had kept him hidden for fifty centuries, simply because —
somewhere beyond his world, beyond that mysterious headland
that would soon be called Cape of the Virgins, and which did
indeed mark the entrance to the great guessed-at Strait — two of
his canoes had been swept away by Ayayema twenty years apart, in
the din of a stormy night, while he slept ashore. They had drifted
to Nuremberg across space and time.

With small precise strokes of the fine brush in his hand,
Behaïm himself added the final graphic confirmation of infor-
mation he now knew to be certain to the first terrestrial globe
ever conceived. He gave no name to the cape where this land
ended and where none had ever set foot, but he drew it in such a
way, hatched with lines and dots to indicate snow and rain, that
Magellan would not be mistaken. Then he considered the
aggressive thrust of that current, several times described to him,
and the violence of the flow of water coming out from that cape:
It could truly be explained only if it was the gateway to a narrow, a
strait, a passage communicating with another free mass of water
butting in from the west with all its formidable weight. So he

drew an island, to the south, facing the cape. It was no longer quite a vision, as it had been when Don Enrique the Navigator *prophesied* Tierra del Fuego, nor was it quite a hypothesis. None had ever seen this land. None had suspected its presence. None had ever spoken to him of it. The cape, yes. This island, no. But it was the last piece of the puzzle and he knew it had to fit there, like the keystone of a cathedral, because the globe's architecture could not be conceived otherwise. He did not invent it. He had only to close his eyes and immerse himself in his thoughts for this very island to leap into view. Then, amid strokes evoking foaming billows that faded into the dotted lines of the coast of *terra incognita,* he drew twenty-seven Gothic letters: PASSAGE TO THE GREAT WESTERN SEA. Finally, obedient to the fine romantic dictates of an age in love with primitive imagery, amid whale flukes bursting from turbulent oceans and seals rearing on rocks like heraldic beasts, he drew in, at the entrance to the strait, a tiny canoe manned by naked savages whose leader resembled Lafko.

Behaïm felt a small stab at his heart, a surge of pity, at the thought that the caravels even now readying for departure would be crowded with soldiers and monks, with chaplains and gunners, with crucifixes, scapulars, chaplets, and saints' statues, with gold chasubles, with chalices, with coffers filled with hosts — enough to convert all the earth under the menacing stare of the arquebuses. All except Lafko. But that Behaïm did not know, for he could not know the divine plan. With a small sad smile he drew in a cross on a tiny island he depicted with a quick stroke, somewhere in the middle of the Strait. It was there that Magellan would raise it . . .

Then he stepped back and considered his work. It was truly his life's work. In the secret cabinet next to his library, lit by chandeliers that threw their own shadows on the walls, the fabulous sphere sat in state, a monument, a forbidden representation of this world, the North Pole almost touching the ceiling, the equator girdled with a gallery you reached by climbing a ladder. A miracle of cabinetwork, with a parchment skin on which not a single detail of the geography of the globe had not been verified several times by Behaïm, from the mouths of several captains, before he himself set it down there with the fastidious tip of his brush. Nobody entered this room except the master himself and the very greatest of the captains, those he judged worthy of the revelation.

They were very few: Diego Cam, Bartholomew Diaz, Vasco da Gama, Pedro Cabral, Christopher Columbus, Nuñez de Balboa, Magellan . . . They had the financial backing of princes of genius — Manuel I of Portugal, in Spain Queen Isabella, then Ferdinand of Aragon, and Charles V. It would not be whalers or vulgar spice traders but true lords of the sea who would take possession of the world within twenty years of dividing it up between them. They knew much more about it than the others, they sensed many of its unknowns, but all made the pilgrimage to Nuremberg, because there alone lay the key to their success: certainties. In this age of untrammeled greed, when princely gold flowed like water to build the fairest ships, hire the finest pilots, acquire the newest portolans and the most precise products of seagoing lore, the disinterestedness of the master of Nuremberg was staggering. So was the fact that in this welter of murderous rivalries his life was spared: because he was irreplaceable, unique; because the only reward he expected from science was to see it vindicated by fact.

And it would be vindicated, at least twice in his lifetime. When Vasco da Gama, in the wake of Cam and Diaz, gobbled up the degrees of latitude in his southward run down the African coast to the Cape of Good Hope, and decided to round the Cape and set sail for the Moluccas despite the pleas of his terrified crew, he gave proof of little merit, merely that of endurance. He *knew*. His entire course had been plotted for him by Behaïm at Nuremberg. When Christopher Columbus, faced with a mutinous crew, swore to them that in a given number of days land would appear on the horizon, he had already seen that land, and almost its exact position, on the Nuremberg globe. When it finally appeared he was admittedly relieved, but not surprised. He too *knew*.

There had been no discoverers, merely brave, well-informed seamen. Or rather there was but one discoverer: Behaïm.

*   *   *

Behaïm died in 1507. But he survived in two men. In a way, each of them sealed Lafko's fate in Martin Behaïm's name.

The first was Balboa. In 1513 he landed at Darien on the Atlantic coast at the precise point of minimum width of what would later be called the Isthmus of Panama. How did he know it was an isthmus, and that it separated him by a few days' march from a vast ocean whose waters bathed the whole western coast of South America? Because he had once been one of Martin Behaïm's inner circle at Nuremberg. Balboa immediately struck through the jungle by the shortest route and discovered the Pacific. Others followed him. They came like wolves. Their road south was strewn with crosses and spattered with blood. Pizarro in Peru. Almagro in Chile. Finally Pedro de Valdivia, who in 1550 reached the desolate Gulf of Penas, but ventured no farther. This was where the somber Messier Channel began, and the watery green world of the archipelagoes where Lafko and his canoes had vanished, willingly obliterating themselves, to escape those who came behind — those who were still coming and who, later on, would catch up with them again . . .

The second was Magellan. Fernão de Magalhães. The overland progress of those coming from the north had been slow, hesitant, almost reluctant, bogged down by the cruel climate, by the emptiness and the insensate configuration of these thousands of uninhabited islands. But Magellan's irruption through the eastern portals of the *Tchas,* the great strait of the Kaweskar — a happening so inconceivable that it shattered their whole conception of the world — at once told Lafko and his people that they were doomed. The miracle was that having realized it, having understood it, having acknowledged it, they would survive another five hundred years.

On August 10, 1519, five Spanish ships set sail from Seville under Magellan's command with 260 men aboard. All had confessed and taken communion. The bells rang out from every church. The banks of the Guadalquivir thundered out a salvo to the royal banner fluttering from the highest mast of Magellan's flagship, the *Trinidad*. Charles I, King of Spain, Emperor of Germany, King of Sicily, Duke of Burgundy, Prince of the Netherlands, had financed the expedition. The Grand Council of the Indies had drawn up its secret instructions. Magellan sailed with the double rank of admiral and captain-general. An officer of no means, poor and from the ranks of the petty nobility, Magellan loathed money and despised courtiers; he was dry, scathing, stiff-necked, of foul character, a shabby dresser, swarthy, dirty, puny, ugly, lame, and Portuguese to boot. Yet alone, and supported only by his own arguments, he had won over the world's most powerful king! Why?

Because the earth was round!

The earth was round, and could be circumnavigated. It was an idea current among the initiate, a heretical whisper in the air, but Magellan alone possessed the demonstration of it that had convinced the king: a terrestrial globe, a small one this, made at Nuremberg to his precise specifications by another German geographer, Johann Schoener, a pupil of Behaïm and by spiritual affiliation of Don Enrique the Navigator. The southern passage was marked on it. This globe would be shipped aboard the *Trinidad* and unveiled to the incredulous ship's officers as soon as the secret was lifted.

"And these?" King Charles had asked the day before they sailed, pointing to a tiny canoe manned by naked hairy savages that Johann Schoener and Magellan had likewise copied from Behaïm's sphere, at the mouth of his *Passage to the Great Western Sea*.

"These, Sire," Magellan replied, "are Your Majesty's first subjects in these regions, and the first Christians of your future conquests."

Only in the latter claim was he wrong.

In an almost metaphysical sense, the past was Lafko's refuge. He would often be encountered there, but never cornered.

CHAPTER FIVE

MAGELLAN

In this southern winter of the year 1520, it still required four degrees of south latitude and a remarkable telescoping of fate before Lafko's canoe, adrift in the Stone Age, could meet Magellan's caravels in the second narrow of the great Strait — an encounter that would trigger something comparable to the splitting of the atom in Lafko's primitive brain. It also required four months, time for everyone to emerge safe and sound from this hell of snow and wind endured in almost total darkness and in an end-of-the-world solitude. Three hundred nautical miles apart, 340 miles undisturbed by a single living soul, two small groups of fires flickered pathetically, like dying stars struggling to pierce the endless night. Magellan was wintering at Puerto San Julian, an uninhabited and barren gulf on the Patagonian coast. Lafko was roaming with two other clans between the first two narrows in the eastern reaches of the Strait.

Magellan had raised a cross on a wind-buffeted dune. The first of a long series, it was blessed by chaplains blue with cold. The seamen were terrified. The drop in the temperature had struck them like a divine curse. No man had ever sailed so far south. Twenty years earlier, Vasco da Gama had rounded the point of

Africa at the thirty-fifth parallel south. God had barely forgiven him for it. These men were at the forty-ninth parallel, and there was no strait in sight. Why did this continent refuse to end? The wind had laid the cross low and they had raised it again. Was that not a sign? An order to flee at once and head back for Seville, calling on God for forgiveness? The admiral had quelled two mutinies, turned several seamen over to the executioners, and clapped one captain in irons.

Now the very earth was freezing. The soil cracked open as if from underground explosions. Ice sheathed the rigging. Sails splintered like glass. In September they were still there. Fresh water was rationed. The ship's biscuits were hard as stone. Salt meat rotted, and whenever they were able to kill a seal, its greasy flesh made the sailors ill. They became anemic; their skin was covered with sores. Their teeth fell out. Some, incapable of digesting anything, starved. Others died of sorrow or discouragement. All were distressed at their inability to adapt morally and physically to conditions that Lafko—but he did not know it—had been overcoming for over five thousand years with all the arrested resources of his stubborn intelligence.

For a time the appearance of Patagonians in the camp distracted the sailors. To these small-statured Latins, they looked like giants, like a species of big monkey clad in animal skins that wrapped around their feet and legs and left tracks like those of a bear in the snow. Their women were big and fat, with enormous sagging breasts that aroused unhealthy laughter. They came from inland, and approached the shore only with terror and revulsion. Water was not their element. They were not the people of the canoe pictured by Behaïm and designated by Magellan as "Your Majesty's first subjects." Were they even human? To find out, they captured one who let himself be dragged off, terrified, while the others fled to watch the scene from a distance. They taught the name of Jesus to the giant, who repeated it in a huge voice, then the Paternoster, which he recited with frightened eyes but without skipping a single word. They made him kneel at the foot of the cross, where the chaplain baptized him and christened him Juan. They gave him a coat and trousers to wear, they set a

hat on his head, and gave him bells, which he tinkled foolishly as
he went off to join his tribe. Magellan shrugged. The crew
laughed without comprehending the darkness of the scene they
had just witnessed. The chaplain praised the Lord. To each
according to his estate: prince, pauper, priest. The result was not
long in coming. They heard horrible noises. It was Juan, dying,
slaughtered and cut up by his fellows. The others continued
to prowl around the strangers' camp, fascinated by their own
fear, devoured by curiosity. The females with their enormous
breasts made the crews restive. There were clashes, with deaths
on both sides, and astonishing couplings between these women-
mountains on all fours and these pale Christians, the spearhead
of the West, humping upright in the snow like goats, their
breeches round their ankles. The children born later from these
unions would be smothered by their mothers as soon as the
umbilical cords were cut . . .

From then on, the Patagonians would retreat behind a cloud
of arrows and vanish from the landscape, herding their monstrous females before them like cattle. The sailors fell back into
their moral torpor, as if these women had taken away with them
what was most human in their souls. Two prisoners remained in
the camp, two savages Magellan intended to present to the King
of Spain. Refusing all nourishment, they quickly allowed themselves to die.

The days grew longer. The cold bit less savagely. The admiral
gave orders to prepare to weigh anchor. One of the five ships was
lost, driven on to the rocks by a storm. Another fled back to
Spain to spread word of the admiral's madness: Locked in his
room aboard the *Trinidad,* he sat face to face with the terrestrial
globe, contemplating it for hours, the only one aboard who still
stubbornly believed in it. On the heads of his assembled crews
Magellan had sworn, "I will not turn back before the seventy-
fifth parallel!" Which meant, "Beyond death . . ." The mutinies
began again. The head of a second captain fell on the block that
had served for all the previous executions. Fifty-eight years later,
facing down a mutiny triggered by similar causes in this same
Puerto San Julian, Sir Francis Drake would order the supreme

penalty to be carried out on the very same block, found lying on the shore, still bloodstained. No trace of the cross remained . . .

Three ships continued the journey: *Concepcion, Victoria, Trinidad.* The admiral's iron will had triumphed over every obstacle and all opposition. In the name of the King? That was mere appearance. In the name of imagination, which always invents a pretext for itself, since the most gifted of men grow bored between the past and the future, between memory and intuition, and burn to hasten the course of events. Perpetual motion. The dazzling flight forward . . . To find out what was happening on the other side of the known, right up to the day when that other side would erupt with the thunder of divine anger . . .

Which was exactly what Magellan's men feared — the punishment awaiting them just around that ominous headland looming through the rain squalls. It was surrounded as far as the eye could see by reefs and breaking seas and clouds of spray flying heavenward like white ghosts. Fifty-two degrees south . . . Another storm roared in. Yardarms toppled and killed men. Keels shrieked against underwater rocks. Enormous seas combed the decks, buckling capstans, shattering boats. Anchors were swept away. The admiral had himself lashed to the foot of the mizzenmast beside the helmsman, similarly bound. Inside the three ships it was hell. The crews' quarters were awash with floating gear and ruptured barrels that bounced from bulkhead to bulkhead, mowing down everyone in their path. Sailors plugged their ears to shut out the awful crashing of waves against the hulls. The chaplain crawled across the decks, granting absolution to one man after another. A powerful current surged out from the distant headland, driving the enormous seas even higher and sweeping the small squadron out to sea, the ships cascading down the slopes of waves as if dropping into bottomless wells. Magellan's officers begged him to give up, to retreat, to turn back once and for all. But the admiral — the sternest, most poker-faced man in the world — was smiling! Drenched, numb to the marrow, his sickly frame shot through with pain, gazing out at a devastated fleet beyond help and thousands of leagues from Spain, he was smiling. He gave an order. Five colored flags in

Spanish naval code fluttered to the masthead. The message was
read aboard the *Concepcion* and the *Victoria* in funereal gloom:
"Two more hours. Keep in sight." An hour went by. Three flags
rose: "One more hour." The admiral was still smiling. He had
identified this cape. He recognized this current. It was the tide
race Martin Behaïm had depicted on his terrestrial globe in
Nuremberg at the very mouth of his *Passage to the Great Western
Sea*. Within the hour it would change direction and carry them in
toward the Strait . . .

Four hours later, and almost a flat calm. Floating in the lee of
the headland, now within clear sight of the three ships as they
rode the current westward inside what appeared to be a gulf
walled in on all sides by mountains . . . Pigafetta, the *Trinidad's*
historian, noted in his journal: "Without the knowledge possessed by the admiral, who would have dreamed of seeking out a
channel here . . . ?"

The place was utterly deserted. The only sounds were the roar
of the seas and the cries of big black cormorants wheeling
curiously over the *Trinidad*. Forms like reclining giants stirred on
the rocks. They were only sea lions, which soon dived to safety.
No trace of human life. They had lost sight of the fleeter
Concepcion and *Victoria,* which had gone on ahead to reconnoiter
the inner reaches of the gulf. Suddenly a cannon boomed to
westward, where they had last been seen. Then another, echoed
by the mountains, its reverberations rolling from cliff to cliff
through the solitude. Now the solitude had been violated — it
was victory! The two caravels had found the entrance to the first
narrow. The crew wept with joy. The admiral fell to his knees. It
was All Saints Day. If this strait led him to the solution of the
enigma, the admiral vowed, he would christen it *Estrecho de Todos
los Santos*. The name never caught on, and the Strait would
forever be known by Magellan's name.

The headland he christened *Cape of the Eleven Thousand Virgins*
because of the thousands of submerged rocks at its feet, which
gave it a retinue of dancing spray, of eternally fluttering white
veils. Today it is called Cape of the Virgins.

For Lafko it had no name. It could have no name. It was a mythical place where the Kaweskar canoes never ventured. Glimpsed only rarely from afar, on unnaturally clement days, it marked the outer limits of a world beyond which nothing existed. You could not name the inconceivable . . .

Yet it was from this *inconceivable* that Magellan's ships sailed in.

From the bows of two longboats, pilots cautiously sounded the first narrow, mile by mile, before the squadron moved in behind them. Looking up to take their bearings from dry land, they made a grim discovery. Its back to a cliff wall, a corpse stared out at them with dead eyes. It was the corpse of a stunted man with short bow legs, long ink-black hair, a sloping forehead, slanting eyes, and a short flat nose above a wide, thick-lipped mouth. He was very ugly, and he was beginning to rot. Around him a ring of red-painted sticks had been stuck into holes in the rock. Weapons lay at his feet — a sharpened stick, a stone club, a bone harpoon. His name was Taw, father of Lafko. The sailors crossed themselves, and hastened onward.

The end of the earth was inhabited!

★   ★   ★

Out of sight of the Strait, halfway between the two narrows, three wigwams stood on a sandy beach in a small, sheltered, almost concealed cove; fresh water cascaded down from a nearby glacier. Two canoes were pulled up to the forest edge. A third canoe was near completion. Yannoek stitched the last row of planks with whale sinew while his wife Kostora pounded at a pulpy mixture of canelo bark and moss for caulking. Lafko was shaping the oars, which he had hacked from a cypress trunk. He worked with a cholga shell shaped to fit his palm. Its edge rapidly dulled, and he had to whet it frequently on a stone. Little Tonko sat watching and crunching his own fleas. From time to time Lafko rose and cut a slice of blubber from the skinned body of a seal, turning it in the flames until the oil began to bubble and flow. He sucked greedily at the oil, which dribbled down his chin, then put the strip back in the flames. Finally, when it was sucked dry of fat, he swallowed the strip in small mouthfuls, cutting it off with the shell as it entered his lips.

Lafko was thinking. It had been a stroke of luck, this seal, a big fat animal they had had to cut up in the water between two canoes before hauling it ashore in chunks. A real stroke of luck, the first for three moons, after a savage winter that had exhausted their reserves. The storm had never let up, and fishing had been impossible. Even Wauda, who was fearless and swam like a fish, had been forced to give up diving. They had lived on fallen birds, blasted dead in mid-flight by the cold. Or else on rats, driven by hunger to leave the forest and attack the camp by night. They had been unable to find the sides of whale meat buried under the sand in preparation for lean days, for the storm had obliterated all markers. Farther south, the men of Tchakwal's clan had eaten an old woman. Then it had rained so hard they had been unable to light the fire. The wood was rotten and refused to kindle, even the little chips of cypress heart they attempted to keep dry by pressing them to their bodies. The kindling bow of hard tepu wood bent and snapped, eaten up by moisture. They had stretched themselves out on the floor of the ice-cold wigwam and sunk into an endless half-sleep, packed tight together under the soaked sealskins, in order to live through the long night. Those who woke screamed in terror at finding themselves still alive in the midst of such terrible deprivation. That was how old Taw had died. Because he was afraid to live. During a lull they carried his body far away from the living to prevent his spirit taking them all with him. If they had not, it would have been the end of the clan. Despite the magic sticks, old Taw (whose name they no longer uttered) often escaped from the rock face where they had left him. He brought them haunting visions and fear, even though better weather had returned. That was why Lafko was troubled. Such was Lafko's memory. Every year saw fresh recollections added to it, changelessly repeating themselves since the dawn of time.

The black clouds parted and sunlight bathed the shore. Shouts of laughter came from a flat rock not far from the beach. It was Kala and Wauda. Yannoek had taken them across in a canoe with a few glowing brands and some wood to build a fire and weave fishing baskets. The rock was a good place for cholgas. Wauda dived, her basket between her teeth. Even Lafko could not hold his breath under water as long as she could. Surfacing, purple with cold, her basket full, she laughed, then went over to warm herself at the fire while Kala took her turn diving. Lafko looked at Wauda, his wife. She was young, and had only just had her first blood. Like all the Kaweskar, she was coated in a thick layer of grime, but Lafko was not aware of it. Her body was firm, her buttocks round, and she had dazzling white, pointed teeth with which she bit the men who attempted to possess her without Lafko's permission. Contrary to clan usage, Lafko never gave permission. Later perhaps, two or three winters from now, when her breasts were as heavy and pendulous as Kala's . . . Wauda could laugh. Wauda could smile. She made up new songs whose heroes were the fish she met down on the seabed. At night, unlike the other women of the clan, she did not moan or whimper. She did not call on the dead in her sleep. When she laid her hand on Lafko's forehead it soothed the terrors of the night. When it was very cold in the wigwam and she came to glue herself to him, her body had the heat and life of a young *huemul* hind. She liked opening her thighs to receive Lafko, cooing like a small animal and nibbling his ear.

Lafko watched Wauda standing on her rock before the flames of the fire, and his penis stiffened. Little Tonko looked down at his own penis with such dismay that Lafko laughed. Kostora approached and lay down in front of Lafko, opening her broad thighs; permission had been granted by Yannoek, who was also laughing. Lafko pushed her aside with his foot and dived. He swam strongly. He took Wauda on the rock. Then he took Kala, whose body was like that of a seal that had grown breasts. Then again Wauda, who guided his tired sex with her hands. Whereupon, having heated three cholgas over the fire and devoured them with a few quick bites, he lay down and fell asleep, sated. Such was the happiness of Lafko, who possessed no word to define it.

Then they rejoined the others at the camp. They ate. They ate until nightfall. Beyond satiety. The memory of their long winter hunger was not yet dead, and the fine days ahead would barely be enough to fatten and strengthen them before calamity returned. The children's bellies swelled. Stomachs crammed with seal meat bulged under stretched skin. Lafko evenly shared out the animal's brains and tongue, the choice morsels. Otherwise, everyone was free to forage in the seal's carcass with his cholga blade. Rivulets of greenish blood trickled from the mutilated body and dried in thick patches on the feet of the eaters. No one spoke, but eyes shone. Eating, more eating: It was a collective resurrection.

Wauda, and Kostora, and Kala, and all the women of the clan busied themselves with storing a part of the meat. They cut the seal's blubber into strips, then into small cubes that they packed tight into a skin sewn shut with a slender vine. When it was stuffed, the skin made a ball about the size of a head. It would be allowed to ferment for a few days in the nearby swamp. Then they would hang it under the wigwam roof; it would give off a fetid smell, but nobody would be aware of this. On the contrary, the stench would comfort them. When your stomach was full you slept better, and the visiting dead relaxed their grip. There was less moaning inside the wigwam. When you woke from a night-mare, you managed to go back to sleep with peace in your heart. All you had to do was dip into the sack swinging overhead and let the beneficent fat melt in your mouth, soothing the pangs of hunger.

Night fell. Ayayema and his accomplices, Kawtcho nosing about underground, and Mwono, the spirit of the mountains, emerged from hiding in the shadows, herding before them their procession of ghosts, sniffing out the Kaweskar. Ayayema had the eyes of a cat. At night nothing escaped him. They carefully buried all the fires except for the one burning inside the wig-wam, invisible from outside. Stretched out on a sealskin, eyes wide open, Lafko thought. They had made their home on this beach for nearly a whole moon now. It was a long time, and sure to draw Ayayema's wrath. But they had all been so tired . . . They had had to recover their strength. They would leave as soon as the third canoe was completed . . . Would they find a stranded whale, so that they could bury its meat, remove its bones and sinews for thread and harpoons? Should they abandon Yerfa, who was getting so old that her nightly howling prevented them from sleeping—for the dead were already in her? No child had been born for twenty moons, and in the same period old Taw had died, and now Yerfa . . . Did they really need this third canoe, if they had not enough arms to handle the long oars? It was always the same fear—the fear of not being sufficiently numerous to dominate the solitude. Lafko's heart tightened. There were no words to explain what he felt, to explain his vision of his people, a people commanded by fate to survive, not to live . . . If Wauda's belly failed to swell, if the baby Kala was bearing died on the day of its birth, like her first, they would have to turn south, toward the great Strait, to procure themselves new women . . . Such was Lafko's fate. Year after year since the beginning of time the same fears arose without ever changing the immutable ordering of their days.

They did not get up next morning. It had rained about dawn, a rain still heavy with snow that turned the air icy around the barely glowing fire. The Kaweskar liked such times. In the pallid light of dawn Ayayema's grip relaxed. The night visitors fled. The moaning died away. They could sleep in peace, skins touching, under the furs. It was now that a sound roused them. Or rather a series of sounds, repeated, identical, at once distant and deafening. A sound they had never heard before, not echoing down from the heavens, like thunder on stormy days, but hurtling along the Strait at wave level and reverberating off the cliffs. Nor was it the familiar din—unfrightening because they knew its cause—of big mountain glaciers breaking off and toppling into the sea. Nor the loud crashing roar of century-old trees felled by the damp, falling amid a crackling tangle of boughs. Speechless with fear, everyone sat bolt upright amid the seal furs. In the silence that followed the children trembled like otters caught in a trap. But the sounds began again and were repeated. They came from the east, from the first narrow. What terrified these unhappy people was that the air vibrated. They felt its effects physically. Lafko's ears hummed. Stupefaction stared from his eyes. He *did not understand*. There was a new silence, another series of noises, then nothing.

This last silence was dreadful, for it endured. Nothing broke the renewed calm save the eternal surge of the wind and of choppy waves breaking on the shore. Those were noises Lafko knew. When they were not whipped up into a fury, he no longer even heard them. They were a harmonious accompaniment to the solitude and slow pace of life. But now the natural order was changed. Something alien had intruded, something so incomprehensible that Lafko and his clan, at once terrified and devoured by curiosity, ached to hear it again. They listened with their whole bodies. They listened not with their ears but with their souls. Finally Lafko could bear it no longer. Since nothing was as it once had been, they had to identify the *thing* so that a kind of order might be restored.

"Arka!" he said. "Up! Who follows me?"

Wauda rose. And Yannoek. Tsefayok and Kanstay, strong oarsmen. Lafko picked up his bow and club. They tossed some provisions into the canoe. They also took fire, a heap of glowing twigs and embers in a clay pot. Some journeys took time. Who knew where this one would lead them?

The canoe pulled away from the shore. Wauda was at the tiller, a shorter, flatter oar pivoting between two pegs. (We should pause to take note of this technical development, arrived at some five thousand years earlier. The sea people: They never even invented the sail.) The men rowed hard against the current flowing from the great Strait. There were no farewells, no wishes for a safe journey. The others remained behind in the wigwam, huddled like frightened animals. Already the women were wailing. Their distress would be unrelieved. They would not even peep outside the wigwam; they would merely keep up a small fire and chew on the seal meat Lafko had thrown them as he left. They were no longer alive. They were waiting.

*   *   *

The officers were assembled on the *Trinidad*'s deck. Normally unwashed and unkempt, the little Portuguese now flaunted all his rank. Clad in black velvet, the chain of the Golden Fleece around his neck, the staff of command in his hand, he lorded over them all. He had almost won. They had just come through the first narrow. The ship's guns had fired off a broadside that set the whole vessel shuddering. And *Concepcion* and *Victoria,* following in the flagship's wake, replied with their own cannon. Liquor was doled out to the crews, a fiery rotgut that dulled the memory of the corpse on the cliff. The chaplains sprinkled the wind with holy water and incense, swinging their aspergilla with sweeping exorcist gestures at the apocalyptic landscape.

It was indeed truly sinister, overcharged with savage majesty. Too many glaciers, mountains, and forests, too many successions of black clouds bursting open without a hint of what they would let fall — rain, snow, hail, perhaps even an occasional thin shaft of ashen sunlight. The air was laden with the chill smell of decomposing loam. And on top of all that, unheard-of numbers of flat rocks just breaking the surface, of reefs, of needles, of rock pinnacles, of coves and spits and sounds barring the way to land. The flotilla was riding a small, enclosed body of water between the first and second narrows, which the admiral christened Philip Sound. He had chosen a median course. He noted the currents and tidal swirls, scrutinizing every eddy, seeking the meaning of every shift in the wind, every change in the swaying motion of the kelp. He never left his ship's forecastle. He supervised everything. He shortened the sails to the strict minimum that would permit steering. The fleet proceeded with the care of someone entering a swamp where each footstep must be tested. Leadmen tossed fishing line weighted with lead ahead of the ship; when the weight was vertically below them, they hauled in the lines to read off the depth, singing out the fathoms in a kind of mournful dirge.

The admiral listened, looked, sniffed the wind and the land, obeyed his intuition. the course he was following — yard by yard, single-handed, without instruments worthy of the name, without any graphic guide save Behaïm's inspired sketch — through the thousand pitfalls of the Strait from the Cape of the Virgins to the Evangelist Islands twenty-seven days ahead, was exactly the same as that figuring on today's charts. It was a course the Chilean Navy did not even begin to mark out until the middle of the nineteenth century! There is no other route, except for the one that pushes northward, up-channel, and opens into the Gulf of Penas — the gate through which Lafko's ancestors had once slipped into the Strait. From time to time the admiral asked:

"Any sign of men?"

The answer — it too was sung out at the top of the lookout's lungs in order to pierce the wind's howling — came down from the crow's nest:

"No no no . . . men men men . . . in in in . . . sight . . . sight . . . sight . . ."

Who could live here? What kind of fortitude could possibly withstand the mysterious curse that sweated from every square inch of this land as if from a skin? There was not a seaman on the three ships who did not commend his soul to God and pray for shipwreck on the high seas rather than slow death in this place.

These were the voices Lafko heard, the voices of the lead-swingers and the lookouts, before he even glimpsed the ships. He recognized men's voices, although, since none other had ventured here for thousands of years, he had believed himself alone on the earth. It took a prodigious effort for him to acknowledge this after so many centuries of solitude. His brain hurt so cruelly that he had to drop his oar for a moment and squeeze his temples between his hands. Lobe by lobe, the inconceivable forced its way in, wreaking irreparable damage. And it was only beginning. For these men who spoke an unknown language were still invisible; at least he could still picture them in his own image, paddling a similar canoe, low in the water, hugging the shore. He knew no other kind of man. His memory was silent on this score. Even the distant Chonos, living north of the Gulf of Penas, his last enemies at the end of the long march, looked exactly like the Kaweskar and built exactly the same canoes. But what was this Lafko saw, just behind the small headland that hid the Strait from him?

It was a canoe, but a monstrous one. Bearing three cliff-high trees whose branches swarmed with more men than all the clans put together. He could not see their skin. They had hair on their chins. A thousand discoveries at once took Lafko by storm, each more painful than the last, annihilating him. Some familiar objects he recognized, of course — ropes, wooden structures. But the ropes, as thick as his arm, and the wood, in huge smooth sections, formed a whole so enormous and so far beyond his experience that he was *technologically* destroyed, if such a term can be employed — Lafko, who labored so long and so hard to stitch three roughly sawn planks together to float a craft quite incapable of sailing like this gigantic canoe that rode over enormous waves right in the center of the tide race. And after that, Lafko grasped nothing. There was no more comparison. No point of similarity. Nothing his conception of things could bear. First of all, the colors. Some men red, others blue, others green, still others black and red at once, not from stripes painted on their skins — like Lafko and his people when they went hunting or held vigil over a dead clan member — but from a total covering of their bodies, arms and legs included. And how did they feed themselves? There were so many of them they must have needed a whale or at least the flayed and butchered carcasses of several seals in their canoe. Lafko saw nothing of the kind. Nor did he see oars. Yet this canoe moved forward, changing course heedless of the current, its weight flattening the waves, its three trees swaying under their foliage of huge white leaves. There were other articles, of a material he could not identify and destined for unknown uses . . . Chains, anchors, winches, pulleys, the main capstan, all shrieking and groaning in a way that tortured Lafko's ears and brain, because none of the sounds was identifiable and none corresponded to anything he knew, while a terrible human voice rose above the wind and the waves: the voice of the admiral himself, amplified by his speaking-trumpet. And now, once more, the same shock to the eardrums, that same inexplicable explosion, accompanied by smoke and by a palpable shuddering of the air, which marked each of the monster's changes of course, and the upward flight of colored objects, which were the code flags rising aloft and signaled by a cannon shot. Two other giant canoes followed, just as heavily laden with men and noises . . .

Lafko and his companions were hidden behind a rock. They had moored their canoe inside a natural haven formed by several small islands from which they usually watched for seal. Lafko said:

"Men!"

"Men, men . . ." the others repeated over and over again, the word becoming a chant of doom, consternation spreading across their features.

For we must understand what was going on inside them, the extent of their psychic disequilibrium in the face of these apparitions from another world. The Kaweskar knew no gods. Ayayema, Kawtcho, Mwono, powerful spirits of terror, created death, not life. Life had not been created. It was. There had been no Creator. In consequence, no such being could be conceived in any human or living form whatever. The afterlife? A desert from which nothing could spring. Faced with the crushing superiority of those who now came, who were human creatures — and in the absence of any divine aid — faced with the manifold prodigies that accompanied these canoes up the Strait, they saw their weakness in a twinkling. Their foolishness. Their nothingness. Their isolation. Their tragic inferiority. Until that day, they had not known it. They had been their only standard of comparison. Only today, from the instant they realized they were not alone on this earth, had they become aware. Others had come. At that precise moment an unbridgeable abyss had yawned, an abyss that would grow wider and wider. On one side, those who could do everything, who were movement and change, who were never the same, who were always new. On the other those who were nothing, past and future confused, static, but who were eaten up by curiosity, driven desperately to compare, lured by an irrational attraction made up of fear and of envy that sometimes led them into confrontation. The two would never meet. Whenever it seemed possible, or about to happen, the Kaweskar would flee. To forget their solitude by seeking solitude again. Leaving behind them pillars of salt — the living dead, struck down because they had turned to gaze at the others . . .

★   ★   ★

The others.

They were very close now. The first vessel had veered and run in alongside the rock where Lafko and his companions were hidden. Soon she would change course and pull away again. Risking a peep between two rocks, Lafko could now distinguish faces. First of all the skin — colorless, repellent-looking. Eyes — deepset and round, some of them frighteningly blue or green, eyes he did not understand, eyes that held nothing familiar. He saw hands similar to his own, but thick, broad, covered with hair. Not knowing that he was very small, he found the size of some of these men terrifying. They never stopped moving. Their harsh voices called from one end to the other of the big canoe.

Wauda was shivering, although she was brave. She said:

"*They* have no women."

Her heart began to pound. Those who came were stronger than Lafko, more numerous and more powerful than all the clans, and they had no women . . . Her belly shook with a fear that shot deep into her thighs. She knew that others would come, that it could be no other way, and that one day . . . Wauda closed her eyes on the future. A tear rolled down her cheek. Squatting, her arms folded over the nape of her neck, she began to chant. A dirge full of names: Kyewa, Yerfa, Kostora, Kala, Wauda . . . *Akwal,* many. Many tribulations. Because of these unknown men. Wauda would have to open her thighs, as she did for Lafko. Horror and love of life . . . *Akwal aswal yerfalay. Akwal,* many. Many moons and many suns shone down on Wauda's grief. The song of the world of the Kaweskar, the great song of lamentation . . . Until this day Wauda had never sung it. She left that to the aged mourners of the clan. Lafko's hand fell on her, heavily.

"Be quiet! They have seen us!"

Bunches of men were clustered in the rigging of the three vessels. Every man not working the ships was staring wide-eyed. Up in the crow's nest the lookout was screaming at the top of his lungs: "Five savages! A canoe!" The admiral raised his speaking-trumpet, then shrugged and changed his mind: What could he say to them? He too gauged the width of the abyss separating him from this little man, naked, ridiculous, dirty, ugly, with crooked legs and a repulsive countenance, a kind of human animal that did not even seem to fear the cold, and that stood on its rock brandishing a bow so crude a five-year-old in Spain could have done better. It was Lafko.

Lafko had mastered his fear. Lafko had chosen anger.

"Pektchévés!" he yelled. "Pektchévés!"

This name was no longer uttered, except in the wigwams during the long night in the light of the hidden fire. The elders dragged it up from deep in their memories: *Pektchévés,* strangers . . . The clans had walked all the way across the earth to escape them.

Lafko mimed his rage. He stamped the rock with his heel, waved his arms, tore like a madman at his hair.

"Lord God, how comely he is!" said the admiral to his officers, forgetting that he himself was small, halting, humpbacked, and ugly.

The men up in the rigging roared with laughter. Lafko yelled. *"Pektchévés! Pektchévés!"*

The forgotten war cry of the clans, if they chose to fight. Their cry of distress if they had to retreat, marking the rhythm of their long march since the beginning of time. Anger, terror. *Pektchévés!* Lafko puffed out his chest, flexed his muscles, bent his bow, aimed with care. The arrow fell pathetically into the sea, far, far short of the great canoe, and sank amid gales of laughter. Another arrow, then another, piercing only the waves, as the ship, which had tacked away, returned.

Aboard the *Trinidad* the admiral gave an order.

"Let us frighten these savages a little to teach them manners. We must push on, but it will serve those who follow us."

A whistling like a williwaw, flying splinters of rock, a water spout, and worst of all that terrifying sound from the canoe's belly, accompanied by a cloud of smoke. First message to the Kaweskar from the first ships of the West . . . Lafko stood rooted to the spot. A little blood flowed down his thigh where a splinter had struck. It was only a scratch, but Lafko did not understand. He looked at this blood, then at the ship. He had seen the big round black stone bounce off the rock. If the strangers could throw such big stones so far, then why not he? Howling his rage, he selected a large smooth rock and hoisted it above his head. Never in his life had he thrown such a big stone so far! Yet it merely fell into the water. Defeated, he hung his head. *Akwal aswal yerfalay. Akwal,* many. Many suns and many moons shone down on Lafko's distress.

But why this fresh burst of laughter, these leers on the white faces aboard the great canoes? Wauda had joined Lafko. At first on all fours, until she was able to master her terror, then upright, bravely facing them, greeted by obscene yells and gibes from the rigging and yardarms. She had the hairless pubis of a little girl, her nipples were black and gritty looking, and her flat feet were greasy with dirt. Hopping from one foot to the other, her thick lips curled back, she mimed the act of biting. Her bowlegs were covered with scabs from wounds made by rocks while she was fishing, wounds that healed slowly in salt water. Her wet hair hung down to her yellow backside like a dirty rag. But she was a human creature, a female! She was naked! In the rigging the seamen leaped about like monkeys. They shouted lewd comments and propositions the prostitutes of Seville would have refused even to hear, unknown words carried on the wind and yet, in a certain sense, *understood* by Wauda. Brutality. Coercion. Second message from the ships of the West . . . Wauda folded her hands across her sex and sank to the ground with a whimper. Lafko dropped his bow, which lay useless at his feet. *Akwal aswal yerfalay. Akwal,* many. Many suns and many moons over a world that had suddenly changed . . .

★ ★ ★

The ships moved on. They no longer heard the thundering voice. One after another the three vessels vanished into the second narrow. Cowering on their rock, motionless, wordless, Lafko and his companions stared after them until they had completely disappeared, then went on staring sightlessly, retaining against their will those images whose every detail terrified them, doomed them. This inner fascination would henceforth be part of their lives.

Lafko thought. Farther on, beyond the second narrow, was Tchakwal's clan. Farther still, the clan of Yuras. Beyond that, Petayem's, and beyond the high mountain guarding the bend in the Strait, the clans of Tereskat and Kyewaytçaloes. Kyasto's wigwams were even farther west, on a little seal rockery that the strangers would find smack in their path.

Lafko said: "Fire!"

Everyone understood. *Akwal,* many fires must be lit, high up on the slopes, almost at the foot of the glaciers, so that they could be seen from a great distance. Alarm beacons, not rallying signals. Fires with high flames to carry through the night as far as Tchakwal's outlying wigwams.

Yannoek blew on the embers in the bottom of the canoe. Not one of them was dead. They all glowed. The first sign of clemency in all this long day. They covered them with a piece of sealskin while the canoe raced toward a beach they knew, where wigwam ribs still stood at the foot of a cliff overlooking the second narrow. Upright in the canoe, the men labored frantically at the oars, for evening was beginning to blur all their landmarks. Scanning the dark water, Lafko let himself be guided by the wiro, the giant submarine weed whose tips undulated on the surface, betraying the direction of the inshore currents. Luckily it was not raining. The wind was gentle.

Once they had reached the shore and hauled out their canoe, the task facing them was too much for what little courage remained to them after the day's revelations. They had to cross the realm of the dead, almost at nightfall, braving Ayayema, then Kawtcho, and above all Mwono, watching them from the mountainside with his red eyes and sending his avalanches thundering

down . . . But they went forward anyway. They could scarcely
see their feet on the path that climbed to the dry part of the
forest. They knew this path well. It led to the big cypresses they
used for the planking of their canoes, but generally they took it
only at noon, *Oykyemma* — sun above — the hour when evil spirits
hid because they feared broad daylight.

Whereas now it was night.

On the shore, all alone by the beached canoe, Wauda waited.
She had hastily thrown sealskins over the wigwam ribs, then
sunk to her knees, without a fire, trembling with cold and fear
and staring wide-eyed into the night. If Lafko did not return she
would let herself die where she knelt. Time was no longer time.
It no longer existed for Wauda.

It was a smell seeping into the wigwam that gave time back to
her. Her nostrils twitched. She rose. Pushing aside the skin flaps
of the wigwam, she saw a red glow at the top of the cliff. The
flames were licking up a deep wooded fissure all the way up to
the glacier.

That night, when they had all come back down, they ate
enormously. Half the stores they had brought with them, a
whole bag of grease heated over the fire Yannoek kindled, for
they had to rebuild life, which had lost all meaning this day. Then
they talked and talked, huddled tight against one another, sniffing each other like animals, squeezing their own flesh until it
hurt to make sure they were alive. Lafko told of the flames he had
seen bursting out in the west in response to their fire, the flames
rising almost to the heavens: Tchakwal had received the message
and would pass it on to Yuras at once . . . The solitude was
retreating. Kanstay had seen another fire even farther west that he
could not possibly have seen, that of Tereskat's clan: He was
inventing. They all gravely approved his words to help push the
solitude back . . . Lafko mimed his fight on the rock, the gigantic stone he had hurled, putting the three vessels to flight. The
others nodded again and again to confirm that they remembered
and that it had happened thus — otherwise how could they forget
how weak they knew themselves to be? Yannoek and Tsefayok,
who had not climbed onto the rock but had stayed huddled in

the bottom of the canoe, the diarrhea of fear running down their legs, recounted their own battle and the clouds of arrows they had loosed off to drive the three vessels away. Lafko nodded. Lafko thanked them. How else could he give those who knew they were conquered the courage to live?

Wauda said nothing. Wauda brooded. Each of them in his heart despaired. Their inventions masked a desolation it would be hard to forget. Then Lafko looked at Wauda, who followed him into the depths of the wigwam. Only between her wide-spread thighs could he regain his taste for life. There was nothing else to warm their ice-cold hearts. Wauda knew it. Lafko gave permission. Then Wauda looked at Yannoek, because Yannoek too needed this warmth in order to live. After Yannoek, Kanstay. Then, after Kanstay, Tsefayok. There was no other appeasement in the world of the Kaweskar. No benevolent female divinity.

Only Wauda, who was life.

★   ★   ★

Magellan saw no other human beings the entire length of the Strait. Not the smallest rainswept canoe. Abandoned wigwams. Flames leaping into life ahead of his ships, calling to each other from shore to shore. But he knew he was followed, observed, spied on. Mooring for the night, he doubled the deck watches, and Wauda inhabited his seamen's bestial dreams. He thought of the little man on whom he had turned his cannon. He felt no remorse. The little man had been so ugly . . .

At the Charles Islands, named after his sovereign, which no ship could miss since they formed a narrow double portal at the southern entrance to the last channel, he raised a lofty cross with a carved wooden Christ. Its ivory skin was mottled Spanish style with trickles of red blood. There was a gaping wound in its side, its eyes were open but blinded by more blood flowing down from the crown of thorns for the salvation and edification of the savages. Third message to the Kaweskar from the ships of the West . . .

Ten days later, rounding a group of four rocks rising from the sea off the last of the land, which he christened the Evangelists, Magellan discovered the ill-named Pacific. He would die there, along with most of his men. Only one ship, with seventeen living corpses aboard, would find her way back to the Cape of Good Hope and Spain. These seventeen sailors would be enough to spread the word. The time of secrets was over . . .

And what did Lafko do now? All the clans were on the move the moment Magellan's ships faded from sight. The Strait suddenly grew animated, like the forest when every animal emerges from its burrow after a storm. They were hungry to exchange news, to count their numbers, to bolster their courage by seeing one another still alive. Rowing hard, no matter how harsh the weather, the canoes converged on their rallying points to the south, between that wind-buffeted mountain at the crossroads of all storms, today known as Cape Froward, and the Charles Islands, at the confluence of the great Strait and the sinister Barbara Channel, which begins at Santa Ines Island where Magellan raised his cross.

Lafko met Tchakwal in the lee of Isabel Island, at the exit from the second narrow. Together they sought out Yuras at the foot of Mount Felipe, where Port Famine would be built fifty years later. Petayem, a savage among savages — he encountered the other clans scarcely once every twenty moons; he could not even tolerate the company of his own sons and set up his wigwams far to the south, beneath the icy walls of Mount Sarmiento — Petayem the solitary rowed out of the Magdalen Channel and headed for the Charles Islands. From the Skyring and Otway Seas came the clans of Tereskat and Kyewaytçaloes. They had seen nothing, except for signal fires relayed by one of their canoes several days' journey from camp. They had been camped beside a stranded whale, hurrying to devour it before its meat was altogether putrid. The last arrivals at the Charles Islands were the members of Kyasto's clan, who had fled when the ships appeared and had not dared return alone under the gaze of the motionless silhouette the strangers had left there, at the top of a small hill, attached to a kind of tree.

It was Lafko who ventured closest to it.

The white man was almost naked. His colorless skin had the same repellent look as that of the other strangers. He did not move. He had no voice.

Lafko squatted at the foot of the cross. He did not question, he thought of nothing, he did not know why he squatted there. He simply waited.

He had daubed his body with red mud, the color that protected against the unknown. Around his head he had tied a band of bird skin covered with white down that was the mark of the shaman. On the ground beside him he had set the little carved spearhead from the seal-gut bag containing the sacred treasure. A dot — the head — a long line — the body — two lines twice — the legs, the arms — and a diamond pattern of four dots just above the head . . . Then God, watching the Kaweskar from high in the heavens, murmured: "This is my beloved Son . . ." In such deliberately low tones, muffled by the cloud layers and the howling of the wind, that Lafko did not hear Him.

Lafko studied the white man. There seemed to be something around his forehead too . . .

The waiting lasted three days.

On the morning of the third day, the white man still had not moved. Lafko rose and said, "Pektchévé! He is dead." Snatching up handfuls of stones, he threw them with all his force and shouted at the white man who was dead: "Leave us in peace!" Then he stuck red sticks in the ground in a circle around the hill, which was henceforth taboo.

They at once moved to new beaches — there were countless beaches on the Charles Islands — for the Kaweskar fled from the dead, rejecting even their memory. There were great orgies of seal-eating and exchanging of women between the clans, accompanied by bloody fights. The unity of the Kaweskar never lasted very long. Soon they separated, dispersing their solitude in the labyrinths of the great Strait.

Life began again.

They did not forget the white men, the ones who had left, still alive, and who might return one day. They would never forget them. But the dead man on the hill did not haunt their dreams. He was not of their family, not of their people, not of their clan. He was, so to speak, a *dead* dead man.

Many years later, when Magellan's cross had rotted and blown away to dust, Lafko, son of Taw who was the son of Lafko, son of Taw, met the first Chilean missionaries. They spoke to him of a dead god nailed to a cross and resurrected on the third day for the salvation of all men persecuted by Ayayema. Lafko answered with indifference:

"I know him. He is the *dead* dead man."

He never changed his mind.

CHAPTER SIX

PORT FAMINE

You needed more than luck to negotiate the Strait of Magellan.

Every rule of nature is violated there at once. The tide rises and falls three times in a single morning, unleashing violent currents that collide head-on and generate enormous serried waves that fall on ships' decks like the blows of a woodcutter's axe. Mad winds dash into one another and spiral off in an infernal merry-go-round that drills a funnel in the sea, sucking everything still afloat to the bottom. Other winds hurtle down from the mountains with hellish roars, descending like furious raptors to devastate decks and splinter masts: These are the williwaws, Mwono's terrible pranks. Night falls at noon, at two, at three. Ships go blind twenty times a day under clouds of sleet and snow. And with the wind comes fog, a glutinous, glacial, opaque drizzle gravid with decomposing forest vegetation. Enormous blocks split off from the glaciers and fall into the sea, displacing mountains of water that brawl down the channels like tidal waves. And nothing, nothing as far as the eye can see for hundreds of miles save this same landscape of sodden forests, of dripping rocks, of unscalable, snow-covered mountains.

When he saw how utterly empty of life it was, Admiral Sarmiento de Gamboa judged it inhumanly, crushingly sad. Sometimes a fleeing canoe blending into the rocks . . . Shadowy forms along the shore, brandishing burning sticks with threatening gestures, then vanishing . . . The abandoned ribs of a wigwam on a beach, a fire smoking in the distance in response to another fire, the cold ashes of a hearth, the stinking carcass of a seal hanging from a tree, without any living being *really* showing itself . . . Just an accumulation of eeriness that weighed intolerably on seamen, settlers, and soldiers.

Much more than luck, indeed . . . And luck had truly deserted Gamboa, by the grace of King Philip of Spain *Captain General of the Strait of Magellan.* Through the quirks of the sea, through desertions, mutinies, and rivalries, he had already lost twenty of the twenty-five ships of his command. And now the storm had blown the surviving vessels away one by one — dismasted, harried out of the Strait by the hammering of the northwest wind toward the liquid deserts of the south where they vanished without trace. All except the smallest of them, the *Maria,* lying at anchor off his "capital."

Nombre de Jesus, Name of Jesus, in Possession Bay, between the Cape of the Virgins and the first narrow: a ghoulish metropolis, scarcely born yet already, like its namesake, nailed to the cross. Christians died there every day, from among the 500 landed in Gamboa's wake on February 6, 1584; thirty women, twenty-three children, judges, priests, soldiers, three executioners, a bishop and a glittering retinue of civilian and military dignitaries bearing sonorous titles that had lost all meaning in the general misery. Not to mention eighty dogs, nearly all devoured by their masters: The few survivors had fled and howled mournfully around the city.

Philip II had decreed: "The city shall be as a chessboard. Its streets laid out straight with ropes. There shall be a cathedral, a gibbet, a citadel, a palace for the governor, a convent, stores, wharves, warehouses, a barracks, and suitable houses for married couples . . ." The might and majesty of the State.

A muddy majesty. A stillborn might. Nothing had arisen from this mudhole. Cathedral, palace, convent: shacks that hugged the ground, rotting on the spot like the forest trees, sheltering starved beings with gray skins, shivering in sodden garments, stiff with cold. The streets looked like peat bogs. No boot had withstood the corrosion of the mud. Uniforms were in rags, their colors faded and running. Leather deteriorated like paper. Breastplates rusted. The crops they had planted rotted. The ground was a plague spot of piled-up vegetable debris, unfit for cultivation. They lived on barely edible mussels, on seal flesh that began to rot the instant the animal was killed. Lacking five thousand years of acclimatization, their constitutions gave up the struggle. They lived in prostration, without strength, without hope. The strongest of them rebelled, attempting to seize the *Maria* and flee. The revolt was quelled. Gamboa put up new gibbets and hanged half of them for the edification of the other half. Around the cross, the cemetery grew. The bishop died of sorrow beside the body of the last of the children, a little girl. Now Gamboa had left them. The roadstead was empty. He had gone to seek help at the colony of La Plata. He would never return.

Another city had been founded at the same time, a little to the south in the direction of Cape Froward. A more sheltered site, with a beach and stream; it was fortified to close the Strait, reconnoitered five years earlier by an English flotilla under Sir Francis Drake. There too they had cleared the land, raised a cross and a gallows, laid out streets, and dug foundations instantly flooded in the waterlogged soil. And they had given up.

Ciudad del Rey Felipe was its name. The City of King Philip . . . Huddled inside their shacks, its fifty surviving settlers no longer had the spirit to get up off their cots. A fascine fort, with thirty soldiers and six iron cannon trained on the Strait. A few dogs. For the survivors of *Nombre de Jesus,* hope . . . When everything was lost, the only hope of salvation lay in movement. Things could not be worse elsewhere; soon you began to believe that they might even be better; and then the imagination took over. The other side of the mountain . . .

It was winter. The long night. Governor of the void, viceroy of the inhuman outer limits, Viedma, the new captain general, abandoned Nombre de Jesus and set off on foot for the second of his two cities, marching along beaches or through forests broken by precipices and glaciers. Whoever could walk followed. Those who fell were not picked up. Corpses littered their passage. The gold and red standard of the King changed hands a hundred times, handed on from the dead to the dying. At the end of their calvary, ten survivors stumbled into the arms of an army of ghosts. Hope was twice betrayed: One group believed help had arrived; the other believed it had found help. The commander of the city was skin and bone. His eyes had a madman's glitter. Pointing to an offshore rock within cannon-range of the beach, he said to Viedma:

"I fire several rounds every day. I will not let them sit there in peace and watch us die."

"Of whom do you speak?"

"Of the savages, Excellency. At first they were invisible. Now they grow bold. You smell them before you see them, for they stink most fearfully! Their ugliness matches their stench. Hairless grease-smeared monkeys. And they live, Excellency, they live!" (The city commander spat on the ground, a sick man's blood-streaked phlegm.) "While we ourselves, creatures of God, perish one after the other; soon we shall all be dead . . . And they have females with them, whereas all of ours are dead! Where is God's justice in that? What kills us helps them to live! Do you understand that, Excellency? In the last few days they have thrown caution to the winds. They approach in their canoes; it is as if they were counting us. Every day there are more of them. They call to each other with the smoke of fires. Sometimes they stone us. They are skilled in the use of slings. They also have javelins, some of them with old knife blades for points. Perhaps Drake armed them? Yesterday they ambushed two of my men by the stream. They killed them and stole their dirks and swords. They fight furiously at first, then flee with howls of terror. It is as if their very courage frightens them. Their behavior is beyond reason, like that of the beasts. I pity the last among us to survive, and I pray to the Lord that I shall not be one of them. Their end will not be a pretty sight. But there they are, Excellency!"

Viedma looked. The offshore rock was crowded. Five canoes were moored there; from them scrambled little monkeylike men, penises in the air, naked beneath short sealskin capes. Females crouched in the bottoms of the canoes, clutching small yellow bales of flesh, their babies, between their sagging breasts. One of them was suckling a puppy, a repulsive sight.

"They have dogs?" asked Viedma.

"They are ours," the city commander answered despairingly. "Our last dogs are leaving us. They know where life lies. For that vermin lives, Excellency!"

The city commander was weeping with rage. He bellowed at his gunners:

"Mow that rabble down!"

Viedma raised his arm.

"I will speak with them. But what can I say that will have meaning for them?"

Magellan had already asked himself this question sixty-four years earlier. And its inverse was also valid. Between the white men and the Alacalufs, it would not be the last time the question was asked.

The chaplain had joined them. "In the name of Our Lord Jesus Christ," he prompted, "peace on this Spanish earth to men of goodwill."

Viedma hesitated. The words seemed ill-chosen. He had been thinking of a different kind of address, almost as if he were speaking to dogs.

"God created man in His image, Father, and look at that litter of rats! Could they possess souls? Unlikely, from their appearance."

"Be not of little faith, Excellency," said the chaplain.

Spanish earth? A gloomy strip of beach. Faith, certainties? Thirty ghosts grouped around Andres Viedma on the water's edge. Everyone who could still walk. Halberdiers leaning on their pikes. Musketeers using their muskets as crutches. Seamen orphaned of their ships. Settlers from Andalusia dreaming of the misery they had left behind them as of a paradise lost. Younger sons of noble families dressed in rags, wrinkled old men of twenty, their minds tottering, ready to give up, dissolving in the icy rain, bodies flapping in wind squalls that cut the weaker ones down and set them on all fours, weeping helplessly. But all of them were gazing at that offshore rock, like sunflowers drinking in the light of the sun, or like a prisoner watching for the slightest sign from the outside world to remind him that he is still alive. What was in their hearts? None could have said for sure. Filled with a repulsive vitality, dirty and ugly, these dreadful gnomes were mocking them as they approached death. And yet their presence was proof that life was indeed possible in this accursed land . . .

Viedma took a few steps forward to the water's edge. Taking a deep breath, he articulated each word with care:

"In the name of Our Lord Jesus Christ . . ."

There was a long moment of silence. On the rock across the water a little yellow man listened gravely. In his hand was a spear tipped with a Spanish dirk stolen from a corpse. His forehead was bound with a white band from which an otter tail dangled: He seemed to be the leader. He had stood up. What was he saying? Astounded, Viedma heard his own words come back to him like an echo:

"In the name . . . of Our Lord . . . Jesus Christ . . ."

The accent, the inflection, nothing was missing. A carbon-copy reply. The strange dialogue continued:

"Peace on this . . . Spanish earth . . . to men . . . of good will . . ."

"Parrots!" the city commander snorted in contempt. "But without feathers, alas!"

It was almost true. Every conqueror of the Strait would make the same discovery: The Kaweskar were prodigious mimics, but they attached no meaning to words if a stranger was addressing them. Even after they had grasped a few rudiments of Spanish — no abstract concepts, simply sounds to designate concrete things — it would remain merely a mechanism unrelated to their thought processes. An instinctive incommunicability. An absolute refusal. The first to refuse was Lafko. He threw the words back like a ball, like an unwanted object to be discarded as quickly as possible on pain of some curse.

"Let us praise God," said the chaplain. "It is at least a beginning."

Strident howls from the rock cut him short. The little naked men were no longer listening. They were leaping grotesquely. Their chief was furiously shaking his lance. Others were hammering the air with their clubs or appeared to be struggling on the ground with an invisible foe. Whatever spell there had been was broken. Some of them clawed their faces. Blood flowed. Flights of arrows lost themselves in the waves and were hailed with wild shouts as if they had reached their mark.

"You see what awaits us once we are beyond defending ourselves?" said the city commander. "We can expect no quarter from such vermin!"

Turning to the fascine works through which his cannon muzzles stared, he bellowed:

"Fire! Fire, I say!"

This time Viedma consented. The chaplain muttered a prayer. Five geysers ringed the rock. The sixth shot scored a direct hit on a canoe. Yerfa the younger, who was the wife of Taw, gazed wonderingly at the blood spurting from her shoulder. She was looking for her severed arm, and for the baby it had been cradling. The child had disappeared, but its image surfaced. Now the creature of Ayayema, it dragged its mother to the bottom. The little men leaped helter-skelter into the canoes. Tumbling over one another in a comic tangle of naked waving legs, catching their feet in bark buckets, colliding with one another, knocking one another down like ninepins as they struggled to ply the long oars, yelping in terror. Demented monkeys . . . Lafko was screaming, "Pektchévés! Pektchévés!", hopping round and round like a top before diving headfirst into the canoe as if he were diving into water. How the Spaniards laughed, slapping their thighs by the water's edge, their emaciated bodies shaken by spasms of mirth. It would be their last laugh . . .

Making a wide detour, well out of cannon range, the four canoes disappeared in the lee of a rocky headland just as the long night once more took possession of everything. The day had been but a reprieve. It would be twenty hours before it returned. Snow was falling. On the shore the little Spanish throng contemplated the deserted Strait. No one spoke. Life had departed. They returned to the dead city, every man bowed down by the weight of his own solitude. When eyes met they offered each other no hope, merely the reflection of defeat. When you see yourself dying in your neighbor's eye, you hate him. The trap had closed again. So had their hearts. That night their dying would cry in vain for something to drink. When day returned, and every day after that, the dead would remain without burial, the settlers folded in upon themselves like fetuses in the gloom of their shacks, soldiers face down on the ground at their posts by the guns, and the chaplain at the foot of the crucified Christ, where the church was to have been built.

The savages did not come back.

Viedma, by now insane, imposed iron discipline on his men. Every morning, in morion and rusty breastplate, girdled with his commander's scarf whose silver tassels were tarnished black, his admiral's staff in his hand, the Captain General of the Strait of Magellan saluted the red and gold standard of the king with a salvo. Dead or alive, the settlers were no longer of the slightest importance to him. He no longer left the fortress perimeter. He had erected more gallows, from which the bodies of his last seamen, hanged for desertion, were swinging. On his orders, the raft they had built to get away was destroyed.

One morning the guns finally fell silent. Stretched out on the damp sod floor of his palace, the Captain General of the Strait of Magellan folded his hands on his breastplate and commended his soul to God. He closed his eyes. He saw sumptuous fleets maneuvering offshore. Troops with glittering weapons paraded down the avenues of *La Ciudad del Rey Felipe,* his capital. The King of Spain appointed him Viceroy. He heard the triumphal fanfares, and the bells of the cathedral ringing out the *Te Deum.* Then nothing. Merely the grimacing visage of a small, yellow man with long black hair whose mouth kept repeating the same word over and over again: "Pektchévés . . .!" It was Lafko.

A short time later the English privateer Cavendish found these ruins peopled by the dead and christened the place *Port Famine*. The name stuck. No one would ever dream of building a city here again . . .

★   ★   ★

Lafko was thinking.

He was carefully plucking his chin, tearing out his rare whiskers with a small mussel shell he handled like a tweezers. Wauda picked the lice from his hair and sang the song of the rat — *aw aw aw* — which runs along cutting the grass with its teeth for its young. She sang bravely, for like everyone else here in the camp, she was afraid.

This morning they had not heard the distant thunder of the giant sling rolling across the Strait from the stranger's camp. No one knew why. Everyone was afraid. Everyone was waiting. None of them was proof against the fascination that had halted them in their flight a mere half day's journey away, despite the deaths of Yerfa the younger and of little Lafko, son of Taw, son of Lafko. On the contrary: Other clans had arrived, forcing the pace of their canoes, the clans of Yuras, of Petayem, of Tchakwal and of Tereskat, of Kyasto and of Yatse, and the clan of Kyewaytçaloes, which had come all the way from the broad Otway Sea and had never laid eyes on strangers, even though ten vessels had sailed by, at long intervals — the time it took a child to grow up — since Lafko, son of Taw, son of Lafko, had first crossed the path of the white men and heard the Pektchévés laugh as they stared at Wauda.

His belly full, Lafko reflected. He had eaten tern eggs heated in the ashes. Taw had uncovered several eggs while climbing on the cliffs. The beach they were camped on was a good one. There were large numbers of otters, whose meat is so disgusting that you swallow it without breathing, but tender for those whose teeth are falling out. There were enough cholgas under the rocks to feed the whole clan, and fat, sweet maggots the children picked from under the bark of the trees at the forest edge.

His canoe loaded with blubber and sides of seal meat, Yuras put up his wigwam not far from Lafko's. They made *tchas,* or barter. Everyone took what he needed from the food stores of the others. Yuras had brought Waka, his daughter, who belonged to no man. She would live in Lafko's clan, harvest cholgas for Taw, and open her thighs for Taw, since Yerfa the younger was dead. She was a good girl, but silent. She never laughed, never sang, never complained in the wigwam. You never knew what she was thinking, for she looked behind her eyes, *ktakso aswalek,* into the past. And yet she was still young, born in the year of the ten beached whales, remembered by every clan because they had eaten and eaten. She was never angry, unless you touched her necklace. It was not a shell necklace, but one of round colored objects given to her by white men. Yuras told Waka's story . . .

Five summers before, Yuras was camped on the Strait in a sheltered bay on Clarence Island, beyond Cape Froward. The clans also remembered that summer: *akwal,* much, much sun. It showed itself almost every day, and warmed your skin like a fire. Game abounded. They slept on the sand, ate, and slept again. They kept no lookout. Since the time of Waka's birth, and for many moons before that, they had seen no strangers. Those that Yuras remembered — he had then been only just a man able to bear down on the long oar — had gone past without stopping, without sending boats ashore.* But they had trembled, and then they had forgotten, despite the elders who insisted that the Pektchévés would return because they had no women. The day they returned the Kaweskar were sleeping, their stomachs full of a plump penguin of which only the feet and beak remained . . .

Lafko looked at Waka. She looked like Wauda, his wife, at the time of her first blood. A smooth body, glistening with seal blubber, sturdy thighs circled with white paint, with white circles around the nipples as clan custom demanded. Crouched

---

* This was probably Juan Ladrillero, a Spanish captain from Chile, around 1557.

over the fire, she poked with a long stick at the head and flippers of the seal whose skin was slowly splitting open, revealing the white flesh beneath. Taw would eat them before he slept. This was the custom of the women of the clan when they submitted to a man. Waka sucked big mouthfuls of water from a bucket and spat them out in a thin stream to prevent the fat catching fire, for the meat had to be crackling, not burned. Lafko said, *"Yefenawon kaya . . .* that is good." Taw also said, "That is good . . ." But Waka, who heard them, fingered her necklace without replying.

Yuras told the story. Twenty men had surrounded them; they were from a big ship at anchor in the mouth of the bay. The first Yuras had ever seen from so close. Very tall, with yellow hair and loud voices. The clan was terrified. They killed no one. They proposed *tchas,* barter. Yuras gave five seal pelts and a bagful of red mud. He showed his listeners what he received: an iron comb, an old knife he had turned into a spearpoint, nails, an empty bottle, a piece of barrel hoop he had fitted with a handle and turned into a scraper, a length of rope so supple to the touch that it mesmerized him. By now half the clans possessed one or more similar objects, taken from solitary, savagely butchered strangers, or picked up along the beaches . . . old barrels, empty flasks. A use for them would come only later, and slowly. There would not always be opportunities for *tchas,* or the carcasses of wrecked ships. They would fight for these treasures. They would kill. They would steal. They would invade moored ships at night, braving Ayayema as well as the Pektchévés. They would conquer the fear the strangers inspired in them, the smell of death emanating from their bodies, the abyss of mutual incomprehension that would never be bridged. They would offer ten otter pelts, twenty, then thirty, for a rusty axe head that would soon become indispensable in this blind alley of the Stone Age. For a necklace of glass beads, women would willingly follow the stranger. Women would remember . . .

Yuras told the story. The strangers gave them drink. A red water (rum) that burned the throat like canelo fruit and exploded inside the head like a thousand suns. *Kyayefna,* drunk, after three swallows, instantly, totally! The canelo also made you drunk, but

much less so, and very slowly, if you chewed it in quantities
sufficient to give you a stomachache. They sang. Fought. Ksefal
killed himself by diving onto a rock, arms outspread like wings,
mouth mimicking the cormorant's call. They also gave drink to
the dogs. Imitating his drunken dog, Yuras tottered about on all
fours. Crazed old women opened their thighs for young boys.
Akwal, much much laughter. Yuras laughed as he recalled it.
When they came to their senses the ship had disappeared. They
found Waka five days later. The strangers had left her on a beach.
It was snowing. She was cold. Her body was no longer smeared
with fat, but her lips had turned red and her hair was piled on top
of her head with one of these things (Yuras showed them the
iron comb). She simply stared fixedly down the Strait where the
vessel had disappeared. She was clutching the necklace with both
hands. She was also wearing bracelets on the ankles and wrists.
The other women of the clan attacked her. Waka bit. She tore off
part of an ear with one bite. Finally she gave up the bracelets, but
she kept the necklace. She never took it off. She was still staring
down the Strait as Yuras's canoe bore her away . . .

Wauda, who was Lafko's wife, asked:

"And after, her womb?"

"When the nine months were past no child was born," Yuras
said.

"Taw will make one," said Lafko.

There was no other choice. As so often in their history, the
Kaweskar were short of women.

And Waka, rolling the glass beads of her necklace in her
fingers, turned her absent gaze on Taw. She would accept him,
but she would go on thinking of the man with yellow hair . . .

★ ★ ★

At about the same time in this year 1586, Sir Francis Drake was
telling a story at a banquet in his London residence in honor of
Queen Elizabeth, who enjoyed a salty tale.

"It was a wager, Your Majesty, I should most assuredly have lost
had I entertained the dreadful notion of accepting it. We had

already encountered a number of these savages at divers places in the Strait. With their skins daubed with rancid grease, they stank at a hundred paces. They slipped between our fingers when we tried to catch them. Dirty, ugly little desperadoes, who might be decidedly unpleasant if they were ten to one against Christian men. Their women were like barrels mounted on bowlegs: They had the flat countenances of seals. Never have I seen uglier feet. But — particularly those of tender age — with dugs and buttocks that might strike a mighty spark in a topman from the Welsh valleys as excitable as a billygoat and as wanting in discrimination as a swineherd. Alas, just such a rare bird strutted among my crew. I learned that he had struck a wager with his messmates: If they managed to seize one of these females, he promised to honor her 'without,' he said, 'any need to black her eye or stave in her teeth' — which, it seemed to me, must be his principal weapons of seduction. I ought to have forbidden the exercise in the name of piety and religion, or at least in the name of cleanliness, but in the name of curiosity I felt compelled to let it take its course. So we laid hold of one of these amiable creatures. I had her presented to me on the bridge, while my Welsh topman sluiced her down with the hose pump. Seal blubber rolled from her in such quantities that we were soon floundering on the deck, but still she stank. Perhaps a little less, however. Indeed I descried a certain envy of the Welshman in the eyes of some of his shipmates . . ."

A man who lived life with gusto, Sir Francis. He had merely been passing through the Strait: It was the quickest route to his objective, which was to pillage the Spanish coast of Peru. He was a fighting mariner, a greyhound of the seas. He was founding no empire in the land of rain and storms. All he wanted was the galleons' gold. He scorned the clumsy Spaniards who needed cannon to ward off savages his own men toyed with. He raised no crosses. He loved life too much for that. He did not even have an official chaplain on board, merely a minister of the Reformed faith, a defrocked Catholic priest dragooned aboard against his will for indecent behavior, a spiritual parent of the Welsh topman and of all the other clothed monkeys howling their approval from the rigging in Gaelic as they surveyed the bride's ablutions.

"For the minister joined them in holy wedlock, Your Majesty! In the Magellan Strait sacrilege was winked at. It was enough to thank God for keeping one alive! The ship was tugging at her moorings. I had ordered the crew to triple the anchor chains. The wind was howling infernally, and the cold, Your Majesty, would have discouraged the best-hung of your gentlemen. But Taffy was no gentleman. He grunted 'Amen' and dragged his savage bride — still nauseating but clean — to the crew's quarters, followed by my petty officers with orders to report on events. And he had decked her out! In his own way, of course, Your Majesty, smacking more of wharfside doxies than of the ladies gracing this table. Who knows where he procured the unguents! A Flemish carnival mask . . . I had promised him a hundred lashes if he failed — enough to kill him — and a gold shilling if he prevailed. When he rose from that stinking female's loins, all fell silent, amazed. The Welshman had the face of a seraph, as blissful as if he had deflowered a nun in legitimate wedlock. The savage woman gazed upon him with something human in her eyes, something approaching — I scarce dare use the word, Your Majesty — something resembling love. Yet the scene had not lent itself to such exalted sentiments. The witnesses were slapping their thighs. Their laughter exploded. The poor topman stood there with his wilted pizzle in his hand, looking about for the breeches they had hidden from him. The female was on all fours, uttering little whimpers. They kicked her to her feet. She did not wish to leave. I had the victor clapped in irons in the bilges, to give him time to meditate. He was like a man waking from a dream. Again and again he said that he had never known such a woman. He said that the stews of Carmarthen, Cardiff, and Swansea would do well to recruit their strumpets in the Strait of Magellan. It was I, Your Majesty, who meditated — on love. When we dropped the savage woman, with a necklace and some tawdry bracelets for her pains, she wailed out mournful lamentations more difficult to escape than the mists invading the rigging. Even our own English ladies, Your Majesty — by no means reticent in love — could not have uttered such heartrending adieux . . ."

The company applauded Sir Francis, and raised a glass to the Welshman's health.

★   ★   ★

After the giant sling fell silent they listened for its thunder every morning, but it never returned. Taw stole down to the stream by the stranger's camp, slipping along the shoreline under cover of the rocks. The stream was deserted. No one came there for water any more.

Then Lafko lit a great fire. He threw wet leaves onto it, sending up thick smoke that the wind swiftly carried into the clouds. Wauda kneaded red mud and daubed it over Lafko, who felt his courage return. Other smoke columns answered, and soon the water was covered with canoes. *Akwal,* many, perhaps a score. Yatse's clan came from the north, from the other entrance to the great Strait where in Yatse's father's time they had fought the stranger. Aksa the younger steered. She too wore a necklace of glass beads, but it was a stolen necklace. Strangers had given it to her, but she had escaped. She had violated the *tchas. Tchas* with the Pektchévés should always be violated. What the Kaweskar gave was good; what the strangers gave was bad. Upright in the stern of the canoe, she was singing the song of Yatse the elder, father of Yatse, who had killed two strangers the year Yatse was born; the clan had eaten them.[*] Other women were singing in the canoes, celebrating fictitious battles, but it had taken the clans so much courage, so much cunning, to master their terror and shed a little of the blood of these all-powerful strangers who came ashore from their thundering ships . . . Advancing on Port Famine, the men painted red and whirling their slings around their heads, the women chanting in harsh voices, the Kaweskar

---

[*] Probably two shipwrecked followers of Cortes Ojea, a lieutenant of Ladrillero, who beached his crippled ship on Wellington Island in 1557, then built a longboat from its timbers and miraculously reached safety in Chile.

grew drunk on words. Wherever their canoes ventured, there was only silence and death. They sensed it, but they were still afraid.

Lafko was the first to enter the city.

In front of him a soldier still stood upright, supported by the lower branches of a tree. He was skeleton-thin. The bones of his hands had broken through the skin, which oozed a pink liquid. Lafko bent his bow and fired. Instead of embedding itself in the stranger's breast, the arrow glanced off before Lafko's startled eyes: Poised to flee, he watched as the soldier tottered. Thrown off balance by the impact, his body pitched forward. His breast-plate detached itself with a squeak and fell beside him. "Pektchévé! He is dead dead!" Lafko selected a big stone, the heaviest stone he could raise above his head, and smashed it down with both hands on the stranger's head, bursting it open in a froth of white porridge. Lafko had won. Pektchévé! For 20,000 years he had been running from those who were stronger and who had never shown him mercy. Now that he knew he was doomed, since they had caught up with him, he could at least take revenge. He would not let his only chance slip by. He was avenging Lafko, the last of his race, who would have no more descendants and who would take the last Kaweskar canoe to the beach where he would die, deep inside the Barbara Channel, after surviving another four hundred years . . .

The Kaweskar poured into the city, miming battle. They too took revenge. It was madness . . . Their arrows transfixed corpses. Their clubs shattered dead limbs. They ran howling from hut to hut. They dragged out the corpses they found inside and smashed their heads in. Few among them had yellow hair. But God Himself would have trouble on Judgment Day repairing those who had. Armed with a Spanish axe he found in one of the shacks, Lafko cut them up like seal carcasses and hung the pieces from every tree. Speechless with terror, Waka followed him, still fingering her necklace. More than ever, her absent gaze was turning inward.

Other corpses they dug up. The last of them had been so hastily buried that an arm was sticking up out of the ground, betraying the cemetery; the horde fell upon it with cries that

were no longer human. Only the gibbets, mobbed by flights of
gulls fiercely defending their prey, were respected. The last
posthumous victim of their ferocity was a woman. She was the
first they had seen. She too had yellow hair. They annihilated her
womb. She paid for every other white woman on the other side
of the world who had given birth to Pektchévés.

It was Lafko who found Christ on the cross at the top of the
hill where the Port Famine church was to have stood. The white
man was almost naked. He did not move. He was wooden. This
time Lafko knew who the man was. Lafko, the father of Taw, his
own father, had already named him the "Dead-Dead Man." He
came with the strangers from their distant land, but never went
back with them. Just before they left him behind, the Pektchévés
always gathered around him and sang on bent knees. Lafko knew
what to do. He wrapped the white down shaman's headband
around his forehead and set the little carved spearhead on the
ground. Then, from high in the heavens where He was watching
this terrible butchery, God murmured, "All is forgiven," but in
such a deliberately low voice that Lafko did not hear Him. He
stuck red sticks in the ground around the little hill, threw
handfuls of stones, and shouted at the white man who was dead
dead: "Leave us in peace!" Then he went back to his people.
They were preparing to leave Port Famine, carrying a vast booty
in ironware. They were already beginning to squabble over it; the
unity of the Kaweskar never lasted long . . .

"Pektchévés!" came a frightened voice from the shore where
the canoes were beached.

A great vessel had just entered the bay. It had done them no
good to reduce the yellow-haired woman's womb to a bloody
jelly. It had not taken her two days to give birth to a hundred
strangers armed with firesticks. They had already launched their
longboats and were pulling strongly for the shore; some of them
were firing at the little naked men scurrying for the safety of the
forest, shooting them down like rabbits. It was Cavendish, the
English privateer. He had sighted the ruined fort and the Spanish
flag floating over the dead city. Cavendish had seen many horrors; he had himself committed many horrors; but what he

discovered in the city was worse than anything he had even seen. Wordless, his gorge rising, he stalked the streets of the charnel house. He had knotted a rum-soaked kerchief over his nose and mouth. His surgeon walked behind him, assuring him that these people were already dead when . . . He could not finish his sentence.

"You are sure?" asked Cavendish.

"Certainly the great majority. Even that one, who is somewhat fresher. You can tell simply by their expressions. Dead of starvation, of hopelessness, of sorrow, of dysentery, but not by violence."

"Then it is even worse!" said Cavendish. "Ghouls! Hyenas! Animals . . .!"

How could Cavendish understand? He too was just passing through. He would never even exchange a glance with one of these savages. He longed to be back on board, where French wine and a Moorish slave-woman were waiting to help him forget this slaughterhouse. He gave orders to burn the canoes and sent men to beat the forest for the scavengers. He dispatched them himself with a pistol, standing among his officers as if at the hunt. He killed the last of them, a female, as they were climbing back into the boats. He barely glanced at her—barely long enough to kill her, without regret, because of the Spanish woman's body and what they had done to it. He did not even wonder why the abject creature had been running straight for the shore, heading of her own will into the trap. How could he have known that his own fair hair was the answer?

Waka ran on her short bowlegs. She had seen the man with the yellow hair preparing to leave with the others. He did not seem to recognize her, and Waka did not understand. She reddened her lips with a mixture of grease and mud, which the rain washed over her chin and then down her neck in bloodlike rivulets. She combed her thick hair upward with her iron comb. The bead necklace bobbed and swung with her breasts, from which she had secretly rubbed off the circles of white paint. She washed herself in sea water, as she had done on the deck of the strangers' ship. Then Waka, who never spoke, called out. Two precisely enunciated syllables. For the Welshman had told her his name! Who knows at what peak of their unspeakable embrace he had uttered his Christian name, Bryan, for her to repeat to him through her moans. A name she had not hurled back in rejection, but accepted as a gift. The poor woman was shouting "Bryan!" as she raced toward the muskets. She was still shouting "Bryan!" in a slowly fading voice, as her life ebbed through a gaping wound and the strangers' longboat pulled away toward the great vessel.

Waka, first of the pillars of salt, because she had turned toward the world of the Pektchévés . . .

★ ★ ★

The night was black inside the wigwams. Ayayema reigned over the dead the clans had abandoned beside the burned-out carcasses of their canoes, after hastily embedding a few sticks along the shore at high-water mark. They would never go back there. They would pull back into the Strait between the Gulf of Penas and the Charles Islands where the maze of channels would protect them; Cape Froward would be their outmost frontier.

The dead haunting their dreams were now more numerous than the living. They had managed to save five canoes, plus five others left behind at the camps, along with women and children and old people, as well as a few young men — barely half the number that had come ashore in this bay. Lafko was alive. Wauda too. And Taw, who would seek another woman, a second, then a third — now an easy undertaking. Lafko would also take Kala, since Tsefayok was dead, and he would make a son for her as soon as possible, with his last ounces of strength, who would be called Tsefayok. Of Petayem's clans, two boys only survived; they were adopted by Yatse. But how many generations would it take before Petayem could once again man the four long oars of a canoe with strong arms? Tchakwal too was dead, and Kyasto took in the survivors of his clan. Tereskat and Kyewaytçaloes fled in a single canoe to the farthest reaches of the Otway Sea. Inside the wigwams, the dogs squeezed in among the thinned ranks of the

sleepers. Perhaps the dreams of men and animals merged . . .
For from that day on, the Alacaluf dogs would burn with fierce
hatred for the white men, often saving their masters by the
savagery of their attacks. Wretched, hardly ever fed, beaten,
abandoned, never caressed, unloved except for the warmth they
provided in the wigwam at night and for their otter-hunting
instincts, formerly the dogs of the whites and now the little
yellow men's dogs, they never again changed camps. The
Kaweskar's only allies on this earth. God's dogs . . .

The clans were now armed with many sharp-edged iron
objects, picked up at Port Famine. Many things now took less
time, such as felling a cypress, shaping the planks for a canoe, or
splitting a seal's skull and extracting the brains intact. Soon they
began to hollow out their canoes in one piece out of big coigué
trunks. No more need to caulk. Perfect watertightness. The only
technical advance they ever made. The first and the last in more
than five thousand years. Otherwise, abandoning cholga shells
in favor of knives or axes (except for plucking their whiskers)
merely meant a lessening of labor and a gaining of time. They
continued to produce the same articles, the same narrow range
to which they added nothing—except that their work was
henceforth faster and cruder, sometimes even botched, leading
to increasing idleness that often bordered on apathy. These iron
implements, these iron weapons, the need to procure them (but
also the memory of the orgies of "red water," tirelessly recalled
in the wigwams at night), the "fashion" for bead necklaces, soon
the taste for tobacco—little desires that would become the very
fabric of their lives—and most of all their unconscious fascination with the white men, would all impel them fatally into
contact with the ships that used the Strait more frequently with
each passing year.

Once they had acquired the habit of bartering, then of stealing, then of wheedling and begging, and finally of subsisting
through begging alone, their canoes becoming refuse containers
for the miscellaneous trash tossed to them from the ships, their
fate was sealed.

It would take another three hundred years . . .

CHAPTER SEVEN

A CIVILIZED
GENTLEMAN

"And what are they doing now, Mister Morriss?"

His eyes glued to a ship's spyglass, the very latest product of English ingenuity, a fair-haired young midshipman scanned some fifty savages stuffing themselves around a beached whale on the shore of Charles Island. The sight sickened him, but he abstained from any remark that might betray his disgust. The officers and middies of Sir John Byron's staff all knew that the commodore, tolerant on so many other matters, did not suffer the expression of any judgment whatsoever on these horrible stark naked little yellow men they had been watching for the last three days as though there was nothing better to do in the middle of the Strait of Magellan than waste time on these savages. Commodore Byron, a man of about forty, sat among his officers on the poop deck of the frigate HMS *Dolphin,* his legs crossed, sipping from a bowl of steaming tea served by his man, who also passed ship's biscuits around on a silver salver. At least it was not raining. The wind had died somewhat. Every now and then a shaft of sunlight stole through the clouds to remind them that God's purpose in creating the earth had not been wholly malevolent. The frigate pulled gently on her moorings.

"Well, sir," the midshipman cautiously answered, "they are going about it with a certain want of decorum. Their faces are dabbled with blood. They are tearing meat in chunks from the animal's ribs. Never seen anything like it, sir, upon my word, sir! The beast must weigh at least 400 pounds. Do they really mean to wolf it down tail and all?"

Nor did anyone on the poop deck dare complain of the stench of putrefaction wafted in so generously from the shore, so faithfully accompanying each mouthful of tea that the fine black suchong from the commodore's personal stores was soon unrecognizable. Even Captain Lovecraft, master of the *Dolphin,* held his peace. Instead he strove to create the picture of a man inhaling healthy sea breezes.

The commodore gave an exquisite sniff.

"It stinks, of course," he observed.

No one said a word. Byron went on:

"Indeed it stinks most dreadfully, but not yet sufficiently to discourage them. I swallowed worse twenty years ago." Then, apologetically, "Of course, I had a young man's appetite then . . ."

They smiled. As much to acknowledge his bantering tone as to mask the spasms of stomachs rebelling at this disgusting revelation. All of them knew that Commodore Byron, then a midshipman aboard HMS *Wager,* Captain Cheap in command, of Admiral Anson's squadron, had been shipwrecked north of the Strait in 1714 and had escaped certain death only by living among the savages with four other castaways. He rarely mentioned it. No one questioned him. From time to time a memory erupted, and the middies listened in awe. Who could imagine that this man in lace ruffle and glittering gold braid, whose pigtail was curled with a hot iron every morning, who changed his clothes twice a day, who had brought aboard a servant whose sole duty was to take care of his wardrobe, who was fastidious to the point of idiosyncracy, who braved storms in three-cornered hat and embroidered waistcoat, had once himself lived nearly naked for six months, sleeping in the savages' wigwams, sharing their lice and rotten meat, smearing himself with seal blubber in order not to perish from the cold? No one knew what he thought about this return to the savage state. No one knew how he looked upon *himself*, or whether the exaggerated care he took of his dignified person was not perhaps a way of wiping out certain shame-fraught memories.

"What are they at now, Mister Morriss?" he asked again. "Do you still see the fellow I pointed out to you yesterday?"

A savage every bit as disgusting as his fellows, but wearing a white headband, a man the commodore himself had closely scrutinized as he left his canoe to join the grisly banquet.

Five times already since the *Dolphin* had entered the Strait the commodore had given an abrupt order to heave to, in squally weather, often taking risks that raised a cold sweat on Captain Lovecraft's forehead and alarmed the crew, simply to allow these wretches to bring their canoes out of the wind alongside the frigate, a maneuver they accomplished with surpassing skill. But their stench, the savage cast of their countenances, their ridiculous little sealskin capes that failed to cover a repellent state of nakedness, instantly neutralized whatever claims to humanity their skillful boat-handling might have supported.

In the first of these canoes, encountered off Cape Froward, a female had been standing at the steering-oar, breasts sagging over a protuberant stomach that could as easily have indicated pregnancy as some nameless purulence. The crew roared with laughter. Some shouted out coarse jokes. On Commodore Byron's orders it had not happened again, on pain of the lash. They had lowered baskets on ropes to these poor devils, filled with articles ordered by the commodore himself—axe heads, knives, nails, beads, hemp ropes, molasses, a little rum, sides of salt beef. Midshipman Morriss himself had made a collection of castoff clothing donated by middies anxious to please the commodore, who had merely shrugged. "I salvaged my uniform almost intact from the wreck," he commented. "It was soaked through, and never dried. It was as cold as a shroud. It froze my body instead of protecting it. Those clothes would have meant my death had I not discarded them . . ." None of these savages had come aboard. The commodore had forbidden it. He had studied them one by one, leaning over the railing, then returned alone to his bedroom where his steward had prepared a big bowl of flaming punch. On such days Sir John Byron drank heavily, and did not show his face again until morning.

"The one who interests you, sir," replied Midshipman Morriss, "is no longer hungry. He is squatting some distance from the others."

"What is he doing?"

"He is looking in our direction, sir. I believe he is even thinking."

"And what makes you think so, middy?"

"He is scratching, sir, an activity ever favorable to meditation."

The commodore permitted himself a smile.

"Disabuse yourself, middy. When these savages scratch, they think of nothing but soothing the itch. Indeed, in their condition and in these latitudes it is wiser not to think, or else you would simply lie down and die. I did it myself twenty years ago, squatting in the same way and scratching myself on the same kind of beach."

Captain Lovecraft stared into the bottom of his cup. The other officers, as if turned to stone, strove to eliminate from their features any hint of expression that might pass for surprise, or even disapproval, at the idea of the honorable gentleman squatting stark naked and scratching himself.

"May I ask you a question, sir?" the midshipman said shyly.

"Very well, Mister Morriss, since you are the ship's baby. You shall speak for these other gentlemen. They too are dying to ask."

The midshipman hesitated, then caught Byron's encouraging gaze and took the plunge.

"How did you do it, sir? How could you? Was it not beneath the capacities of a . . ." (He struggled for words, wondering if he dared, then, blushing scarlet, he blurted it out.) ". . . a civilized gentleman?"

"Quite simply by forgetting that I was the gentleman you speak of, Mister Morriss. But it was not quite so simple. The instinct for survival, however strong, was not enough. You had to strip yourself of the tiniest particle of memory, of any hint of comparison with previous ways of life. All my companions in misfortune perished, not of hunger nor even of cold — we shared the same lodgings, after all — but of shame, sobbing as helplessly as babes over the gentlemen they had once been. Seeing themselves reduced to living like beasts, aping the behavior of other beasts — since that was how they judged the savages around us — their souls naturally gave up before their bodies. I saw things differently. Once I had made of myself a *tabula rasa,* so to speak, my conduct no longer seemed anything but normal to me. That, clearly, was the key . . ."

The commodore took from his pocket something that looked like a white shell, its hinges bound with a thread. Thoughtfully, he toyed with it.

"It was with this that I plucked out my beard, whisker by whisker," he said, "the more to resemble them. It was no easy task, for my beard was tough and much thicker than theirs, and while at it I spent more time bloodying my chin than I have spent on the poop of this ship. Here, Mister Morriss, you try. The shell serves as a tweezer."

"Er, well, the fact is . . ."

The midshipman was as beardless as a girl. Everyone laughed. The atmosphere grew less strained.

"For you see, gentlemen," the commodore went on, "we all made the same mistake. Conscientious officers that we were, we read the accounts by our predecessors before we set sail for these parts — and took for gospel what the earlier navigators of the Strait passed on to us (and which is confirmed, alas, by scenes such as Mister Morriss is surveying through his spyglass, scenes most damning to these poor people). One hundred and eighty years ago Cavendish had already judged them animals and attempted to exterminate them. Forty years later, Admiral Jacob L'Hermitte of the Dutch navy declared quite seriously that these savages were nearer to beasts than to men, and that he discerned among them not the slightest evidence of religion or of government — and then bombarded them with cannon for the amusement of his Batavian bullies. Another unspeakable Dutch brute, the privateer De Weert, kidnapped a girl, a mere child, civilized her after his fashion, and carried her back to Amsterdam where he sold her to a bawd. He claimed to have felt no remorse because he saw no tear in the unhappy creature's eye, any more than he had seen one in her mother's eye when he stole the child. Perhaps he was unaware that terror prevents one from weeping. Even our own countryman Narborough, to whom we owe our first charts of these waters, as you well know, and who was a gentleman, found little to comment on save the stench of these savages, their ugliness upon reaching man's estate, their trick of squatting like monkeys, of devouring rotten meat, of repeating everything stupidly without making the smallest effort to understand, and of behaving in society as if bereft of human intelligence. From such a perspective, what an endless history of contempt is unraveled! And yet . . ."

Once more he saw himself in Lafko's hut, his naked body close enough to the fire to roast his skin, turning shellfish under the hot ashes with a long stick, and sucking seal blubber. Even the dogs had grown used to him. They no longer smelled his characteristic white man's scent. It mingled with the smell of the others, and even he no longer noticed it. Since his hair was black, only the whiteness of his skin set him apart from the savages, as well as his bushy pubic hair, dense tufts in which Waka the younger, the daughter of Tsefayok, liked to wriggle her broken-nailed fingers. She emitted an endless stream of chuckles that resembled a hen's clucking and that stopped only when his penis, stirring of its own will, decreed that he put an end to the game or else bring it to a conclusion in conditions utterly unworthy of a civilized gentleman, to borrow Midshipman Morriss's expression — and Commodore Sir John Byron, seated among his officers on the poop of the good ship *Dolphin,* blushed at the memory . . .

"Mister Morriss," the commodore asked again, "what further news of the naked gentleman? Is he still scratching?"

Consternation among the officers. Had Sir John lost his reason? His lips wore a faint smile. He had lied just now in saying that his thoughts had been empty as he gave himself over to that monkeylike exercise. He recalled that in truth he had applied his last vestiges of humor and philosophy to that particular circumstance; in the course of it he had promised himself—if he should ever get away and see London again—that he would have himself painted in this posture, but with a ceremonial tricorn on his head over the gold-lettered legend: "English Gentleman Scratching . . ." Anything rather than lose heart. The project had never borne fruit.

"No, sir," the midshipman replied. "There seems to be a conference between the man with the white headband and the itch and four other savages, among them, God forgive me, two women."

"And what should God forgive you, middy?"

"My lack of Christian charity, sir. They are really most abominably ugly; what is more, they appear to be engaged in some kind of *toilette*, painting their bodies—and most particularly their bosoms, sir—with white lines and circles."

"And the men, Mister Morriss—are they not daubing themselves red?"

Midshipman Morriss fiddled with the eyepiece to refine the focus of the spyglass: He was slowly beginning to realize that the instrument was like the light of a star moving backward in the fraction of a second across thousands of years.

"You are right, sir!"

Byron rose. His officers followed suit. He was no longer smiling. He had waited so long—and so fearfully—for this moment. Since the occupation of the Malouin Islands (he had rechristened them the Falklands), he possessed no royal charter to linger in this Strait, in this inhospitable waterway that was as much a ships' graveyard as a passage for navigation. On the contrary, he was supposed to break out with all speed into the Pacific, and there lay claim to as many islands as possible in the name of His Majesty King George III. He had tarried here past the end of the short summer season in order to meet Lafko again. Meanwhile, the ebullient Captain Wallis, the commodore's second-in-command and master of the corvette *Tamar*, was reconnoitering the Skyring and Otway Seas: Byron had sent him there so that he could pursue his own quest in peace and without having to explain himself. Next day, at dawn, they would have to resume their mission, in consort with *Tamar,* which would be standing by some twenty miles to the west, at the mouth of the Otway Sea.

"Gentlemen," the commodore announced, "we are about to have visitors, and this time we shall receive them."

There followed a series of orders and instructions, delivered in the courteous but inflexible tones that were the style of command in the Royal Navy, and which indicated that the commodore spoke in earnest despite the seeming folly of his words. A wave of disbelief flowed over the assembled officers, stemmed only by Byron's towering reputation as a seaman, as a darling of the Lords of the Admiralty, and as an "original." Captain Lovecraft's scarlet visage betrayed the inner struggle he was waging to bite back the comments his superior's remarks inspired.

"Gentlemen," the commodore went on, "as Midshipman Morriss has just informed you, the savages have taken some care over their appearance for this visit. Their effort merits some small zeal from us in return. Have the goodness to put on your dress uniforms and observe, as gentlemen, every customary courtesy, even if it appears not to be understood. For the rest, simply see that you model your demeanor on mine, and that you make no move toward our callers that I have not myself approved. Mister Stanhope . . ."

He addressed another midshipman, who at the sound of his name strove to compose his features into a mask that hid his amazement.

"Yes, sir."

"You have cold hands, I believe, like the rest of us? Your fingers are a little stiff . . ."

"Yes, sir."

"Go and warm them in the galley. I want your fingers to be supple enough for you to play us a little air on your fiddle."

"My . . . fiddle? Yes, sir."

"As for you, Mister Lovecraft," said the commodore to the captain, "You will oblige me by advising the crew of their comportment toward these savages. They have the right, like all of us, to a minimum of respect."

"Respect, sir?" said the captain, tearing his eyes from the canoe, now halfway between the frigate and the shore. "Respect? And how should I explain that to them? What I see through my own eyes is exactly what they see through theirs! And you would need damnably sharp eyesight to see anything deserving of even a particle of respect in the physiognomy and general aspect of the beings in that canoe. But look at them for yourself, sir!"

His outburst relieved him. His scarlet hue gave place to his normal complexion.

The commodore walked to the rail and looked. There were five people in the canoe, two of them women. Could the savage with the white headband be Lafko? The commodore closed his eyes to bring his memories into focus. They had been about the same age — if indeed these savages knew their age, counting their years as they did by summers and on ten fingers. Beyond ten, it had been simply *akwal,* many, many summers . . . How long had Midshipman Byron wandered alone, without fire, feeding on roots and raw shellfish, shivering beneath a shelter of boughs, not far from an encampment of savages? The nauseating smell of the smoke rising from their wigwams represented the castaway's only hope. Yet none of them had approached him. Not the slightest curiosity about this destitute stranger who came unattended by any prodigy. Several times he had tried to approach, but had been driven off by a pack of dogs before the savages' uncaring eyes. They always had meat, which they tore from seals' bodies and draped in disarray from the trees. But they also had human meat, for they had eaten an old woman a fortnight earlier; the dogs were still squabbling over her bones. One stormy night, at the end of his resources, his shelter blown away, his sodden clothing stiff with ice, realizing that he would die before the night was over, Midshipman Byron crawled to the nearest hut. A skin flap sealed the entrance; beyond it the dogs were snarling. Then the flap was raised and he saw a little naked man, his eyes reddened by the smoke the wind drove back into the wigwam. There were ten of them, men and women, around the fire, all

naked, their glistening bodies snuggled one against the other,
and about an equal number of dogs. The master of the house
lashed vigorously at them with a stick. Then Midshipman Byron
of His Majesty's Navy, younger son of a baronet, left his frozen
clothes at the entrance and crawled naked, as if in some dream of
earthly delights, to the fire deep inside the wigwam, slipping
between two savage bodies that closed around him in an envel-
ope of skin that radiated a beneficent warmth in which he fell
asleep, his heart brimming with contentment, exactly like a lost
baby that had finally found its mother . . . Next morning they
fed him. Then he fell asleep again, and slept throughout the day,
the women taking turns to lie beside him, and the dogs, no
longer snarling, to warm him with their bodies. At last, that
evening, he opened his eyes and saw Lafko watching him. The
brown gaze expressed no feeling, except perhaps for a vague
contentment: Lafko with his white-down headband, as well as all
the other inhabitants of the wigwam whose names he gradually
learned: Wauda who had warmed him, and Yerfa the younger and
Kyewa, and Yannoek, and Kostora, Taw the elder who was Lafko's
father, Kanstay who never spoke and who killed snared birds
with a single bite, and Waka, Waka the younger with her fishing
scars, one of them star-shaped, on her thigh, Waka the younger
who liked to lie next to him, and Tsefayok who was her father,
and who had insisted on the custom, a seal's head cooked by
Waka, which the midshipman had been obliged to eat. He had
not found them filthy, or ugly, or stinking. Or even savage. He
was no longer able to judge them in such terms, unless he was
also to judge himself filthy and stinking, and ugly with his
unkempt lice-ridden hair, his calloused feet, his blackened nails,
his language, made up of the thirty or so gutturals whose
meaning he managed to grasp, and which he repeated as vac-
uously as a backward child who has just learned to speak . . .

When he answered Captain Lovecraft, the commodore raised
his voice so that everyone should hear; he spoke in icy tones
quite unlike his normal delivery:

"The same respect that is due me, Mister Lovecraft, as commander of this squadron. I want it known that I shall consider

any mark of disrespect toward these savages as being directed against my own person."

The former Midshipman Byron, castaway, meant exactly what he said. He had been one of these savages. He did not intend to be mocked. He would tolerate it from no man aboard his ship. The privilege of command absolved him from explanation. How many noble souls among these scourings of the Portsmouth back streets would understand? And his officers? Even with them, he could not reveal himself beyond certain limits consistent with his dignity . . . He saw himself once again in Lafko's canoe, hands bloody, teeth clenched, mastering his weariness to take part in the communal effort, and Waka rowing beside him with a ferocious energy that seemed close to despair. It was for him that the whole clan was straining on the four heavy oars against the terrible north wind. They were fighting their way up the Messier Channel toward the Gulf of Penas, far outside their usual territory. A region that was now dangerous, the hunting ground for the past few years of Chilotan *loberos* from Chiloé, half-breed seal-hunters who showed the Kaweskar no mercy and habitually stole their women. The clan had set him down on the island that now bears his name, Byron Island, and immediately fled back to the depths of its watery labyrinth, terrified at having dared venture beyond the confines of the world. With the promise of gold for their pains, the *loberos* had taken him back with them to Chiloé, and from there he had been taken to Puerto Montt, the most southerly port in Chile.

The officers obeyed. In dress scarlet, in tricorns and powdered wigs, they lined up silently on the poop deck, while a fearful smell rose from the foot of the gangway where Midshipman Morriss was waiting.

"Ah, our company has arrived, sir," said the unrelenting Lovecraft. "Shall I have the boatswain pipe them aboard?"

"Mister Lovecraft," said the commodore in a strangely altered voice, "I beg of you . . ."

"My God! How dirty and ugly they are!" he thought in spite of himself; the abyss he had hoped to fill in by gathering his memories reconstituted itself with blinding speed. Now he would have been unable to answer Midshipman Morriss's question: How could he have done it? He watched with horror and revulsion as the five miserable creatures scampered over the frigate's deck, bellies to the ground like dogs, grabbing at brooms, buckets, ends of rope, and other trivial articles, catching the apple cores, onion peelings, and rotten ship's biscuits the laughing seamen tossed at them in defiance of the captain's orders, wolfing down the lard used for greasing the capstan, without a single glance of awe or even of curiosity at the universe of masts and spars soaring above their heads — because for those no explanation existed, or any use they could comprehend. The Pektchévés had always entered the Strait attended by such prodigies — the unimaginable height of the masts hung with white sails that blazed as if they reflected the sea, the disproportionate size of the longboats. Just like the moon and the stars: another world, commonplace by virtue of its crushing superiority, situated elsewhere, outside life . . .

Some seamen held their noses. Others, jostled by these naked glistening savages fluttering as frantically among them as moths, tried to wipe spreading stains of seal blubber from their clothing. Sir John Byron contemplated the disaster. All philosophy had deserted him. All humor too. He denied himself. Midshipman Byron denied himself. On the thigh of one of the females he had seen the star-shaped scar. Waka! Could it be? Could it really be? His stomach turned. His whole body rebelled. She was not a woman, she was a monkey, an aged monkey with flat, grotesquely swinging dugs and the face of a stupid animal, staring at the commodore without the slightest sign of intelligence. An immense distress flooded over him. A maelstrom of confused thoughts from which nothing human emerged, not even the wreckage of a soul in which to recognize himself — a castaway rescued, warmed, brought back to life by the touch of this obscene body whose memory, he realized with horror, had never left him. He thrust away from him the score of words remaining to him of their language; words which would assuredly have made it possible for him to link past and present, to awaken their memory. He no longer wished to do so. He was even terror-stricken lest it happen.

Midshipman Morriss would go far. Indeed, he would end his career as an admiral, in warm seas where warm girls anointed their hair with palm oil and gave off a spicy perfume. It was he who saved his commodore. He saw him standing undone, his face drained of blood, as the little troop of savages gradually calmed and came to a halt in front of him. Their stench was unbearable. They heard a trickling sound, and a small puddle formed at the feet of one of the two females. It was Waka. She was urinating where she stood, like a cow. The officers bit their lips, but the crew could not contain their laughter. Midshipman Morriss called for a mirror and presented it to the female. She started in fear when she saw herself in it, then walked cautiously behind it in an attempt to solve the puzzle. She came back, saw herself once more, started again, and ran back behind the mirror as if to catch herself by surprise. Not seeing herself there, she began all over again; and finally she directed smiles at herself from her hideously toothless mouth. When her image smiled back, she burst into shouts of laughter, giving every sign of glee.

"Well," commented Captain Lovecraft, who had recovered his aplomb, "we may offer thanks to Providence. I should have thought the sight would kill her."

The commodore forced himself to laugh, and the effort brought him relief. Everyone had now been put back in his place, on opposite sides of the abyss. Midshipman Stanhope was playing his fiddle, sprightly Scottish airs the savages heard with open mouths, their eyes glowing with pleasure. One approached to examine the fiddle. Another laid his ear on it. Who were they? Yannoek? Kanstay? And the other woman, could she be Wauda? It had been more than twenty years, and Byron's memories were blurred. But he was sure about Lafko. He strove to avoid meeting his eye. And at that moment Lafko leapt up, scurried nimbly down the gangway, rummaged in his canoe, and ran up with huge strides bearing a sealskin bag that Byron at once recognized. It was the bag filled with red mud.

The commodore saw it all again. It had happened after he ate the seal's head, crunching into it as if into a monstrous apple, while the whole clan watched him unblinkingly. Once the meal was over, Lafko had taken some red grease from this very bag and applied it with short thumbstrokes to his face and body, taking greater care than when he daubed himself. It was almost — how best to express it? — it was almost brotherly; while he was doing it Wauda, Lafko's wife, was drawing broad white circles on Waka the younger's skin. There had been no abyss then, and the midshipman, surmounting his despair, had reflected that if God willed that he never see his own kind again, at least he would not live alone but would be sure of a measure of human feeling among these savages . . .

An officer shouted an order. Another reached for his pistol. Two seamen restrained the savage waving a grease-smeared hand in the captain's face and delivering a voluble speech, a torrent of guttural words stressed by violent nods.

"Let him be," said the commodore. "He will do me no harm. We have received him. He is thanking me."

Now that Lafko had recognized him, he could not refuse the paint. For Lafko had said several times, "Tonko!" It was the name they gave him the day he ate the seal's head. And there was another word, repeated over and over again: *"Tinikit, tinikit,* I do not understand." He said: "Tonko wished to leave. *Akwal,* many, many days we rowed hard to the strangers' land. *Akwal,* many, many summers went by and we stopped dreaming of Tonko. Why has Tonko returned? *Tinikit, tinikit,* I do not understand . . ." As he drew the lines with a sticky thumb on the commodore's stoically compliant features, Lafko sought a reply. But what in fact could poor Lafko have understood? Why did so many ships follow one another through the Strait? What did he know of the world's movement? Of that gigantic appropriation of hundreds and hundreds of peoples by the vessels of five nations that had determined to divide the earth between them? And why did this man dressed in red, whom he had taken in half dead, not answer a single word in the language of the Kaweskar? *Tinikit,* I do not understand . . .

Suddenly Lafko stepped back, abandoning the unfinished painting like a child done with playing. Standing squarely before the commodore, upright on his little bowlegs, he studied him gravely. It lasted only an instant. This time he no longer said "Tonko." He simply said, "Pektchévé!" then turned to fling himself on the baskets that had been set out on the bridge. He filled his arms with knives, ropes, necklaces, noisily sniffing everything edible, surrounded by the others who behaved like a troop of chimpanzees quarreling over bananas. Neither he nor his fellows gave one more glance at the Englishmen. Soon they dashed away, like thieves, leaving a trail of dropped trinkets in their wake, jostling one another down the gangway and finding their voices again only when their canoe was loaded down to the waterline. Then, standing upright to man the oars, they shouted: "Pektchévés!"

"Are you enlightened, sir?" asked Captain Lovecraft. "We receive them like princes, we heap them with gifts, we play music for them, and they take their leave without a word of thanks! Why such a hasty departure? It makes no sense. In any case, good riddance!"

The commodore gave a long sigh of relief. If there had been enlightenment — and he was by no means sure there had been — it had come from the mouth of that savage: He, Tonko, the castaway, had been given back his true identity.

"Lend me your looking glass, Mister Morriss, if you please."

Only half his face had been painted red. The other half was still white. It might have been comic, but it was tragic, for an identical sadness stared from the eye on the red side and the eye on the white side. The commodore turned his head several times, presenting the red profile, Tonko's, to the glass; then the white, Sir John Byron's, of His Majesty's Navy. Finally, almost reluctantly, he wiped off the last traces of Tonko's passage on this earth. The handkerchief stank, soiled beyond redemption. He tossed it overboard. In the distance the canoe was vanishing on a sea shot with funereal hues; the sky suddenly burst asunder to drown everything that dared breathe in an icy downpour. Soon they could hardly see it, then it disappeared completely, liberating an immense solitude and a soul taking its leave.

"Mister Morriss," said the commodore. "May I offer you a present? A mere keepsake. A small thing."

He handed him the mussel-shell, the one he had used to pluck his beard, and added in fading tones:

"I believe I shall have no more need of it."

HMS *Dolphin* weighed anchor at dawn. Drunk as a lord, Commodore Byron handed over command of the flotilla to Captain Wallis of the corvette *Tamar*. He did not reappear on deck until they had passed the Evangelists, the four rocks off the mouth of the Strait which mark the gate to the Pacific.

★   ★   ★

In this year 1768 the Kaweskar received a name. For more than three centuries no one had troubled to name them, although they heaped mountains, capes, islands, channels, and straits with the names of every prince in Europe and of all their admirals — double or triple appellations, in English, French, Spanish. But not the men who lived there. No one judged it needful. They counted for nothing. They were "the savages," nothing more. Not a people or a tribe, not even bands or clans. A subspecies on the margins of the animal kingdom, undeserving of classification.

They used their true name only among themselves. It would remain a secret for many years. Finally, in the second half of the twentieth century, the last survivors of the clans were questioned by a French ethnologist* who had taken the trouble to learn their language. They revealed to him that they were simply the Kaweskar, the People. An index of the contempt of the outside world, and of the strange reticence of this people, who remained hidden in a silence that lasted almost until the extinction of their race . . .

But in 1768 they were called, for the first time, Pécherais. They

---

* José Emperaire, in 1947.

were given the name almost simultaneously, and for identical reasons, by Midshipman Morriss and by the French explorer Louis-Antoine de Bougainville who, hearing them shout "Pektchévés," had turned it first into a nickname, then a name. It was clearly a contradiction, but Byron, the only one to know the truth, did not enlighten them. Tonko-Byron, the castaway, a Kaweskar of the clan of Lafko, a refugee from the Old Stone Age, had severed the last link . . .

In 1768, too, their reputation was finally established. Leaving Fortescue Sound opposite the Charles Islands, Bougainville, who had also "received" them aboard the *Boudeuse,* noted: "The females piss upright, but the men stoop: Could this be the most natural way of pissing? If this is the case then Jean-Jacques Rousseau, who pisses very ill in his fashion, should adopt their manner. He recommends the noble savage to us so eagerly . . . The Pécherais are in what one might call a most precise state of nature; and in truth, if one were to pity the fate of a free man, master of his own soul, content with what he owns because he knows no better, then I should pity these men; deprived of all that makes life comfortable, they have still to endure the harshness of the most fearful climate in the universe . . ." Then he added, less kindly: "These savages are small, ugly, thin, and they stink unbearably. They devoured everything we offered them, showing a particular affection for candle tallow. They showed no surprise either at sight of the ships or of the equipment we showed them. This doubtless because it is necessary to possess rudimentary ideas about civilized handiwork before you can be surprised by it. These brutish people treated the masterpieces of human industry as they treated the laws and phenomena of nature. We had some difficulty ridding ourselves of these disgusting and inconvenient guests . . ."

From Cook, a few months later, the sentence would be without appeal: "Their emotional life is much nearer to that of the beasts than to that of any other nation. We were unable to discern whether they had leaders or any kind of government. In a word, they are perhaps as miserable a set of People as are this day on earth."

CHAPTER EIGHT

WAKA THE YOUNGER RETURNS FROM ENGLAND

On the cover of the notebook was a neatly underlined title: *Pécherais-English Dictionary;* beneath it, in proud simplicity, a cross composed of two intersecting lines. The goose quill squeaked busily across the paper. In the smoky light of the kerosene lamps in the midshipmen's berth between decks, where you had to duck to avoid hitting your head on the overhead bulkhead, the Reverend Watkin kept an anxious eye on the inkwell, whose level bobbed like a mobile black eye to the pitching and rolling of the ship. He sighed. The golden-haired Galahad of the Patagonian Missionary Society was already somewhat discouraged. His charges, Harry Froward and Fuegia Virgin, were being decidedly unhelpful.

Fuegia Virgin scarcely bothered to answer his questions any more. Yet she was a nice girl, meek, shy, gifted with an open mind, quite unlike the savage female captured three years earlier, along with Harry Froward, by Captain Fitz Roy during HMS *Beagle*'s first expedition along the shores of Dawson Island at the mouth of the Magdalen Channel. No one knew her savage name. She had never revealed it. Fitz Roy had christened her Fuegia, from the Spanish Tierra del Fuego, and Virgin for Cape of the Virgins; her companion had taken the name of Cape Froward and the captain's Christian name. She spoke almost faultless English. Yet from the moment the Cape of the Virgins had appeared on the horizon to mark the entrance to the great Strait, she had turned inward upon herself. Perhaps she had liked England, and would have preferred to stay there? Was it not perhaps cruel to force this child to make a second crossing of the sidereal reaches of time separating the civilized world from the primitive universe of the Pécherais—where she was about to be tossed back again? But the Reverend Watkin had plans for Fuegia. He meant to make her his wife in the eyes of God and for the edification of the heathen. Thus, by the Christian virtue of example, he would convert the Pécherais; they would become men worthy of the name. Stroking his golden beard, he contemplated his beloved. True, she was not beautiful, but she was clean and healthy, modestly dressed like an English girl, her black hair in braids, her body well nourished, and her mind considerably refined by the two years she had spent at the vicarage in Walthamstow near London. Her smooth face had copper highlights that excited the minister, and whenever he met her brown gaze he sought in it—against his better instincts, and begging God's forgiveness—the promise of forbidden delights. She was the only woman on board, and he had been the object of many envious looks.

God . . . The notes for Reverend Watkin's dictionary lay open at the letter G. His work was flagging. The page was blank. How could he bring the word of God to the savages—his future flock in the Strait—if they had no name for Him? Not a single Pécherais word for God! Nor for soul, for good and evil, for abnegation, charity, goodness, respect, humility, not the hint of a religious term, nothing that expressed the slightest notion of morality. A language silent on the emotions. And love? She did not understand the word. How did you say love in Péchera⸱⸱ man, a woman . . . Once, venturing beyond the limit⸱ ate to a man of the cloth, he had asked her to ⸱ "Oh yes," she replied, "we say *tsochak tyako,* op⸱

He had blushed to the roots of his hair and called God's forgiveness down on this simple child.

For the tenth time he repeated his question:

"How do you say 'God,' Fuegia? I have frequently spoken to you of Him. We must find Him a name our brothers and sisters will understand. Let us look at the pictures again."

His cheek brushed against her thick hair. He leaned close to inhale the powerful smell of her skin. The illustrations were of the kind used to teach the Bible to children. In one, a bearded figure was admonishing Adam and Eve. In another he sat in the clouds as a lightning bolt illuminating the tablets with the Ten Commandments zigzagged from the heavens. Elsewhere the same figure was stretching a protective hand over a newborn baby, or watching from the heavens as another bearded figure died on a cross. Fuegia maintained a stubborn silence. That night she had had a dream. But it had been Waka the younger, daughter of Yannoek, who had dreamed the dream as she slept in a Royal Navy hammock. For the first time in three years, Ayayema had reappeared, his face covered with blood, and with the features of a golden-bearded man who looked like Reverend Watkin.

"How do you say 'God,' Fuegia?"

The midshipmen sitting around them roared with laughter. It never failed. A young man busily writing at the other end of the table raised his head and smiled. He was Charles Darwin, sailing as naturalist aboard the *Beagle* with Captain Fitz Roy. He had already noted this talent for mimicry. Watkin's voice and intonation, even the sugary way he said "Fuegia," everything was there — but it was Harry Froward who had spoken.

Reverend Watkin disliked Harry. Was he Fuegia's brother? Her cousin? No one knew. When they conversed in their own language, coughing out those sonorous gutturals so grating to the ear, they seemed to be quarreling. They had quarreled more and more frequently since reaching the Strait. Harry spent hours up on deck staring at the empty coastline, then came back down wildly waving his arms. The minister considered him sly and malicious. Harry used to feign sympathy for the many people ˋboard who suffered from seasickness. "Poor, poor fellow," he would say commiseratively in his halting English; but when he thought himself unobserved he would turn away, still saying "Poor, poor fellow," to hide his laughter. Every night Reverend Watkin begged God to shine His light on Harry's soul and bathe in Christian love the mission he was to found on Dawson Island.

Harry Froward was small, round, and fat. He had done nothing but eat in England. He had mastered fewer than a hundred English words, most of them concerned exclusively with his appearance. He was extremely vain, almost foppish, and the nearer they came to their destination the greater care he took of his turnout. He wore kid gloves day and night, tugged constantly at his frock-coat to eliminate wrinkles, gazed tirelessly into the mirror in ecstatic contemplation of the four chin whiskers he proudly called "my beard," and flew into a violent rage if he dirtied his highly polished shoes — a gift from the good ladies of Walthamstow who had taken him to their bosom and regularly entertained him at tea. The finger he poked at the picture of Christ on the Cross was almost clean.

"Him I know," he said.

"What does our brother Harry know?" asked Reverend Watkin, his voice vibrant with affection as he turned his luminous blue gaze on the young man.

"What does our brother Harry know?"

New roars of laughter from the middies. Even the pair of youthful acolytes accompanying Reverend Watkin, full of dreams of a martyr's crown, Messrs. Christopher Young and Michael Wilson, could not suppress a smile for which they sheepishly apologized. Thoughtfully, Darwin studied young Harry. The words he had just uttered were once again a perfect imitation of Reverend Watkin, right down to the slightly forced tone. Could it be that Harry's ear had discerned what his primitive brain was incapable of descrying? For four months now, the *Beagle's* naturalist had been studying the young Pécherais, who had been left to roam freely within the narrow confines of the frigate; and he was beginning to realize that nothing had really penetrated his obtuse brain. Harry's smattering of English was mere appearance, his gestures and posturing a mere overlay, as if he sought concealment and protection within the alien, imposed model. For instance, Harry often said, "Savages, very stupid, very dirty, I no like . . ."

Reverend Watkin was losing patience.

"Well, we are waiting, Harry."

The answer erupted in two short words. Harry's voice, his look . . . this time Darwin was not mistaken. It was the savage who spoke:

"*Lâlat Lâlat!*"

Reverend Watkin snatched up his quill.

"Do I understand correctly?" he asked. "Is it thus we say 'God,' Harry?"

"*Lâlat Lâlat!*" Harry shouted.

He seemed very angry. Jabbing his finger at Christ on the Cross, he repeated in great agitation:

"Him! Him! *Lâlat Lâlat!*"

Tugging a handkerchief from his pocket, he bound it round his forehead and sank to his haunches, heedless of his fine frock coat whose tails trailed in the dust. Then he let loose a volley of raucous words — "*Ofsic tcawhs atktaal kuterek, Lâlat Lâlat*" — which he stubbornly refused to translate and which, in the language of the clans, meant: "And now leave us in peace, Dead-Dead Man!" Thus Lafko had spoken. All Harry lacked was the red sticks to mark the Dead-Dead Man off as taboo.

"Most edifying!" said Reverend Watkin, misreading the scene. "See how the spectacle of the Crucifixion saddens and disturbs him. Is this not a mark of strong religious feeling? The birth of a simple soul? We must give thanks to God."

"We give thanks, Mister Watkin," said the cautious Darwin, stroking his mustache doubtfully.

Harry had recovered his calm. He was absorbed in brushing off his coat with the back of his hand.

"*Lâlat Lâlat: God,*" said the minister, his blue gaze alight with seraphic joy as his quill squeaked across the page.

"*Lâlat Lâlat,*" repeated the two acolytes, gazing on their brother Harry with high hearts.

"Jesus Christ, *Lâlat Lâlat,*" Harry repeated dutifully.

So it was that Jesus Christ, Son of God, Very God of Very God, the second member of the Trinity, took His place under the letter *G,* for God, in the Reverend Wilfred Watkin's *English-Pécherais Dictionary.* But what Reverend Watkin did not know was the true meaning of this double word handed down by the Kaweskar from Lafko to Taw, from Taw to Lafko, ever since the first cross Magellan had raised three centuries earlier on Charles Island: *Dead-Dead.* The misunderstanding would never be cleared up . . .

A blessed day for Reverend Watkin! His minister's heart melted in mystical bliss. His man's heart overbrimmed with love. The spiritual father of these savages, divinely invested with their care, he would also commune with their flesh once he married Fuegia and made her Christ's bride in His minister's embraces. What could she be thinking? She sat with downcast eyes beneath heavy, slanting, half-closed lids. Ugly? She was no longer ugly, since God had chosen her and given her to him. The thick everted lips under the flat nose were faintly blue in the pallid lamplight. He would teach them the kiss the slave queen gave to Solomon. Her neck was thick and short but smooth and round, like the rest of her sturdy body. He guessed at the voluptuous young female breasts beneath the folds of her dress. He imagined them glowing soft and yellow and firm, with animal nipples heaving with animal lust. His whole being shuddered; through his head ran a verse from the Song of Solomon, a verse he used to recite to himself in London as he secretly ogled his female parishioners, fair and utterly inaccessible to a minister awash in hidden desires: "This thy stature is like to a palm tree, and thy breasts to clusters of grapes. I said, I will go up to the palm tree, I will take hold of the boughs thereof: Now also thy breasts shall be as clusters of the vine, and the smell of thy nose like apples. . . . There will I give thee my loves." He covered his beloved's hand with his fevered palm.

The hand he squeezed remained lifeless. The eyes in which he sought a response were empty. It was precisely this animal absence that was new in Fuegia and that had reawakened in him unbearable desires. Could he not say, "Open your thighs," in

Fuegia's savage language? The Reverend Wilfred Watkin could not ask that. Not yet. Nor could he suspect that the same mute prayer was rising, like the silent call of a drowning woman, on the opposite brink of the abyss. Waka was thinking, "Open my thighs." Everything else was beyond her. *Tinikit, tinikit,* she did not understand — words, looks, sighs, sentiments, cheeks brushing together, the pressure of fingers. What she wanted was to have this white man introduce himself into her body to awaken her from death, as others had already done on this ship. She had seen crowds in England — *akwal,* many people, countless people — whereas here in the land of the People she had seen only a few wigwams on the shore since her return, none of them of her own clan. Poor Fuegia, she too was discovering the solitude she had been unaware of before the *pektchévés* took her away. To live among her own people again, lost in this world of death, she had to be Waka, Waka the younger, daughter of Yannoek. Fuegia Virgin was not equal to it. And Waka was afraid. What was the best way of clinging to life? She herself could not express it. Hidden behind her half-closed eyes, the progress of her thoughts owed nothing to words and everything to instincts buried deep in her belly. That was why she opened her thighs beneath old damp sails in the small forward locker where the seamen took her; yet Fuegia had not acquiesced in this until that black overcast day, swept by rain and snow squalls, when the ship had entered the Strait and met the wind howling down from its gleaming glaciers.

Who among Fuegia's traveling companions might have guessed at this? Darwin?

He was a man without indulgence, without kindness, highly intelligent, sarcastic, full of his own superiority. Three days ago he had focused his small inquiring eyes on the first naked savages they had encountered, manning a wretched canoe. He noted: "I had not measured the enormity of the difference separating the savage from civilized man, a difference surely greater than that separating wild and domesticated beasts. Beholding these men and women, hideous of countenance, their skins unwashed and greasy, their hair unkempt, their voices discordant, their gestures violent, it is hard to believe that they are human creatures inhabiting the same world as ourselves. Poor Reverend Watkin can go on stubbornly noting down what he takes for intelligible words as long as he likes, but nothing leads one to believe that the language of this people deserves the name of an articulated tongue. Captain Cook compared it to the noise a man makes clearing his throat, but most assuredly no European ever emitted such harsh sounds, such guttural notes, while clearing his throat."

This was his first judgment. He never revised it. A silent witness of the scene between Fuegia and the minister, sitting at the far end of the midshipmen's table, he quietly noted: "There is no more intercourse between them. Just like stupid Harry, who repeats words parrot-fashion, Fuegia now confines herself to mimicry. She is returning to her primitive ways. It is a subconscious rejection of all they were able to teach her. The English words she knows have petrified. They no longer penetrate her mind. Soon she will have forgotten their very meaning—always supposing, which I doubt, that she ever truly assimilated them. There can be no remission for thousands of years of changeless stupidity. Species that do not evolve die. The Pécherais are a stillborn branch, incapable of further growth. Fuegia Virgin's remission was quite superficial. It seems to me that she has begun to stink—a sure sign. I wager that since we entered this Strait (finding herself so to speak at home), she has ceased to wash, just as that other poor devil, Harry, cares for his clothing only because we care for ours."

There was the sound of pipes and running feet on deck. Sails flapped noisily. The midshipmen, hailed aloft, scampered up the ladder with Harry, looking busy, on their heels. It was an hour before nightfall. The ship was preparing to drop anchor as she did every night.

"God willing, we land tomorrow," Reverend Watkin said to the two earnest young acolytes, Wilson and Young. "I burn to build God's kingdom. Go up and see how things stand, my friends. I shall follow you."

Fuegia rose. She wanted to go with them. The smell of decomposing soil was spreading through the ship. They could not be far from shore. And that other smell? Fuegia sniffed like a dog. Short, sharp movements of her head accompanied each sniff. It must be a still-fresh seal carcass, into which the men would already be thrusting their hands.

"Pray stay with me, Fuegia," Reverend Watkin ordered. "Sit here, next to me. We must learn to live together, one for the other. You must grow accustomed to me. First, do not call me *Father* any more. You must call me Wilfred now."

"Call me Wilfred now," Fuegia meekly repeated, mechanically aping the minister.

He smiled indulgently. What might he not persuade her to say if he were imbued with the spirit of sin? Then there would be but a short leap from words to action . . . This kind of wild submissiveness frightened and attracted him at once. Slipping his hand under the table, he seized Fuegia's knee. Seeing Darwin's eyes on him, he began to justify himself in tones of pathos. He was probably telling the truth.

"All this is new to me. Love declares itself first through words, particularly in a minister bound by the proprieties. But how am I to go about it with this child? And yet I must make her understand that I will love her, that I do love her . . ."

Darwin nodded wordlessly, assuming the air of gravity appropriate to this singular state of affairs, but he smiled into his mustache. Who could have believed when they left London four months ago that the Reverend Wilfred Watkin, of the irreproachably respectable Patagonian Missionary Society, would abruptly become a subject of study almost as abject as the savages inhabiting this end of the world? He wrote:

"Here we have an upstanding young missionary of impeccable morals, the son of a bishop, as worthy as he is brave, borne along by the purest intentions, yet who appears for the past few days to have been mesmerized by the animal qualities of this young Pécherais female. This is the more astonishing when one remembers that throughout the crossing he behaved toward Fuegia in the cramped confines of this ship as he would toward any English girl—and that the most naturally in the world, without effort or artifice, as befits his estate. Everything changed the first time we went ashore. It was on a beach in Rosa Sound, just north of Cape Froward, where we visited an encampment of naked savages. On seeing us they behaved like monkeys, without a hint of hostility but in a tumult of gestures and behavior in which it was impossible to discern a meaning. There are human races as well as animal ones whose instinct compels them to live in society: They are most capable of improvement if they obey a chief. The Pécherais obey no one.

"There were some forty of them, including a few females of quite monstrous appearance, uniting in a kind of caricature of the human form all the attributes of the female body (and abundantly so, I must add) with pure animality of feature, gaze, and comportment. One of these women ate raw a bird we had shot in order to frighten these people. It chanced to land at her feet. She threw away its heart and entrails, and then, after plucking it, devoured it whole with sickening sounds of chewing and swallowing; she even consumed the gizzard, turning it inside out with her teeth, like a glove, in order to scrape its insides. Blood flowed from her mouth and ran down her neck and bosom. Setting aside the repulsive nature of the repast and the woman's simian features, I must confess that in a Portsmouth whore her youthful, voluptuous figure might readily have found favor with an illiterate tavern drunkard. But surely not with a minister in holy orders! Yet what did I see? Reverend Watkin captivated to the point of abandoning all restraint in his rapt contemplation of this creature. Nor did he appear to trouble himself over the judgment of those who witnessed this fascination. The precise direction of the looks he cast upon her person left no doubt as to the nature of his curiosity. And when he turned away to gaze at Fuegia—who had accompanied us to see whether these people were of her family—it was as if he were discovering her for the first time. Here again, there was no mistaking the nature of his looks. It was in the state and the nakedness of the bird-devouring Fuegian female that he now beheld Fuegia, almost to the extent of losing all self-control. He caught himself quickly enough; but he is forever fondling her under a show of protective affection, seizing her hand, her neck, her chin, all those little bundles of naked flesh, stroking her hair (and in this very instant her knee); and he speaks of nothing else but marrying her in order to reconcile the high aim of his mission, his estate, his dignity, his authority over those two blockheads Young and Wilson, with the terrible slope down which his senses are hurtling him. Unhappy Reverend Watkin!

"Nor is he aware that even as he burns with unrequited passion, some of the roughest of the seamen are taking shameless advantage of his charge's altered frame of mind. Human nature is so constituted: Ever since we came upon these people, so generously offering us the spectacle of their females, certain of the crew have found them to their taste; and they have vented the urgency of their monstrous desires on Fuegia Virgin! Our surgeon, Doctor MacCormick, has told me all about it. It takes place forward, in a locker at the bottom of the hold where they stow old sails and worn ropes. The seaman he surprised there in Fuegia's company begged him to say nothing to Captain Fitz Roy. Otherwise it would have been the lash, irons, confinement, and the hulks on his return. In exchange, he talked. The first among the seamen to take the plunge had encountered no resistance — yet never before that, throughout the long crossing, would the idea of such an attempt have occurred to him. She had allowed herself to be led as a dog follows its master. Since then all who share this shameful taste, which to me smacks of zoophilia, have taken turns to enjoy her favors. They simply make her a sign, and she trots off to wait beneath her heap of sails. She asks nothing in return. And she says not a word, she shows no enthusiasm of any kind that might suggest sexual connivance; she merely disrobes and spreads her thighs. Then she lies quite still, as dejectedly as a dumb beast. Which led Doctor MacCormick to wonder why the men ran the risk of a flogging with a lead-tipped lash, of a court martial, of the hulks, perhaps even of hanging, for an exercise so disappointing and so wanting in human warmth. He put this very question to the seaman, who replied: 'That's just it, sir! She's ugly, her legs are crooked, she smells, and when you stick your pizzle in her it's not like entering a real woman at all — and then all of a sudden you're fetching off like a madman without even understanding why . . .' Doctor MacCormick believes this reply confirms the existence of a very intimate particular of the physiological configuration of these females; the same physical peculiarity can be discerned, between the lines, in certain accounts by Cavendish, by Sir John Byron, by Cook, and by Weddell only ten years ago when he discovered two of these women aboard his ship, the *Beaufroy*. They had been spirited aboard by his crew and appeared to have resigned themselves most happily to their fate, as if these particular physical dispositions of theirs had been revealed to them by their frequentation of brutish seafarers. Again, this does not answer the question as to how, in the absence of all previous experience, in the mutual ignorance of these inadmissible revelations, certain of these women give themselves so readily, and why certain men of the white race (who ought to recoil from them in horror) lower themselves to feast on these creatures. For myself, I believe that these lovers of savage carnality obey an unconscious instinct that compels them to redescend the ladder of human improvement and rediscover the bridled animality lurking within every one of us — and which is the only reality of the species. Perhaps, without knowing it, they regret its loss, which should not surprise us excessively on the part of some of the particularly simple beings recruited into His Majesty's Navy. Born and reared as they are on the margins of English society, there is no doubt that without the example of numbers and without religious and social coercion, they would never have evolved one whit. They have changed only superficially; so that in discovering and then appropriating these females they have, so to speak, unburdened themselves of a dignity that was onerous to them. But Reverend Watkin?

"His case is remarkable in that it cannot be separated from Fuegia's. In the past three days, watching the minister's unworthy show of love — and the melancholy looks from Fuegia which I take to be a manifestation of acquiescence — I have formed the dreadful impression that they are exactly made for one another; that each has embarked on his separate journey merely in order

to give himself to the other. She by undergoing an apprentice-
ship in white males in her sail locker — since she has submitted
in her flesh to men separated from her by at least fifty centuries.
He by liberating his unconscious instincts in the same way — and
now he is off in minister's guise to brave savage shores. They
make a fine doomsday pair, summarizing all of humanity in a
monstrous confusion of the two extreme limits of its evolution.
It is fated. It will assuredly be pitiful . . ."

Darwin crossed the *t* in "pitiful" with a flourish and set down
his pen. He was not a modest man. He was very pleased with
himself. He had a right to be. He had come close to the truth.

They heard the rumble of the anchor chain being payed out,
and the chimes of the mooring bell on which the officer of the
watch read the fathoms. Reverend Watkin seemed lost in silent
contemplation of Fuegia.

"Are you coming?" Darwin asked him. "The spectacle is on
deck now."

The Magdalen Channel is a wide, dark corridor cutting its
tumultuous way between Dawson Island and its western neighbor, still unchristened at the time; it then butts violently into the
bulk of Mount Sarmiento, on the very southernmost tip of
Tierra del Fuego. The first glimpse of Mount Sarmiento invariably produces a shock of anguish. Indeed, the headland in whose
lee Captain Fitz Roy was mooring the *Beagle* was called Cape
Anxious. He had named it himself three years earlier in a rare fit
of discouragement. Given Captain Fitz Roy's stoutness of heart,
the reader can imagine the desolation of the spot. The vast mass
of rock was bare and leaden-hued; the outcrops jutting from it
into the sea looked like sarcophagi whose ice lids had been
whittled to perfect smoothness by the wind. Beyond the coast lay
a world even more forbidding than the one they had left behind
on their southward run from Cape Froward. A world that
seemed walled in, without the smallest hopeful gap in the black
clouds rolling down from the mountain, for when they opened
for a second they revealed only snow cones, blue glaciers, and a
jagged line of peaks, some near, some distant, looming and
fading at different elevations and seemingly suspended in the

lowering sky. The colors were harsh, the shadows deep black, the toothed walls of the valleys seemed about to snap shut like the jaws of deadly traps. There was nowhere for the eye to rest. Nothing but craters, precipices, hideously misshapen rocks. There was no perspective. Planes clashed and jarred in an opposition that even distance failed to reconcile. There were nearly 200 men aboard the frigate *Beagle,* tough, stolid, horny-handed seafaring men, not given to flights of fancy. But not one of them dared utter a word to break the funereal spell the sight cast over them. Whenever a squall blew up — brief but of extreme violence, with gusts of sleet and snow that lashed their faces and made the ship heel even though her masts were bare — not one of them sought shelter. All were gazing at four round wigwams on a narrow beach at the foot of a dark forest. Two canoes, and the gutted carcass of a seal, had been pulled up on shore. A fire gave off thick smoke, with occasional flames throwing flickering shadows into the gloom where a score of forms were standing, as motionless as the *Beagle's* crew on the other side of the abyss.

At that precise moment, with night about to fall, two glittering horns of ice suddenly towered through a break in the clouds at a height the absence of perspective made impossible to guess — two glittering horns inexplicably suspended above the indecipherable. Then the wind ripped through the veil of clouds that masks this southern holy of holies from one year's end to the next, stripping bare the prince of solitudes from its twin peaks to the green-black water at its base: Mount Sarmiento! A ten-thousand-foot iceberg floating motionless over the sea. A vertiginous sheerness in which not the slightest roughness, not the smallest break in the rock face could be seen. It was a mountain not of this world. When it deigned to put on flesh, to take on material shape, it was to tell men of their nothingness. Whereupon, its message delivered, it withdrew into itself like a mythological beast withdrawing into the depths of its cloud cavern, leaving the witness of its apparition gasping in awe. None who saw Mount Sarmiento found the taste for life again.

"Poor devils," a seaman muttered as night blotted out the small encampment on the beach.

Reverend Watkin shuddered. He had seen his destiny. It was here that he would be set ashore, armed with the collective will and the bulky stores of the Patagonian Missionary Society.

It had started to rain. Only Reverend Watkin, Fuegia Virgin, and Harry Froward remained on deck in the dim light of the flares at the foot of the mast. Reverend Watkin leaned on his elbows on the poop rail, while Fuegia and Harry stood side by side a little farther off. All three were scanning the darkness for some still-visible sign of the camp. Curfew had not yet been tolled. Belowdecks the ship buzzed with the sounds of life. Men were singing. There were smells of soup, of pipe tobacco, of rum doled out by the quartermaster to keep the crew's spirits up. From the captain's room came the strains of music. It was Darwin with his flute, accompanied by a midshipman on his fiddle and the fine grave voice of Doctor MacCormick singing a Haydn melody. Life . . . From the shore not a sign, not a sound, not a glimmer . . .

Harry's handsome frock coat was drenched. He no longer gave a thought to his boots or to the kid gloves presented to him by King William IV in his brilliantly lit palace. His memories of England were growing dim. The good ladies of Walthamstow who had taught him how to eat with a spoon, how to dress, how to greet people, who had stuffed him with cakes and made him recite English words until his head was spinning; and the one who had smelled of old women and had taught him how to wash and who, by opening her thighs for Lafko, had taken Waka's place without even cooking a seal's head for him . . . A short while ago he had recognized Taw, his father, and Yannoek, Waka's father, and Kostora, who was her mother, Kanstay and Tsefayok, and Kala, Kyewa, and Wauda the younger who had neither breasts nor pubic hair the day he had been seized by Captain Fitz Roy's white men on a rock where he was eating the mussels Waka brought up to him. Life . . . He remembered his terror when they were tossed, naked and dirty, on the deck of the great ship in the middle of a crowd of Pektchévés. That terror had never left him. It had stayed with him day and night through the hubbub of all those strange voices; even through the peaceful streets of Walthamstow where too many people smiled at him; and in the huge hut full of people where they had taken him and Waka, dressed in white, to splash water on their foreheads at the foot of the Dead-Dead Man on the cross . . . He had done everything they asked him, he had obeyed as best he could, he had watched and mimicked their every move, he had washed his backside and penis, he had stopped squatting on his heels, he had sung *O Lord My God* at the top of his voice, he had opened the thighs of Pektchévé the elder without nibbling her ears; he had polished his shoes, brushed his clothes, picked up his hat in the street, stopped strangling pet canaries, desisted from beating dogs, had spoken to Waka only in English — disconnected words that made people laugh, whereupon he too would laugh. And all this because he was afraid, because everything, starting with the fact that he was there, terrified him. Only eating calmed him. He had eaten enormously. His terror had circumnavigated the globe. He had carried it with him all the way to this beach where the people of his clan, naked and dirty as he had once been, would rediscover Lafko on the morrow, dressed as a Pektchévé. His fear had circumnavigated the earth. It had also circumnavigated his head. It was before him and behind him. He was still afraid of the Pektchévés, of Father Watkin, of the captain. But now he feared Taw, and Yannoek, and all the others, and Wauda the younger whom he recognized although she had grown breasts. He said to Waka:

"*Akwal,* many, many moons have come and gone. There is a big seal on the beach. Unless Taw permits it, we will not be allowed to eat any . . ."

Waka did not reply. She was sad, and her belly was hot with fear. *Akwal,* many, many suns and many moons, *akwal aswal yerfalay,* the song of the world of the Kaweskar, the great song of lamentation, began deep in her throat and rose to pierce the night with its one strident note. Anxiously, Reverend Watkin drew near. He had never heard this dirge.

"Oh no, my children, not tonight. Let us rather sing *O Lord My God,* and then we must go to bed. Tomorrow is a great day."

"Tomorrow is a great day," Waka meekly repeated; then, in the guise of Fuegia Virgin, she led her lovelorn swain down through the bowels of the ship to the musty sail locker where they made mutual exchange of their fear.

Darwin added a few lines to his notes before climbing into his hammock: "On a desert island Man would doubtless use a goat for a woman, and I even believe, God forgive me, that the goat would not be insensible to the honor . . ."

★ ★ ★

Crack of dawn and action stations. The entire ship's company on deck. The captain issued arms to the *Beagle*'s marines, who saluted the hoisting of the colors with a musket volley, on the principle that you must first show your strength to the weak if you want to avoid having to use it. His orders were firm: "No savages on board." Their unruly manners, their tendency to steal, to poke their noses everywhere, to behave with neither reason nor restraint—had they not seen one of them, in Rosa Sound, attack a precious water cask in order to rip off its iron hoops?—were likely to lead to a confrontation. It would naturally be to the detriment of these poor devils, and would therefore compromise the peaceful establishment of the mission.

Canoes pulled alongside. There were two of them, with their usual naked, hirsute, lice-ridden cargo. The winter must have been harsh. They were haggard; some had open wounds on elbows or knees through which the joints protruded. Their bodies were striped with fresh red and white paint.

"Come on, Harry, speak to them!" said Reverend Watkin. "They do not even appear to recognize you."

In hat and frock coat, standing twenty feet above them on the frigate's deck, Harry stared his crushing contempt at the savages. They were peering stupidly up at this stranger who resembled them, and it was in English that he shouted:

"My name Harry Froward, I your brother, your son."

It was grotesque, pathetic. Harry grew angry. He stamped on

the deck. He turned to the officers who were trying to hold back
their laughter.

"Savages very dirty, damned fools! No understand!"

The minister persisted.

"Speak to them in their language, Harry. Tell them of your joy
at seeing them again."

"Me forget," said Harry stubbornly.

Lafko had forgotten nothing. He was floating like a lost soul
between the two brinks of the abyss. Squatting for the first time
in two years, elbows on knees, shoulders hunched forward, he
took temporary leave of them all. He waited. Suddenly there was
a commotion aboard the canoes. The women were uttering
guttural cries, particularly a small crone who hopped about
frantically and shouted, "Waka!" over and over again, her desiccated dugs flopping about on her chest. This time the ship's
company could no longer hold back: "Waka! Waka!" A hundred
voices joined that of the old woman, poor old Kostora, wife of
Yannoek, calling on her daughter Waka whom she had hesitated
to recognize in this stranger's disguise — until Waka . . . In the
confusion aboard the frigate, none had noticed that Fuegia,
despairing of being recognized, had torn off her dress, her stock-
ings, her shoes, in her haste ripping buttons and reducing to
tatters her fine layered petticoats, her chaste corset, her chemise
of embroidered white cotton, a gift from the ladies of Walthamstow, who intended their protégée to be a model for her
long-lost sisters. The model had just broken. The crew fell
suddenly silent. Even Darwin, impressed by the will implicit in
this sudden mutation, desisted from one of his usual disagreeable
sallies. Fuegia Virgin threw a leg over the rail. They saw her
plump yellow body (well known to at least five seamen, all
mechanically addressing a heartfelt if silent farewell to her) cleave
the air and dive straight between the two canoes. A second later
she was in Yannoek's canoe, dripping water and trembling with
cold, with a seal cape on her shoulders that Kyewa had wordlessly
removed from her own. Had it not been for her two long black
braids (which she now undid with upraised arms, in a gesture
whose grace was a last echo of Walthamstow), and the roundness

of her body (in painful contrast with the leanness of the others), no one would have guessed that Waka the younger had just returned from England.

When they saw that they would not be allowed aboard, the savages pulled away and rowed back to their camp. As soon as she stepped ashore Fuegia Virgin walked up to the seal carcass. Tearing off a piece of blubber, she heated it over the fire and then began to chew, squatting, her gaze empty, slicing the strip off with a mussel shell as it entered her mouth. Lined up on the beach like monkeys, the other women followed suit.

"Afternoon tea, Mister Watkin!" said Darwin cheerfully, following every move through his small folding spyglass. "I fear her visit to Europe has not much served her. And what a strange reunion! Do you think they are speaking to each other? No. Apparently they have nothing to say. This positively historic encounter seems to me even less interesting than that of two mares in a meadow. At least she has a mind of her own; and she seems less backward than her sisters. If you manage from time to time to make her dress again — to divide herself, as it were — she will be your stoutest ally. But you may also decide to give up. In your place I should not hesitate. Everyone will know these savages for what they really are, and you will return to London with your head held high. No one will reproach you, I will see to that."

"Too late," Reverend Watkin answered gloomily. "My fate is in God's hands."

"God's hands? That would surprise me; but he is right: It is too late," thought Darwin, recalling the two empty hammocks in the midshipmen's berth after curfew last night; he recalled too the minister's sheepish form creeping in an hour later, doing its best not to waken the other sleepers, followed by Fuegia's shadow with its odor of mildewed sails.

"In that case, Mister Watkin, I believe the moment is at hand. The two longboats are already in the water, and I see that they are taking on your baggage."

★   ★   ★

Fitz Roy gave himself three days. For once the weather was fine — meaning that no snow or hail fell from the pallid, shrouded sky — and they found a firm, flat stretch of ground above the beach suitable for putting up four small buildings. But the site under the eternally menacing ice phantom of Mount Sarmiento was as sinister as ever. The captain had felt duty-bound to urge Reverend Watkin to give up his plans, even though the minister's instructions from the Patagonian Missionary Society specified that the mission be set up exactly where the family of the two "civilized" savages was established. The minister had refused. So, to ensure him the best possible chances of survival after his departure, Fitz Roy drove himself and his men as hard as he could. He sent carpenters, a cook, a detachment of marines, and his most skilled seamen, for there were a thousand things to do; and he decided to camp ashore with his men in order to impress the Pécherais, because other canoes were arriving, shooting out of the maze of channels as if by spontaneous generation.

First he had to restore order. Everything not tied down was immediately stolen and taken off to the wigwams, or else irreparably damaged in the bickering that erupted. They saved the pig, the two sheep, and the chickens just as the savages were making ready to slaughter and devour them on the spot. Crates were ripped open and crockery smashed, and the fragments strewn all over the campsite. For in addition to the bundles of clothes, the stores, books, tools of every kind, folding beds, blankets and sheets, there was crockery in these crates, a generous gift from the good-hearted people of Walthamstow! Several services of fine English china for the table of the Pécherais . . . Harry Froward, still wearing shoes, gloves, and hat, lashed out with a stick in defense of what he considered to be his own property. He shouted, "Them no civilized, savages very stupid, thieves!" He fought with his family, and they had to be pulled apart. They almost killed one another when Taw, his own father, supported by Yannoek and Kanstay, leaped on him brandishing a small mussel shell to pluck out the four whiskers he so proudly called "my beard." Fuegia, apparently indifferent to the uproar, roamed from one camp to the other. She had put

her dress on again, but over her bare skin, without corset or
petticoats, and her feet were bare. Dressed in this way, unbut-
toned, her bosom exposed, she looked like a poor woman of the
slums. One of the two youthful acolytes, Young, was almost
stripped of his clothes. Fitz Roy had to step in constantly.
Reverend Watkin worked like ten men. He managed to impose a
semblance of calm by holding a Bible reading for the savages,
who had been somewhat calmed by the distribution of jars of
honey in which, like monkeys, they dipped their fingers. Psalm
51:

Have mercy upon me, O God, according to thy lovingkindness:

According unto the multitude of thy tender mercies blot out my
transgressions.

Wash me thoroughly of mine iniquity, and cleanse me from my sin.

For I acknowledge my transgressions:

And my sin is ever before me.

Against thee, thee only, have I sinned, and done this evil in thy sight.

He read this text, so appropriate to his own remorse, in a firm
voice. Darwin was almost moved by it. But in an attempt to make
himself more clearly understood, Reverend Watkin underlined
his words with gestures. It was like bad theater. He invoked the
heavens with upraised arms, feelingly pressed his hand to forehead and heart, beat his breast, abruptly bowed his head in
profoundest affliction, then raised eyes radiant with hope to the
firmament. The result was predictable. In a confused drone of
voices mimicking the pastor's, the savages reproduced every one
of his gestures in amplified form. Old Taw thumped his chest.
Yannoek scanned the heavens in search of whatever it was that so
preoccupied the white man. Then they all trooped up to press
their ears to the book, one by one, while Harry stubbornly
repeated, "Savages damned fools. Them no understand."

"No, no, Harry, no, no," said the minister, looking lost, and
striving to hold on to his last shreds of hope. "On the contrary, it
was an excellent beginning. God be praised!"

The reprieve was brief. Captain Fitz Roy was forced to establish a kind of frontier around the mission territory—merely a line dug out with a spade, of purely symbolic value; but it frightened the savages—and like trained animals they respected it, for each time they tried to cross it the marines fired blanks at them with much noise and smoke. Believing themselves hit, the savages screamed and rubbed their foreheads and breasts. Soon there was no need to fire. They stayed meekly lined up on their side of the "frontier," a row of squatting spectators, watching the work from dawn till dusk, and deftly catching everything tossed in their direction. The abyss, the eternal abyss . . . That day Darwin generously noted: "Their degradation could be read even in their postures, and their bestial features clearly expressed astonishment, wonder, envy, and fear."

By the afternoon of the third day everything was more or less ready. One of the four sturdy log-and-plank cabins boasted a small tower with a lovely little bell cast specially for the mission. This was the church. The second was the minister's house. He would live there with Fuegia. The third would be the home of Messrs. Wilson and Young, the acolytes. The fourth, a much cruder affair, would house Harry—if he decided to take a wife and live as he had been taught to do in Europe. It would set an excellent example, but alas, he had made so little progress. However, he stored the gifts from the good people of Walthamstow in the cabin and slept there to keep watch over them, although he scorned the folding bed and slept on the floor, where he almost perished of cold despite his blankets because he missed the clan's animal warmth.

Had it not been for the wretched climate and the crushing sense of isolation, the little settlement would have been a pleasant sight. They had even built a hen-run and an enclosure for the livestock, and had turned a plot of soil for a future vegetable garden. As for the flock of Reverend Watkin's extreme southern parish, it numbered about eighty savages who did not seem truly hostile. There was Petayem—very much at home here, since his camp was in Keats Bay just behind Mount Sarmiento—there were the clans of Yuras and Tchakwal, who had come in from

Rosa Sound just north of Cape Froward; Yatse and his wife Aksa, who had followed a huge dying whale in from the west; the clan of Kyasto; the clan of Tereskat; and even Kyewaytçaloes, in flight from the *loberos,* the dreaded Chilotan seal-hunters who had overrun the Otway Sea. Their ranks were thinner. *Akwal,* many, many white men now passed through the great Strait. Many women and children taken away. Massacres. And orgies of red water served in barrelsful by the white men. Who would ever understand the Pektchévés? They gave, or they slew, with equal indifference. And what could they expect of these strangers in this camp? This unanswered question was what had lured them all here.

An hour before nightfall the work was completed, and Captain Fitz Roy decided to order the ship's company back to the frigate. He would set sail at dawn next day. Only the minister and acolytes would remain ashore, for a first experimental period of three months, while the *Beagle* took soundings up the Cockburn Channel to the ocean and then, on the far side of the Eastern Furies, all the way to the channel soon to be christened Beagle, on the southern coast of Tierra del Fuego. If the experiment failed, and cohabitation of white and savage proved impossible, he would pick up the three members of the mission on his return.

★ ★ ★

Three months later the *Beagle* moored punctually off Cape Anxious. Nothing seemed to have changed, except that the savages were strolling about inside the mission perimeter as if they were at home there. Their garb was striking. Some wore trousers back to front. Others buttonless coats flapping over bare knees; the missing buttons had been turned into necklaces that swung between the women's breasts. As soon as Captain Fitz Roy's longboat, loaded with red-jacketed marines, pulled shoreward from the frigate, they left the mission and lined up on the other side of the "frontier" in their habitual squatting posture.

"I had forgotten how they stink," noted Darwin. "God knows we washed ourselves in the stream before their eyes for three days! The example was not contagious."

It seemed to him that Reverend Watkin also gave off a powerful odor ill-becoming a gentleman. His coat was stained and full of holes. His boots were down at heel and twisted out of shape. The two acolytes looked scarcely better. Young Wilson's hand was bandaged with a dirty bloodstained handkerchief. Nevertheless, they held their heads high. To Captain Fitz Roy's questions concerning his wound, Wilson replied:

"It is nothing. A mere dog bite."

The Pécherais dogs . . . Even armed with sticks, they dared not venture three steps beyond their cabins for fear of being assaulted by the ferociously barking pack, which seemed to enjoy license to torment them with impunity. Then the savages would take over from the dogs, pestering them with their demands, leaving them neither respite nor leisure, gesticulating and grimacing, even threatening them with their slings despite the appeals of Harry, who had remained more or less loyal. At night they had to take refuge in the loft, pulling the ladder up after them. Next morning, to win another day's respite, they tossed clothing, dried meat, and candles through the window; the savages consumed the latter items with a revolting air of contentment.

"It will not do, will it?" said Captain Fitz Roy. "Be frank, Mister Watkin. Besides, you look exhausted."

"Not at all, sir. We have had trying moments, to be sure. Reaching the hearts of these poor wretches requires sacrifice and time. But they show signs of improvement."

That was also true. There was no explaining it. The savages had punished their dogs, which fled, howling. Then they came and squatted comfortably in the ground floor of the white men's cabin, like old friends paying a call. They brought wood for the stove, an otter pelt, a bloody side of seal meat (which made Harry jealous and brought a sneer to his lips: "Savages bad, very dirty. No believe them."). But Harry was gradually weakening. You could sense the division within him, the inner struggle that was

clearly too much for him. Giving up "my beard," he had
plucked his chin. He kept shoes and gloves and hat, but discarded trousers and coat. It was thus that the "civilized" savage
strolled about the camp, almost like his own people once more.
In these intervals of blessed respite, Reverend Watkin captivated
the savages by reading from the Bible, desperately prolonging the
exercise like a snake charmer with a cobra. And equally inexplicably, the savages periodically hurled themselves on the minister and tried to undress him. It was his golden beard that angered
them most. They often tugged at it, attempting to pull it out in
tufts. Then they settled down again, probably recalling their
earlier fear, their worshipful awe of the Pektchévés. The minister
would take advantage of these periods of calm to seek sanctuary
in his loft.

"Er . . . and the young lady?" was the captain's next question.

The minister squared his shoulders. He looked the captain in
the eye. For the sake of the Lord's honor, the acolytes had
promised to remain silent. But how unpleasant the affair had
been . . .

"I have married her before God, sir, as I said I would. A simple,
moving, edifying ceremony . . ."

Wilson had rung the bell and Young had stood outside to
usher the savages into their pews, men on one side, women on
the other. Both wore white surplices. Impressed, the savages had
stood in silence, listening with a kind of wonder to the thin peal
of the bell. Every one of them was there, and they had tied up
their dogs, a sure sign of goodwill. Some of them wore shreds of
clothing; others were naked, particularly (despite the minister's
exhortations) the women, who had white stripes on their limbs
and circles on their stomachs and breasts. There had been one
consolation, though. Fuegia seemed to have recovered some of
her Walthamstow airs. She wore a white wedding dress and a
veil, miraculously retrieved at the bottom of a bundle marked
"Fuegia's Trousseau" by the ladies of Walthamstow. Under the
dress her feet were bare and dirty. She no longer washed, ever.
Two scented candles, which had somehow survived Pécherais
bulimia, added the smell of incense to the terrible stench of seal

filling the chapel. Reverend Watkin read from the Song of
Solomon: "I am black, but comely, O ye daughters of
Jerusalem. . . . Tell me, O thou whom my soul loveth, where
thou feedest, where thou makest thy flock to rest at noon." Poor
Fuegia. She was neither black nor comely, but was yellow and
coated with grease; she had breasts like two great loose bundles
under her white dress, heavy hips, short legs, unruly hair in
which her comb perched like an ornament set on top of her
head. But the besotted minister read the magnificent lines for
her. The reading produced the expected effect — a hubbub of
voices almost like responses — all in all an acceptable litany from
the mouths of these ignorant savages. Then suddenly, with
absolutely no warning, just as he took Fuegia's hand to pro-
nounce the solemn marital oath, "I, Wilfred Watkin, take you,
Fuegia Virgin, to be my wife," he was picked up and thrown aside
by a throng of howling savages who milled around Fuegia. Once
they had torn her wedding dress to shreds, they returned in
orderly fashion to their places, satisfied. Her naked body, which
Reverend Watkin had not seen since that carnal night aboard the
Beagle, was covered with white stripes. It was a discovery — but of
himself. The Reverend Wilfred Watkin of the Patagonian Missionary Society began to shake all over, his forehead burning,
uncontrollable waves surging through his loins. Seizing Fuegia's
hand again, for fear that God might take her from him, he
rushed through the lines that joined them and gave him access,
absolved of sin, to the animal delights of her body. That very
evening, almost by force, he was dragged by Yannoek and Kanstay
to the savages' wigwam where they made him eat a seal's head
cooked by his beloved's own hands. Since then a balance as
uncertain as it was fragile seemed to reign between the white
men and the Pécherais. The savages stole shamelessly. They
killed all the chickens, slaughtered the sheep, and hung the pig
from a tree, polishing it off inside three days. They wandered into
the mission cabins at all hours, pointing out articles they coveted
and uttering high-pitched cries until the minister, exhausted,
handed them over. Later they found the gifts spoiled, broken,
unusable, scattered around the camp. Reverend Watkin lost his

watch, half his books, several excellent pairs of shoes, his folding
bed, all his clothes except for those on his back — which he had
so far managed to salvage, in a last surge of dignity, along with his
beard. It was strange: He would even have sacrificed his clothing
in order to safeguard the golden beard that still set him apart
from the savages. On the other hand, he and his acolytes were
tormented less, their only reward for the disorder they could no
longer control. He spent his days surviving, in increasingly
degraded ways, and his nights waiting for Fuegia; she joined him
in bed almost faithfully, but at unpredictable hours. For these
occasions, she put on her dress. When the minister slipped it off
her, it came to him in his delirium that he was reliving the story
of Genesis somewhere along Ham's cursed line. The rest of the
time she went naked.

Captain Fitz Roy's gaze grew more and more insistent. The
two unfortunate acolytes could no longer keep the distress from
their faces. He noted, too, the sly, stubborn expressions of the
savages squatting on the other side of the "frontier"; among
them was Harry, but shoeless, hatless, without gloves, once again
unclean and repulsive, his long hair tangled, a band of white
down around his forehead. The civilizing experiment? A disaster.
To complete the picture, it was snowing. Insensible to the flakes
whitening her hair, a woman was suckling her naked baby. As it
thawed, the snow trickled down over the grease that coated all
these bodies. Why wear clothes, indeed? In the name of Christian modesty? And why teach them that?

"Mister Watkin," the captain said firmly, "we are taking you
aboard at once. All three of you. You cannot stay here any longer.
Er . . . all four of you, of course." (He began to speak, and
hesitated.) "We shall take care of . . . Mrs. Watkin. She too shall
see England again."

The minister smiled sadly.

"Mrs. Watkin . . ." he murmured sorrowfully, without irony.
"Look at Mrs. Watkin, sir. Do you think her capable of enduring
a third metamorphosis? You should not have taken her away in
the first place. You cannot take her now. This time it was I who
made the journey . . ."

Squatting beside Harry, "Mrs. Watkin" watched the scene. Every now and then she flapped her hand at a snowflake, as if at a fly. Her only clothing was a necklace of silver candle-sockets from the chapel candelabra; the ladies of Walthamstow would have blushed to see them dangling between her enormous yellow breasts. Her eyes were expressionless.

"There is something I must tell you, sir," said Reverend Watkin — and the effort it cost him was visible. "Fuegia is three months pregnant."

"Merciful heavens!" thought a horrified Darwin. "A baby in that belly!"

"All the more reason, Mister Watkin," the captain insisted in fatherly tones. "The child will be born in the Falkland Islands, where it will at least be among good English men and women."

"It will be born here, sir. You would never persuade its mother. You would have to cage her. And how should I travel? Inside the cage, as her husband? Or outside it, as her keeper? My place is here. Here I stay."

"And Mister Young? Mister Wilson?"

"I absolve them of their agreement. They have suffered more than I . . ."

And the minister mysteriously added:

". . . Without joy or reward. Leave, my sons. Never come back."*

Farewells were brief. Young and Wilson ran rather than walked to the captain's pinnace. They were worthy young — very young — men. They would have accepted anything: being tied to a pole and tortured by proud plumed savages; the stake, with a crucifix pressed to their lips; massacre in the chapel, clad in white surplices, Bible in hand, singing psalms of praise to God; all the exalted imagery of martyrdom. But not this abject degradation that had gradually reduced them to the level of the most primitive beings on earth. God had not asked that of them. And of Reverend Watkin? It was a question they henceforth chose to

---

* The Patagonian Missionary Society would return. It would be a series of disasters.

evade. Even Darwin was unable to drag three words on the subject out of them throughout the three months of the return passage.

As the redcoats reembarked, the savages slowly plucked up courage to cross the "frontier" again. The last man to climb into the pinnace, Captain Fitz Roy said:

"I shall return in six months, after careening in the Falklands. But it will be the last time. Meanwhile, God have you in His keeping."

"It will be the last time. God have you in His keeping," was the minister's only reply. Darwin had the sudden impression that he was listening to a Pécherais parroting stupidly and uncomprehendingly, like Harry on the *Beagle*.

"The wheel has turned full cycle," thought Darwin. "If the unhappy child is born, will it all begin again from scratch?"

★   ★   ★

A little more than six months elapsed before the *Beagle* once again dropped anchor off Cape Anxious. It was the time of the long night, the beginning of the southern winter. The sky was more leaden than ever. The bulk of Mount Sarmiento was shrouded in mist, but the unseen giant's physical presence — it diffused a vast chilly irradiation all around it — was tangible. Navigating these waters at this time of year required more than seagoing knowledge: It required much luck, much intuition. Only his word had persuaded Captain Fitz Roy to keep the rendezvous. This time they would pick up Reverend Watkin whether he liked it or not and leave again as quickly as possible. Messrs. Young and Wilson were not part of this pleasure jaunt. Suffering from nervous prostration, they were convalescing in the Falklands.

Captain Fitz Roy scanned the shore through his spyglass. With one exception, nothing but ribs remained of the savages' wigwams. There were no canoes to be seen. And while the mission huts looked intact from this distance, they had the desolate look of abandoned houses.

"This place stinks of death," said the captain. "Make haste."

He ordered his men to hurry with the launching of the pinnace.

At that exact moment Darwin was thinking that on the contrary, the place stank of nothing, in a place where human life ordinarily meant an unbearable stench. He drew the same conclusion from his reflection as the captain.

The marines jumped ashore. They too were in a hurry to be done. Low-lying black clouds, heavy, ominous, formed a roof over their heads so oppressive it weighed physically on their souls.

"Search everywhere, and look sharp!" said the captain.

The ground was strewn with refuse. Everything not blown away by the wind had sunk into the moist soil, from which fragments of books, shreds of clothing, and shapeless bags full of sticky mush that must once have been tea or sugar or flour protruded. A marine raised a shout.

"We've found him, sir."

Reverend Watkin's body was naked and riddled with wounds. A carving knife — a gift from the good ladies of Walthamstow to their worthy young charge, Harry Froward, the "civilized" savage — was still buried in one of the wounds. According to Doctor MacCormick, death might have taken place a fortnight earlier. But what added to the horror, what was the incarnation of horror itself, was the unhappy minister's face. His cheeks, chin, throat, and the corners of his mouth were one enormous bloody blister, a monstrous crust of dry black blood with a few golden whiskers sticking through.

"Oh God!" said the captain in a faint voice. "But why did they attack him with such savagery?"

"Plucking, sir," Darwin heard himself say, his stomach in full rebellion. "A brutal plucking!"

"Such hatred . . ."

"I would not swear to it, sir. But anger, yes. A savage anger. Probably desperate too. Since I cannot resemble you, you shall resemble me . . ."

"But how stupid!"

"Most assuredly, it is stupid. Savages, sir, are intensely stupid
beings . . ."

And he left hurriedly to vomit.

The captain pulled a silver flask from his pocket and passed it
around. Orders went out to the ship for planks and a carpenter.
Fitz Roy wanted to finish quickly.

"Where should we bury him?" he asked.

"Where he lies," said Darwin. "Look at those red sticks. They
must have put them there after he died. The one glimmer of
religious feeling in these brutes. A primitive protective instinct
toward their own dead. Cavendish mentioned it, and so does
Byron. All said and done, they did not deal so badly with him.
They considered him one of their own."

The captain started.

"You think so?"

"Otherwise they would simply have smashed his head in with
stones and sunk his body in a swamp. They might even have
eaten him. Weddell reported such things . . . He lost two men
from the *Beaufroy* in the same way."

Fitz Roy thought the young naturalist had gone too far.

"Just jolly good fellows then, eh? Not as stupid as you say?"

"Oh yes! More than you imagine. They are men, after all . . ."

He did not explain his remark. Just then one of the marines
searching the camp called out.

"Look who's coming, sir!"

It was Fuegia. She had come crawling out of the only wigwam
still covered with skins, stood upright, and was now approaching
them. At once, heavy in the air under the low sky, Darwin
recognized what he called the stench of life. She was not completely naked. A kind of torn and shapeless cloth covered her;
everyone recognized it as the dress she had worn aboard the
Beagle. Darwin was the first to notice the strange arrangement of
her tangled hair. It was almost as if—but it was! She had tried to
braid her hair! And she was speaking. She was even speaking
English. "Good morning, dear Wilfred," she said. The captain
had tears in his eyes.

"Poor woman! What sorrow! And now she is mad!"

"I think not," said Darwin. "Her eyes do not look mad. She is fishing tatters of English from her memory, strings of words she is no longer able to differentiate."

"And the baby?" asked the captain. "How is your baby, Fuegia?"

No reply. She did not understand.

"If you will permit me, sir," said Darwin.

Cupping his hands, he mimed a swollen belly; naturally no one laughed. They were all close to tears.

Then something overwhelming happened. Drawing inspiration from the unhappy Reverend Watkin's readings, and the passages concerning death and the afterlife, she lifted her arms heavenward with gestures that left no doubt as to the child's fate.

"So he too is dead," said Fitz Roy, clearly in the deepest distress. The captain would never be able to forget that he was initially responsible for this tragedy. Why had he taken the two savages back to England? For the unhealthy pride of exhibiting them? As an experiment? Had God authorized him to do it? Now he must judge the results. He had upset the order of things at the cost of irreparable damage. And now what should they do with this unhappy woman? On which brink of the abyss should they leave her this time? Here, in this icy wilderness? Or back in England, more alone in that inhabited desert than ever? Had she not put on a dress, as if expressing a preference?

Choking, the captain growled to Darwin:

"Since you manage it so well, try to ascertain whether she wishes to follow us."

No reply when he asked her in English. Fuegia stared uncomprehendingly at the stranger. Then Darwin took her hand. He was surprised to find it soft despite its layer of dirt. He put his arm around her shoulder as if to show her affection — and indeed it was something of that kind he felt, a sort of grieving pity suddenly irrigating his arid heart. He pointed to the pinnace, then the ship, making gestures to suggest a long voyage. But she pulled away, pushed him aside, and dashed away to crouch at the mouth of her wigwam.

"I believe it is better thus, sir," said Darwin. "Now everyone is back where he belongs."

The hammer blows in the chapel had stopped. Reverend Watkin was laid in his coffin. "Captain! Captain!" someone called. It was Doctor MacCormick's voice. The surgeon had just finished washing, as best he could, the mortal remains of the missionary, who now lay shrouded with the White Ensign of the Royal Navy. He was pointing to some writing no one had noticed, on the wooden wall of the cabin just above the ground. The letters were clumsy and shaky, and appeared to have been written in blood: "Dig Here!"

"Well then, dig!" the captain ordered.

About a foot down a small tin box was buried. Inside was a simple notebook, with the words *Pécherais-English Dictionary* on its cover, and a sheet of paper folded in four. The penciled text was beginning to fade.

"Read it, Mister Darwin, if you please."

Darwin read:

June 10 (?) 1834

The child was well-formed. A fair-haired boy. He cried out as he should, but he did not live an hour. Probably he did not wish to. By dying he sentenced me. They expected at least life from the stranger they had accepted. I engendered only death. Fuegia will not be able to save me. When the child died, they drove her away.

In her way, she loved me. It was thanks to her that I ate enough to stay alive, for they stole everything from me. I have been happy, I say, beyond all probability. With child she became almost beautiful. There was great gentleness in her eyes. I managed at least to teach her to say 'I love you' in English. Childish perhaps, but I so wanted to hear her say it in my own tongue. This has been my contribution to the civilizing work of the Patagonian Missionary Society, together with the attached dictionary, which I bequeath to my superiors in memory of a thundering good run that alas finished badly.

"What was that?" asked Captain Fitz Roy with a start.

"That is exactly what he writes, sir. And the letter ends there. He did not even trouble to sign it."

The captain's gaze wandered around this scene of desolation. The hastily knocked-together plank coffin, the unhappy minister's shape making bumps under the flag (for they had been unable to straighten his stiff knees), the hole the seamen had dug in the damp floor, already filling with water, the snow falling outside and whirling in through the gaping openings, the howling wind . . .

"'A thundering good run', indeed," he murmured. "He must have lost his reason."

"I doubt it, sir. A leap ten thousand years back into the past — is that not a thundering good run? I believe that while writing this letter he fully grasped its absurdity. Whence his nonchalant final salute. I should not have believed him capable of it."

"We will destroy this letter, Mister Darwin, since it is not addressed by name to the Patagonian Missionary Society. We must not discourage missionaries. They are England's conscience."

"We must not discourage them, sir," Darwin agreed sententiously, a brief light of mirth kindling in his sharp little eyes. "And they shall have the dictionary . . ."

The captain recited a prayer. They filled in the hole. Everyone tossed in a handful of earth. A seaman thought of ringing the bell, but it had been stolen. On a wooden cross they wrote:

REV. WILFRED WATKIN
1802–1834

The entrance to Fuegia's wigwam was empty. She must have taken shelter inside. A wisp of smoke rose from the roof.

At dawn next morning a longboat landed a half-dozen sacks of dried meat, cakes of lard, sugar, blankets, clothes, and a demijohn of rum thrown in at the last minute on Captain Fitz Roy's orders; he felt that if the clan returned it might perhaps smooth the reunion between "civilized" and savage. Fuegia did not approach.

But as the *Beagle* unfurled her sails and began to pull seaward, she lit a huge fire on the beach, its smoke shimmering through the mist like a farewell.

Captain Fitz Roy gazed for a long time at that smoke. Clearly, something was troubling him. An unanswered question. That night, having invited Darwin to dine with him, he asked:

"When we returned the first time, six months ago, she was quite naked. Nothing set her apart from the savages. But this morning she was wearing a dress . . . well, the memory of a dress, as she was yesterday, with her hair approximately braided. It was as if she had come over to our side. And yet she declined to join us. How do you explain this?"

Darwin hesitated, and stroked his mustache. He did not like to contradict himself. He would never write down the words he was about to utter. There is no trace of them in his records.

"Indeed I have considered it. All other things being equal, she was of finer stuff than her sisters, and most particularly less frightened by the white man. Or rather truly attracted . . . And she proved it. I believe that that is what she was trying to remind us of—a kind of physical loyalty. She had no wish to go with us. She would like us to return. By us, I mean white men, who come here without females. Now that is utterly astonishing: I believe it is a case of the intuitive reasoning of a woman choosing her own ground and her own weapons! Only here can she seduce. She awaits us."

The captain protested. His whole intelligence rebelled.

"Seduce?"

"There is no other word in English."

"Astounding!"

"Astounding indeed," agreed Darwin.

★   ★   ★

Waka the younger did not wait long. For the past few years whalers had begun to ply the Strait and the coast of Tierra del Fuego, following the great whale down the maze of channels. It was a Nantucket schooner that found Fuegia Virgin standing outside her wigwam on her deserted beach. Womanless for half a year, the big Yankees watched her run to the water's edge, shouting "I love you, Wilfred, I love you!" She stank of rum and seal blubber. A windfall. Reverend Watkin's civilizing mission bore instant fruit. Fuegia changed names again. Christened "I-love-you-Wilfred" by her first admirers, she went from crew to crew, from schooner to schooner, drunk from morning till night, scattering the bounty of her charms and the pox she contracted on her second whaling season. She would die of it on the fifteenth, the disease gnawing through to her brain, an abandoned pillar of salt on that same beach at Cape Anxious, where the chapel had finally rotted away and the flesh of the man she loved had finally dissolved: *"Tsochak tyako,* I opened my thighs."

Reverend Watkin's dictionary was piously received by the clergymen of the Patagonian Missionary Society. They put it out on special paper guaranteed against the damp as a vade mecum for the missionaries who would snatch up the torch on the illusion-fraught quest to further the conquests of the Dead-Dead Man. The results would be disastrous. Like the whole of this absurd mission, they would teem with contradictions.

And Lafko?

He did not remember that he had killed.

He was himself again.

Pushing his canoe to the water's edge, he merely said:

"Arka! Up! We must go . . ."

CHAPTER NINE

ALACALUF

The vise tightened.

A little more than a hundred years now stood between them and extinction. They were, of course, unaware of it, except perhaps as a sad resignation, beyond their understanding, that slowly permeated their campsites. Less singing, less miming. They stopped painting their bodies. The clans dispersed down the length of the great Strait from Cape Froward to the Messier Channel. Their canoes made short forays around their campsites but never put any great distance between themselves and the wigwams. Mass gatherings of the clans were now rare; when they did congregate it was more often to loot a wreck or get dead drunk than to celebrate life around a beached whale carcass. Although unable to reckon their numbers, they sensed that they were fewer, and this awareness deepened their dejection. Their nomadic instincts weakened. The energy that had once driven them on long expeditions — to collect eggs, for example, on the rocks of the Pacific shore, or to hunt cormorant on the cliffs of the Otway Sea — now barely sufficed to take them across the bows of the strangers' ships, which came through in greater numbers every year. On these occasions their vitality was intense.

140

If not already stark naked they stripped to excite curiosity and stimulate compassion. They waved, showed off their women, and revived their talent for mime to indicate their hunger. The strait echoed to their pathetic appeals. They no longer shouted "Pektchévés" as they once had done, but called out the word "Alacaluf! Alacaluf!" over and over again. In the language of the Kaweskar, it meant: "Give! Give me! Give me something, Stranger, *now!*" in tones somewhere between whining and demanding. After "Savages," after "Pécherais," this would be their final name. They never had another. But men's judgment of them did not change.

They were surrounded.

From the north, through the Messier Channel, in ever greater numbers, came seal-killers from Chiloé, the dreaded *loberos*. Six armed men in a rowboat would land and set up a hunting camp; they were kept supplied by an unending stream of schooners that picked up thousands of flayed, salted, and casked sealskins and thousands of newborn pelts. The offspring of white men and of Chono Indians—the same Chonos who had pushed the weak and timid Kaweskar into these frozen solitudes thousands of years ago—they despised the Alacalufs, except for their women and their youths. Pitiless brutes and drunkards. The Alacalufs hated them, and yet . . . They flocked in, dazzled, blinded, mesmerized by the abundance of wealth overflowing from the hunting camps. There were articles of every kind, limitless alcohol, and a different kind of food for which they were developing a taste. First they tried stealing. They were slaughtered. They came back. The *loberos* took their women and press-ganged their boys to row their boats and perform the hardest tasks. Still they came back, giving up all they possessed, their otter-skin capes, their nutria cloaks, in exchange for ragged ponchos or threadbare blankets in which they shivered all night long. Cheated but satisfied, they dug in, setting up their wigwams beside the *lobero* camps. The People became slaves. They worked. All day long they skinned seals and hunted for the *loberos,* in exchange for flour cakes, potatoes, onions, and fig "coffee." In the evenings there was alcohol, which mowed them down in their wigwams while the *loberos* amused themselves with their women. When they finally escaped, sobered, themselves again, their numbers barely sufficient to handle the heavy oars of the canoes, terrorized by Ayayema who came every night to count off the dead in their dreams, they were permanently scarred by the experience. When the new year began they returned. Thus, year by year, the *loberos* devoured them. And there was worse — the fate later meted out to them by a new race of half-breeds, of their own blood this time, who led the life of the *loberos* and pursued the Alacalufs with implacable hatred . . .

In the south, the whalers.

Here their reception was less inhuman, but the damage was no less severe. These seafaring men were generous. They paid well for the women they bought — good steel axes, knives, old guns (the first to appear in the clans' canoes). Admittedly, the seamen pitched in to pay group rates, one woman for the port watch, one for starboard. And you could not really call it purchase, but rather mutually acceptable compensation. The women came aboard willingly, but their husbands and fathers had to be paid off. It simply replaced the "permission" the males of the clans asked one another before exchanging their females — who were invariably consenting. In dealings with white men, the custom had a price tag, but it was still the same custom: The women took the initiative.

Here we have to think back to Wauda, wife of Lafko, and her first sight of Magellan's ships. Not a single woman on board! *Akwal*, many, many white men, their gazes converging on her, yelling wildly, shouting male propositions whose meaning was easy to guess, some of them going so far as to lower their breeches and threaten her with their penises . . . She had screamed in terror, yet at the same time the warmth in her belly told her that the Pektchévés were men and that they needed women, and that one day Wauda and her sisters, Yerfa, Waka and Kostora, Aksa, Kyewa and Kala, would open their thighs for them because they were more numerous and stronger, and because you did not resist life. And that was exactly what had happened. At first the fathers and husbands had opposed it, concealing the youngest of the women whenever a ship appeared, making them hide in the forests or among the rocks if the strangers came ashore. Sometimes they even fought and died with their slings in their hands, but with the growing and contradictory feeling that they were drawing closer to the Pektchévés because the latter had a taste for their women. In the end they gave up; they even began to look on the women who fell into the white men's hands as a sort of bridge or link, the only one that hoisted them across the invisible abyss to the height of the Pektchévés. Of course it was an illusion. With their women, life left them. In the south, too, the clans withered and perished.

Well treated aboard the whalers, many of these women never came back. Some, like Fuegia, ended tragically. The hydrographic vessel *Almirante Hohenlo,* of the Chilean Navy, laying the Strait's very first marker buoys around 1870, came across a number of these luckless women who had died several years earlier on deserted beaches. Was their name Kala, or Kyewa? They were the end of their line, the break in the long genetic chain. Since Chileans are devout folk, they buried the corpses under wooden crosses with these words branded on them: *Unidentified Alacaluf Woman.* Other women were luckier. Arriving in Punta Arenas, the only township in the Strait and, after 1860, the provincial capital, they were taken in by the missions after their "campaigns" aboard the whalers; if necessary they were given medical attention; and then they were fed into the local pool of ready-made spouses for the very first immigrants, lumberjacks and gold prospectors, mainly Yugoslav and of a peculiarly Balkan savagery. They adapted unflinchingly. These women too were lost to the clans. And then there was Yerfa, Yerfa the younger, but she was a rare case. She fell among Frenchmen, good fellows in the main, but serving under a very wicked skipper, an utterly loathesome, rapacious man, who took her all the way back to Paris in 1878, where . . .

But let us return to 1870.

Since the development of steam, traffic through the Strait had accelerated. The ships belched out black smoke but were unafraid of the williwaws, those brutal, unpredictable shifts of wind and current. Only the vagueness of contemporary charts perpetuated the work of death that had made the Strait of Magellan the biggest ships' graveyard in the world. There were losses of men and belongings, of ships impaled on rocks, but the majority of vessels got through; they were coalers for the most part, with a few yachts belonging to millionaires, and a regular passenger liner sailing four times a year between Europe and Valparaiso. All these ships stopped at the Charles Islands, or farther on at Providence Island if weather permitted, or at any rate they slowed down. The Charles Islands, in the middle of the Strait, marked the confluence of the Barbara Channel, which petered out into the labyrinths of Clarence Island, and the narrow twisting channel that empties into the Otway Sea. The Skyring Sea and the northerly waterway leading up to the Messier Channel mingle at Providence Island. In these two places, under snow, rain, and hail, the canoes would lie in wait for the ships. There the last of the clans hung on, at midpoint between north and south, where the two faces of death watched for them.

The scene never varied, but there was not one visitor during this period who did not retain a harrowed memory of it, or who did not describe it in emotion-filled terms.

In this last third of the nineteenth century, the Alacalufs were not very different from those Magellan had first encountered. They still smeared their bodies with the seal blubber that protected them from the cold more effectively than the European castoffs tossed in their direction; they wore these only out of vanity, to resemble the strangers. They retained not a word of any of the languages (usually English and Spanish) they heard. Still fascinated by mirrors, buttons, and beads, and now by matches, which they struck by the boxful, like children, they had no interest at all in the smoke from the ships' stacks, the noise and vibration of the engines, the oil lamps, the steam winches, and other refinements they understood no better than they had earlier understood the principle of sail. They were men of the remote Stone Age. The hawser thrown down to them so that they could tie up alongside accomplished a trajectory of thousands of years in a single second. Whence no doubt the emotion that overcame even the most hardened travelers.

Their reception varied from ship to ship, but it was rarely ill-natured. People might have been entertained by them, but they did not lose their sense of compassion. For steamship passengers, it was at once a distraction and a good deed. They entertained the savages in the ship's dining room and served them plates of meat and bread. It was hilarious to see them sitting naked on chairs, stuffing food into their mouths with their fingers, and rejecting water for wine, which they guzzled down straight from the bottle; but at least it was good to see them eat their fill, poor devils! The ladies dabbed at the corners of their eyes. The powerful odor of their guests was somewhat reminiscent of a circus. It too was part of the show. Then they were led into the stateroom. There, amid the red plush and the upholstered sofas and the elegant passengers, people whispered, "My God, how ugly they are!" Someone would sit down at the piano, for these globetrotters knew, like Shakespeare, that "music soothes the savage breast." It was always the hit of the evening: One of the savages would poke his head into the instrument to see if there was anyone inside; when he found nobody there he looked so baffled the passengers almost died of mirth. Next they were led, hand in hand, into a dance. A farandole with the savages was one of the star attractions of the Cunard South America Line. Passengers and savages mingled freely, one naked, one dressed, and everybody madly gay; but clearly no one realized that the Alacalufs were *miming* gaiety, which they never expressed in this manner—and besides, they were far from feeling gay. Why should they be? No one knew what they were feeling: a break in the crushing unconscious boredom of a life that had lost all meaning upon contact with the strangers. But the passengers honestly believed they had brought a little joy into the lives of these poor people . . . When it was all over, they had to be pushed outside. On deck bartering began. Tobacco and liquor were the strongest currencies. The savages could not resist them, handing over their females' button necklaces in exchange for four packets of tobacco, although they had earlier acquired the necklaces in exchange for the otter and nutria skins that were their only clothing, or even for their women. The passengers also gave them gifts—"Alacaluf! Alacaluf!"—empty food cans, a few loaves, a bottle . . . Everyone rushed off to rummage through his trunks. As the savages pushed off in their canoes, old trousers, torn waistcoats, battered hats, and outmoded dresses rained down on them.

Then came the moment of separation.

As the canoe moved slowly away from the ship's towering hull, everyone would hang over the railings. Its size seemed ridiculous, dwarfed by the hostility of the elements. The passengers fell silent. They saw that they had laughed too much and that they should not have laughed so much. With powerful sweeps of their oars the savages headed back for the shore of pain. Children were sitting at the bottom of the canoe, crouched over a feeble wood fire that gave off more smoke than heat under the whirling snow. The passengers could hardly tear their eyes away. At that moment the Indians' eyes held an unbearable animal melancholy. Then the invisible thread snapped. It snapped without a sound—unless it was the sound in the bottom of everyone's heart as the tumult triggered by the fission of time broke forth.

On board that night, with the ship moored in icy, impenetrable darkness, they would return to the subject. The captain would bring his rolled-up charts and old logbooks down to the stateroom. He would tell them he thought that the number of canoes he met was dwindling each year. Everyone followed the canoes' presumed migration on the chart: Last Hope Bay, Cape Anxious, Desolation Island, Port Famine, the Western and Eastern Furies, Cape of Storms, Sadness Island . . . They would drink more than usual—Dutch gin, flaming punch—as the wind howled outside and they tried vainly to wipe out the image of the lone canoe they had watched fading from sight, an image that remained imprinted on the sea after the canoe had disappeared.

★   ★   ★

In the wigwam, Lafko was thinking.

Taw, his old father, was dead, and it was now Taw, his son, who slept squeezed between two dogs. Taw was ten. He had neither brothers nor sisters. His mother Wauda had grown old when she was taken by *loberos* shortly after Taw's birth. They had kept her for a moon. Then she had escaped. Since then she whimpered in her sleep and awoke with no relief from her pain. Yet Lafko had blown on that pain. Every morning he knotted the shaman's headband of white down around his forehead. With thumb and forefinger he pinched the skin of Wauda's stomach; then, holding her pain in his fingers, he raised it to his mouth and blew as hard as he could to scatter the pain in the air and send it away on the wind. But his medicine was powerless. They had abandoned Wauda, who belonged to Ayayema.

Lafko was thinking. How many moons was it since he had last heard from Petayem in his camp at Mount Sarmiento? From Tereskat whose camp was on the islands of the Skyring Sea? And from Kyewaytçaloes, who used to come down from the far reaches of the Otway Sea every summer for the great gathering on the Charles Islands? Smoke signals were rare nowadays: You no longer saw them beyond the midpoint of the Strait, where they linked the clan of Lafko with Yuras's clan, then Yuras with Tchakwal, then Tchakwal with Kyasto, then Kyasto with Yatse — and then when Yatse lit his fire, no one answered from the south, just as no one answered Lafko from the north.

Lafko was thinking. Kostora the younger, wife of Yannoek, had two children. Kostora the elder had borne four. Many children died these days. *Akwal,* many. An unknown sickness prowled the wigwams. They had to change beaches often to try and shake off the evil, but Ayayema always found them again, and again pointed to the path of evil. Poor Lafko. He did not understand. Kyewa the younger had disappeared. She would give Kanstay no more children. Kala's baby had not lived, but her belly was round again. Waka's belly was also round. Lafko said they must leave; they had tobacco, liquor, new axes, knives, iron harpoons, pointed nails to tip their javelins. He said that the babies that were coming must be born in the land where whales beached themselves, where the waters of the ocean surged up the Barbara Channel. There would be time to return later, but not until the children had eaten their fill of whale meat. In the wigwam everyone sniffed at the forgotten smell of dead whale.

Next morning they lit a big fire on the closest hill. Who would go with Lafko? Who wanted to smell the smell of life again, to sleep the sleep of the well-fed with stomach full to bursting, to hear the singing around the butchered carcass, the children so sleek with fat they played in the icy water like seals, the women with taut glowing skin as snug as dogs in the wigwams? Who would go? Only one smoke column replied: Yatse. The others preferred to beg aboard the white men's ships. "Alacaluf! Alacaluf! Give! Give me! Give me something now, Stranger!"

Two canoes.

Life began again. They sang as they rowed. Yerfa the younger sang the song of the whale, of Palpal the parrot, of Yasoep the great owl, as well as a new song, Tobacco, that made everyone in the canoe laugh: *"Tcoema tcoema kurkwelak alacaluf yekasaka kyelol,* I have run out of tobacco, give me yours or I will steal it . . ."

Lafko gazed at Yerfa the younger, who had just had her first blood and who lay beside him in the wigwam, for Wauda was no longer with them. They had abandoned her to her dreams, to her nightly whimpering that chilled the clan with terror. She would soon die. She was *already* dead.

Today a pale sun bathed the dark forests and made the glaciers glow. Even the wind had dropped. In pristine solitude the canoes slid over calm water as still and transparent as emerald. The first days of man had returned. Countless gulls, terns, and cormorants wheeled and shrieked over a small island where a dark bulk lay. The smell reaching them told them the whale was still edible. They were happy. Of course, they could not tell each other so. There was no word for that in the language of the Alacalufs. They merely said, "We are no longer dying, we are alive."

Their happiness endured for the three moons that came before the long night. Then a vessel came into view, a dirty gray schooner with an auxiliary steam engine; her fishing season was done, and to avoid rounding Cape Horn she was steaming up the

Cockburn Channel toward the great Strait, following the course
originally plotted by the *Beagle* and now marked on all the charts.
But Lafko did not know this. The strangers' ships never used
these waters. This ship was *La Destinée* out of St.-Malo, Captain
Courvalec in command.

It was destiny indeed that led Captain Courvalec to moor off
Fitz Roy Island one night, at the crossroads of the Cockburn,
Barbara, and Magdalen Channels. The island had no name for
Lafko. It was there he had camped. Later, when he was talking
about it, he would say: "The island where I lost Yerfa, and
Kostora, and Yannoek, and also old Tsefayok, taken away by the
Pektchévés . . ."

And he would add, in horror: "We had eaten and eaten, we
were no longer dying, we were alive . . ." He knew no word to
express the injustice of fate. *Akwal,* many, *akwal aswal yerfalay,*
many suns and many moons, Yerfa would never return . . .

CHAPTER TEN

THE CANNIBALS OF
THE GOOD SHIP
JUNON

Monsieur Gaston Lemay was a happy man. It had been years since he recalled having even one day spoiled by any of life's large or small inconveniences. He was at peace with himself—the essential thing for a self-centered bachelor. He lived on a private income on the Rue de l'Evêché, in Carpentras, with his aged housekeeper, on the second floor of a private town house overlooking a shady garden. He played whist on Monday, billiards on Wednesday, set Thursday aside for walking, Friday for going the rounds of a number of specialist bookshops in Avignon, Saturday for visiting friends, Sunday evening for entertaining guests to supper, and the rest of the time shut away in his study with its walls lined with travelers' tales. He planned to write a great work devoted to the French travelers and explorers of his century; everyone in town spoke of it with deference. A work so monumental it would never see the light of day. He knew it. Whenever he began to annotate one of the books in his prized collection — just at present the complete works of Monsieur Alcide d'Orbigny, Patagonian explorer, 1802–1857 — he was carried away by his reading; he at once stopped working and began to dream of distant lands. Monsieur Gaston Lemay was also the special

150

correspondent of *Le Temps,* a member of the Académie of Vaucluse (whose meetings he graced with his presence and erudition), of the Geographic Society of Paris (whither he repaired twice a year to drink at the fountain of knowledge), and above all (his special glory, the bedrock of his reputation) the author of a book recently published by the Parisian publisher Charpentier: *Aboard the Junon, Account of a Voyage from Marseille to Valparaiso via the Strait of Magellan,* previously published in excerpt form by *Le Temps.*

For although at peace with himself, Monsieur Gaston Lemay was not unadventurous. Though of placid habits, he was no stay-at-home. He too had traveled. Of Mediterranean origin, he had a taste for cold climates and desolate ocean wastes. He knew the North Cape, Iceland, Newfoundland, and St. Pierre and Miquelon off the North American coast. He was a collector of the earth's last frontiers — provided they were suitably frozen, sinister, and deserted. And in this respect he had been admirably served aboard the *Junon* in 1876. To the shareholder-passengers on the venture — they had included a photographer, a professor of natural history, a pharmacist, a Belgian baron, and a special correspondent for *Le Temps* (Monsieur Gaston Lemay in person) — the Strait of Magellan had put on one of its most tumultuously Wagnerian extravaganzas, including the irruption of naked savages, hideously ugly, primitive, and cannibalistic to boot. *Cannibals:* He had said so in his book, even though he had not personally witnessed scenes of cannibalism. He had borrowed the terrible term from Darwin, who had it from Cook, who in turn had it from Byron, who had seen the Alacalufs devour an old woman one hundred and forty years earlier. But no one had ever wondered whether this odious gastronomic proclivity, which they accepted as unquestioned fact, might not have been lost over the course of the years. He had written of this encounter, of this straddling of the centuries, with discretion and with the white man's sense of superiority tempered by tolerance. To be sure, he had judged them brutes "justly relegated by Darwin to the lowest rung of the human species," but he had also allowed them "a mixture of mindless good humor and unexpected delicacy of feeling." These "poor devils of cannibals" had come to beg and dance aboard the *Junon*. They had fed them on sardines, of which they were inordinately fond. There were two young women with "quite voluptuous bosoms," round, fleshy, flat faces, and low foreheads beneath bushy hair; there was also a young man with "fine teeth," and others who were most ugly and most dirty, as well as one old man quite horrible to behold: He had been given an old white tropical suit and preened around the stateroom in it, stuffing hands still covered with sardine fragments into the pockets, "even happier than if he had dined off a European — a supposition his age rendered quite probable." The *Junon*'s voyage was supposedly scientific in its aims. While the others amused the savages with a watch whose ticking intrigued them, the professor of natural history examined their jaws, measured their skulls, prodded their limbs; "and I have no doubt," concluded Monsieur Gaston Lemay of the Paris Geographic Society, "that they took this scientific probing as a mark of friendship, for their facial contortions announced that they were smiling amiably . . ."

Aboard the Junon had enjoyed a modest success accompanied by flattering reviews and a medal from the Geographic Society. And yet, on this morning of August, 1878, opening the copy of *Le Temps* his housekeeper had just brought him, Monsieur Gaston Lemay suddenly encountered one of those contrarieties of conscience he had so long been spared. He could not yet define it — a twinge of remorse, a sinking of the heart, a disagreeable sense of unwitting complicity . . . In an advertisement on page 2 he read:

CANNIBALS AT THE
PARIS UNIVERSAL EXPOSITION

Since the Universal Exposition, pride and glory of our City of Light, opened its doors to visitors flocking from all Europe to admire the wonders of the Fairy Electricity, there has been an exhibit at the Exposition Park on the Champ-de-Mars that must be seen by all desirous of measuring the enormous progress accomplished by civilized peoples, in contrast with the night of savagery in which so many other peoples still toil.

Monsieur Maurice, whale hunter, explorer, animal-tamer, has brought back from his latest foray into icy southern seas a complete family of cannibals from Tierra del Fuego. He has put them on public view in a marquee, enclosed for the safety of visitors in a large cage. These savages go unclothed, eat their own lice, speak a guttural language akin to the barking of dogs, and when in good spirits paint themselves red. Monsieur Maurice feeds them twice daily on raw horse meat, whose taste is apparently close to that of the human flesh that forms their diet in the deserted reaches of the Strait of Magellan. A lesson taken from life for the edification of young and old. Entrance fee: 50 centimes. The visitor is staggered at the notion that these wretches belong to the human species.

Running his finger under his collar to give himself air, Monsieur Lemay reread this venal, pimping prose, deploring (not for the first time) the introduction of advertisements in publications as respectable as *Le Temps*. But had he not expressed himself last year, in the columns of this same journal — more elegantly, of course, but in almost identical terms — on the subject of these savages? His palms grew moist. His heart was visited by an ache whose causes he could now identify only too precisely. He knew how he had sinned: through lack of scientific rigor. How much time had he spent in the Strait? Four days and a few hours. How many opportunities had he had to observe these savages at close range? Just two. First a canoe to which they had tossed some old clothes, then another that had come alongside for a brief shipboard visit. Monsieur Lemay had embellished, waxed droll, camouflaged the brevity of his study in the authoritative sweep of his comments. Were these poor Alacalufs really as savage as he had claimed? He was no longer so sure. Were they not unhappy rather than savage, and was their stupidity not simply a product of their ignorance and poverty? Savage? That pathetic naked girl fingering her necklace of red beads and casting looks of scared submission at the *Junon*'s male passengers? Ugly, dirty, malodorous, without the slightest shame, probably of primitive amorality — but savage, had he any right to make such a claim?

What did he know of this woman's thoughts as he stood there judging her? She had brown eyes that were almost beautiful, slightly bulging, and narrowing toward the temples; there was softness in her gaze, softness and much sadness.

Monsieur Gaston Lemay removed some photographs from a drawer and spread them out on his desk. They had been taken aboard the *Junon*. There he was — ludicrous, capering around the stateroom table between the girl with the soft eyes and the young man with fine teeth, although Monsieur Lemay never danced, at Carpentras or anywhere else! A grotesque scene that had made his friends laugh, the way everyone, savages and white men alike, had laughed aboard the *Junon*. How could they know what that laughter really meant to these unhappy creatures exhibiting themselves in exchange for a plate of sardines?

Monsieur Lemay was no longer laughing. Opening his own book and the excerpts from *Le Temps* of which he was so proud, he reread himself with horror. He had behaved, literally, just like this Monsieur Maurice who was exhibiting his "cannibal" troupe on the Champ-de-Mars. He had not deserved his medal from the Geographic Society! Behind a glib screen of words he had engendered contempt, hardness of heart, derision. He could already hear the stupid comments, the coarse laughter, the malevolent barbs of the public in this Monsieur Maurice's marquee. He pictured the poor Indians exposed to the witticisms of the proletariat in the heart of Paris. Into what abyss of desolation were his tragic "dancer's" eyes now gazing as she squatted behind the bars of her cage, confronted, like her companions, with the inconceivable — for Monsieur Lemay did not doubt for a second that these people were Alacalufs . . .

Utterly crushed, Monsieur Gaston Lemay forgot to be selfish. His own shame had run him to earth. This man, who had never shown the slightest real solicitude for his neighbor, was overcome by pity. This quite novel emotion galvanized him. He made up his mind. He rang for his housekeeper.

"Pray pack my bag, Madame Louise. I still have time to catch the eleven-forty-five express to Paris."

★   ★   ★

Toward noon next day, after a twelve-hour journey, he dropped
his bag off at the Hotel de Suède on the Rue des Saints-Pères,
not far from the Geographic Society's headquarters on the Boulevard Saint-Germain. As he washed and spruced himself up, he
pondered the situation. Should he not expose the facts to the
Society's president, Monsieur Poivre de la Mirmande, dis-
tinguished entomologist, member of the French Institute?
Something warned him to proceed with caution. That grand old
lady, the Institute, and its president, Dumont d'Urville, did not
welcome waves — particularly if they originated in the provinces.
There could be unpleasant repercussions. Better to move dis-
creetly at first. There would be plenty of time to decide what
steps to take once the true facts were established.

Monsieur Lemay swallowed a hurried lunch on the terrace of a
crowded café. All Paris was out on the streets, along with throngs
of out-of-towners. The weather was magnificent. The sun shone
down, high in the heavens and warm. The sun, a star unknown
in the Strait of Magellan. How were these unhappy Alacalufs,
torn from their frozen solitudes, enduring the sun, the heat, the
polluted air, the crowds? Monsieur Lemay felt the call to arms.
He quickly finished his meal, grew impatient, waved frantically
for his check. As soon as he had paid, he hailed a cab.

"To the Exposition, coachman! And quickly, if you please. I
am in a hurry."

"In a hurry, he says!" grumbled the driver. "Every boulevard is
clogged. The Republic, my good sir, is playing host to a king a
day. And the people love it! The idiots . . . Today it's the King of
Württemberg."

At the Invalides they were stopped by a line of uniformed
constables. The Esplanade was thronged with armed troops.
Generals in gold braid and cocked hats galloped at the head of
their squadrons. Drums rolled. The King of Württemberg sailed
by in an open carriage, handsome as a demigod in his sky-blue
uniform. Beside him sat a radiant young woman as fair-haired as
the spring, with round bare arms and slender white-gloved

hands, smiling and waving graciously to the crowd. Shouts of
"Bravo!" and of "Long live the queen!" rose from the packed
ranks of applauding onlookers. And there was no denying that
the young woman gliding behind the trotting horses was as
beautiful as a dream. Monsieur Lemay thought of the female
savage, squat, hirsute, thick-lipped, with greasy yellow skin,
black, broken nails, and grime-encrusted feet. Some of his fellow
passengers on the *Junon* had mockingly addressed drawing-room
gallantries to her, even going so far as to bow gravely before the
poor creature as if she had been a visiting princess. That too he
had recorded. A scene not to be missed — and he had not missed
it! Now he blushed at the memory, looking with a kind of
loathing at the blonde fairy-tale creature sanctified and surrounded by a cloud of aides recruited from France's pampered
youth . . .

"The idiots . . ." Monsieur Lemay said in his turn.

To himself he added: "God is not just." And God, who saw all
and knew all, even though Monsieur Lemay did not believe in
His existence, smiled an understanding smile as He murmured
among the clouds: "Not just? Me? Wait until Judgment Day!
They will see!"

The gates opened and the crowds flocked in. The cab dropped
Monsieur Lemay at the main gate of the Exposition. Nothing in
the florid spectacle interested him. Turning his back on the twin
minarets of the Trocadéro Palace; ignoring the Gallery of Industry, where dazzled visitors could watch the manufacture of car-
riages, of electric light bulbs, of textiles, of guns, and where all
kinds of shiny machinery clattered busily; disdaining the cafés
and the pleasure gardens; jostled by the Parisian mob, surely one
of the worst-behaved in existence, he finally reached a village of
fairground marquees where the sideshows were on view. Grotesquely dressed barkers bellowed and gesticulated on stands in
front of each tent: "The headless woman!" "Siamese twins — and
deadly enemies!" He went from stand to stand. Everything
appalled him. The base mob could take its pick . . . and it did
just that. The more lurid the barker's description, the more
eagerly it shoved forward. "The duck-boy, with webbed hands

and feet, housed in an aquarium . . . The ferocious Bulgarian dwarfs . . . The wolf-man — with a wolf's muzzle, ladies and gentlemen: He drinks only blood! . . . And an unforgettable spectacle, not recommended for sensitive stomachs, the wild cannibals of Tierra del Fuego!" There they were, the unhappy Alacalufs, thrown in with fairground freaks and the scum of the earth!

There was an eager crowd in front of the tent. Children itching to get inside tugged at their parents' hands. Children did not have sensitive souls. It would be a mistake to think so. Cruelty and treachery were their two most natural inclinations. Children were monsters. Indeed this was the chief reason Monsieur Lemay had never married.

Tickets were being sold at the window of a small wooden booth by a middle-aged man with a brick-red complexion, small, green, spiteful eyes, and crow's feet wrinkles fanning out to his temples, like someone whose profession had exposed him to many years of bright sunlight. He had enormous hands with sausagelike fingers he was unable to straighten fully, like those of the *Junon*'s oldest seamen who had spent their whole lives hauling on hemp ropes. But he used them very skillfully to make little piles of change; his face expressed a hideous satisfaction. Business was booming . . .

A ticket cost ten sous. Monsieur Lemay paid and went inside. Bleachers rose in a circle around a big iron cage like a circus lion enclosure, its floor strewn with straw and sawdust. At the back of the cage was a long, low cabin of rough logs, with openings at ground level; it looked more like a kennel than the circular sealskin wigwams Monsieur Lemay had glimpsed from afar on the shores of the Strait of Magellan.

Monsieur Maurice — for such was the "animal-tamer's" name — entered the cage with a kind of trident in his hand. He was the one who had been calling up the crowds on the stand outside. Although got up to resemble a deep-sea fisherman, with thick sweater and coarse blue canvas pants stuck into rubber boots, he was clearly a fairground professional. Curiously, he was wearing a gray derby. A sailor this scoundrel had never been. He had neither the gait, nor the hands, nor the eyes; whereas that other one, the ticket seller . . .

"Ladies and gentlemen," Monsieur Maurice began in booming tones, striking just the right note of braggadocio, "when I was hunting the white whale through the outermost reaches of Patagonia, and the ship under my command dropped anchor for the night, savages would approach us in canoes, silent as shadows, stealing aboard to attack my crew in their sleep and carry them off to their lairs, where they wolfed them down raw! I lost several men that way, in circumstances so horrible I'll leave them to your imagination . . ."

Monsieur looked at the crowd around him. Big and small, they were riveted in horror, petrified in their pleasure, already relishing the abomination they pictured crouching inside the log cabin. It was true that when they were at their night moorings aboard the *Junon* they had followed the advice which the Punta Arenas harbormaster gave all foreign skippers, cruelly spreading carpet tacks on the decks to discourage the savages from their larcenous errands. (Unless of course they were trying to set fire to the ship with torches — this had happened twice in the space of twenty years — an ultimate act of war on the part of these wretches.) But devouring seamen — never! Once again Monsieur Lemay was ashamed of the part he had played in suggesting such a thing . . .

"So I set a trap for them," Monsieur Maurice went on. "We captured a whole family. Justly enraged, my crew was all for slaughtering them. But I am not a savage! I spared their lives. Since my ship had to return to St.-Malo without stopping at any port of call in between, I was obliged to bring them back with me. They are henceforth at the service of science. Our greatest minds have pondered their case — in vain. For my part, I did my best during our long return passage to inculcate some rudiments of civilization into them. Alas, ladies and gentlemen — but judge for yourselves . . . Let the show begin!"

Necks craned. Malicious barbs rose to a hundred lips. Stupidity waxed within the spectators' skulls. Monsieur Lemay shrank. He would have given everything he owned for the "savages" to turn out to be imposters.

"Since these savages have no names," Monsieur Maurice went on, "and do not appear to use names among themselves; and since when all is said and done it would be improper to give them Christian names, I have baptized them First, Second, Third, and Fourth — for there are four of them, ladies and gentlemen, four cannibals from Tierra del Fuego! And here comes the first of them — Mister First!"

No one emerged from the cabin.

"He is a little old and deaf," the despicable Monsieur Maurice explained. "We shall have to shout louder. Come on, children, give me a hand! Mis-ter First! Mis-ter First!"

The children? Everyone yelled! It was a Punch-and-Judy exercise in degradation. Suddenly the yelling stopped. From one of the openings in the kennel-like cabin a living form emerged on all fours, its white hair trailing to the ground. It was a man, an old, old man. He struggled upright and stood shakily on short bowlegs. Apart from a loincloth flapping around his thighs, he was naked, and heartbreakingly thin. His yellow skin was lifeless, dry, hatched with wrinkles deep as wounds, so clearly auguring death that Monsieur Lemay realized how vital to the health of these savages was the stinking seal fat with which they covered themselves. For he had recognized beyond all doubt — he had the photograph on his person — the old man they put into a white suit in the *Junon*'s stateroom. Through his slanting Indian eyes the poor man — who had been called Tsefayok when he was free — looked uncomprehendingly at the sea of strange white faces beyond the bars of this inexplicable cage. Monsieur Lemay, in his turn, was going through his own baptism of distress. Although he had not wept for forty years, although he had not wept since the small sorrows of childhood, he now wiped away a tear that trickled down his cheek.

"Mister First," Monsieur Maurice announced triumphantly, "was already born when the explorer Darwin undertook to study Tierra del Fuego's savage cannibals. In other words, this cannibal alone must have gobbled down the equivalent of several ship's companies . . ."

There were horrified oohs and ahs, mingled with some nervous laughter. Flushed with excitement, small boys nudged each other violently in the ribs. Little girls licked their lips, their venomous tongues flickering out between sharp teeth.

"Mister First, pay your respects to the ladies and gentlemen!"

The wretch made no move, but just stood there, arms dangling, swaying as if he was about to fall. Monsieur Maurice struck the ground with his trident.

"Mister First! You are in France now, home of good manners! Pay your respects!" insisted the vile Monsieur Maurice.

Was he about to goad him, the way a tamer goads a recalcitrant wild animal? Monsieur Lemay shuddered, fighting to hold back his indignation, his anger, his despair. From one of the bleachers came a timid protest: "That's enough!"

It was immediately drowned by yells of "Mis-ter First! Pay your respects!" The dissenting voice had been the sole hint of a human soul in this whole Parisian crowd. "An unhoped-for percentage," Monsieur Lemay reflected grimly. Taking the old man's inert hand, Monsieur Maurice hoisted it in the air, like a referee after a fight. The hubbub died and the crowd, feeding on its own shame, vented it in a burst of coarse laughter, while "Mister Second" was called out to take a bow.

This was a much younger man, although he seemed just as bewildered as the first, and it was impossible to read his exact age in his sorrowful eyes. He too was naked apart from a loincloth, but his bones were perhaps a little better covered. That face, those flattened features, that shock of black hair beetling over his eyebrows, those teeth, still inexplicably healthy — Monsieur Lemay recognized the young man "with fine teeth" who had been so fond of sardines, and who had been called Yannoek in the days of his freedom. "Merciful heaven! A whole canoe!" Monsieur Lemay silently groaned. He noticed that Monsieur Maurice did not ask the young man to pay his respects to the crowd, but edged away a little and watched him out of the corner of his eye, exactly like a tamer wary of a vicious animal. The savage uttered an indistinct grunt — in fact he said "Pektchévés," the expression of all his woes — and came forward to grip the bars, causing the front row of spectators to start back in fear.

"Mister Second, sit!" shouted Monsieur Maurice, shaking his trident.

As if in a well-rehearsed scenario, "Mister Second" hesitated before complying, sending a thrill of anxious expectancy through the crowd. Finally, "Mister Second" sank grudgingly to his haunches, his chin on his chest, as if he was contemplating his toes. The crowd relaxed.

"And here is Madame Third!" bellowed the horrible Monsieur Maurice — and his triumphant tones told them this was the star attraction. "Madame Third," Monsieur Maurice went on, "is still a very young woman, but she possesses deadly powers of seduction. Observe her wide mouth, those thick, cruel lips. Like the praying mantis, she has consumed every one of her husbands . . . as well as quite a few seamen rash enough to approach her with amorous intent."

A shudder ran through the crowd. The gentlemen leaned forward for a closer look, some white as sheets, others brick-red as if on the point of suffocation, as a short, stocky girl crawled out of the cage. Her legs were crooked, her thighs heavy and bare under the loincloth that did nothing to conceal her sex, her long, thick, wild hair mantling the breasts everyone was craning (with what is known as "a stir in the audience") to see. Monsieur Maurice proudly waved his hand, in the gesture of a slave dealer showing off his wares.

"Up, if you please, Madame Third, so that we may view you in all your glory!"

As she rose her hair parted to reveal a large hanging bosom like two yellow leather gourds, so incongruous, so abnormally indecent under a ridiculous yellow bead necklace that, after a moment of amazement, the boys, and then the women, burst out laughing. The men quickly followed suit, their laughter a much greater relief to them than to the others. What could they have been imagining? Thank God she was not beautiful! She was even frankly repulsive by white men's standards of beauty. With her flat nose, her bestial face, she seemed only just a woman, a female, a cannibal from the frozen south, lower down the scale than a Negress from France's African colonies, a kind of human animal you could show off without embarrassment, without modesty, without any taint on your honor. Monsieur Lemay heard somebody shout, "Hey! She'd be better lying down!" which released gales of laughter. He stared at her unblinkingly, struggling by the intensity of his gaze to catch the "dancer's" vacant eyes — for this was the woman who had been called Yerfa the younger in the days of her freedom — and get her to recognize him so that he could give her at least a first sign of hope; he stared so hard and so raptly that his neighbor, a fat coarse featured man, gave him a nudge and a sly wink: "Monsieur fancies her, eh? Not too fussy for a man of Monsieur's age! My compliments!"

"And here is Madame Fourth!" Monsieur Maurice went on in his inimitable style.

In the days of her freedom she had been called Kostora. Kostora, wife of Yannoek. She was the other female savage Monsieur Lemay had held by the hand as he "danced" between these two women in the *Junon's* stateroom. "Madame Fourth" immediately scurried over to squat by "Mister Second," in the same woebegone posture.

"A lovely couple, are they not?" commented Monsieur Maurice, as the crowd hooted its mirth. "True love, you see!"

Now they roared out loud. What? These primitive creatures, these gross horrors, loved one another? Then something strangely out of character with the rest of the display occurred. "Mister Second" raised his head and shot the man with the trident a look suddenly alive with true human feeling — hatred. It lasted only a second, but long enough for Monsieur Maurice, surprised, to pretend to threaten Yannoek with his trident, adding hastily, in order to regain his hold over the audience:

"Upon my word, the animal is jealous! What could he be thinking? That we're going to take his woman? Well, ladies and gentlemen, I think I can say for all of us that we willingly surrender her to him!"

The words came out so spitefully that you could have sworn it was a confrontation in which the unfortunate female, crouching as still as a stone, was the stake. The crowd roared and stamped its feet in glee. Monsieur Maurice had carried it off well. The spectators applauded him furiously. Monsieur Lemay was not misled. He sensed a drama of unfathomable origins behind the strange scene. But the "show" was not over. Monsieur Maurice called for silence. What he had to say, he explained, was addressed exclusively to the gentlemen. An unforgettable experience. A leap into the world of the savage. A trip twenty thousand years back into the past . . .

"Come up, gentlemen, come on up!" he said. "Come and touch Madame Third. Come and feel the grain of her skin, as if you were feeling one of the first humans to walk this earth! Come and touch the wild hair of the wife of a prehistoric man! Just imagine — twenty thousand years separate you from this woman! But be warned! No intimacy! No hanky-panky! Unless you want to draw our lovely Madame Third's amorous thunder-bolts down on your head! And then I won't be held responsible! Who wants to try? Who wants a feel? Who'll do it? You, sir?"

In every crowd there is always someone stupid enough to debase himself publicly. A soldier shuffled up — pushed forward by his chums to yells of "Go, Marcel!" — and sheepishly acknowledged the crowd, fists clasped above his head like a boxer as he entered the cage. Yerfa the younger had not moved. She had not twitched a muscle since the beginning of this whole scene. She squatted as if walled in on herself. Nothing, absolutely nothing of what was going on had crossed the threshold of her mind. Without the nightly visits of the white man who had stolen her from Lafko, she would have forgotten that she was alive.

"Go on, Marcel! Tweak her pussy!" shouted one of the soldier's friends.

"Shame on you, Marcel!" shouted another.

"She'll bite your dick off, Marcel!" roared another.

From the midst of her offspring a mother protested: "There are kids here, you know!" But she made no move to leave her

seat, and her ugly little monsters did not miss a split second of
the performance.

Marcel hesitated. Did the idea that he was doing something
wrong penetrate his brain? Was it because there was no reproach
in "Madame Third's" empty eyes that he sensed, however dimly,
that he was dealing with a lost soul without either will or
awareness? Suddenly he wanted only one thing: to get out of
there fast. Salvaging his honor by giving the savage woman a slap
on the buttocks as if he was flattering a cow's backside (it seemed
to him the most decent thing he could do), he fled blushing,
head hung in shame, to the hoots and catcalls of his companions.

"Who else?" asked Monsieur Maurice. "Who else wants to feel
Madame Third? Nobody?"

Monsieur Gaston Lemay rose to his feet. His fat neighbor,
mopping his brow with a checkered handkerchief, shouted after
him: "Can't keep away, eh? Monsieur likes his meat gamey!
Ugghh!" Monsieur Lemay did not hear. He, the eminent special
correspondent of *Le Temps*, member of the worthy Geographic
Society, so in love with respectability that he had never in his life
dared cross the threshold of a house of ill-repute, was striding
resolutely toward the cage, risking reputation and honor, ignoring the converging stares of the crowd and the crude encouragements raining down from the back rows . . .

"Ah, now here's a gentleman who knows what he likes,"
commented the awful Monsieur Maurice as he eyed this dis-
tinguished apparition in gray overcoat and gloves, top hat and
cane. "Has he come to ask her hand in marriage?"

Then, as Monsieur Lemay took "Madame Third's" hand,
holding it a few seconds in his own and murmuring a few words
to her, he elaborated to the roars of the crowd:

"Yes, he has! Our heartiest congratulations, sir! What a lovely
couple you make! Our compliments!"

The crowd rocked. Yerfa the younger sifted through her memories. Where had she seen this stranger? Her memory finally
answered. The hand that now held hers for the second time was
not a hostile hand. *Akwal,* many, many moons had gone by . . .
She looked into the stranger's eyes, and Monsieur Lemay, a lump

in his throat, once again met the gentle brown gaze she had shown him on the *Junon,* a gaze filled with such limpid sadness that the crowd fell into embarrassed silence. "I will help you, do not lose heart," said Monsieur Lemay, knowing that he could not be understood — and Monsieur Lemay who did not believe in God found himself imploring the Most High for a little help in transmitting his message. He would receive it. God heard him.

Monsieur Maurice studied the pair with worried, wicked eyes. There was something going on here he did not understand. Hesitant, frustrated, the crowd was wavering. He had to regain control as quickly as possible. Pity was a rare emotion among Monsieur Maurice's customers, but it sometimes surfaced. Two of the savages had stood up and come over to join "Madame Third." Only the old man remained inert — the man who had been called Tsefayok; no recollection could pierce the fog of his memory.

"A big hand for the gentleman!" bawled Monsieur Maurice, at the same time gripping Monsieur Lemay firmly by the arm and bundling him out of the cage.

Monsieur Lemay offered no resistance. He had exhausted his courage. He merely muttered, "You are a miserable swine! Take your hands off me!" while the other man answered between clenched teeth in the same low voice, "I don't want to see your face around here again, understand, Mister?"

Monsieur Lemay returned to his seat. He had no idea how his legs carried him there. He had been rocked to the bottom of his soul. And what more must he now endure? The very worst!

"And now, ladies and gentlemen!" boomed Monsieur Maurice in triumph, "feeding-time for the cannibals! Rest assured, old and young — it is only horse meat. They gulp it down raw, it's all they'll eat."

A helper brought in a basket heaped with bloody fragments of meat, long badly cut strips with shreds of fat and sinew clinging to them. "Bountiful heaven!" thought Monsieur Lemay, "do they keep these wretches starved until this hour?" And indeed they hurled themselves on the meat with every appearance of hunger, ripping at it with fingers and teeth, blood dribbling from their mouths. The "dancer" no longer looked gentle. She ate, and it was horrible to see. Horrible too were the crowd's comments, as it took vindictive revenge for the flicker of humanity it had surprised in the poor woman's eyes a few moments earlier. Monsieur Lemay closed his own eyes, determined to see and hear no more. He did not open them again until the thunderous final applause and the departure of the spectators. The cage was empty. Monsieur Maurice towered over him threateningly.

"The show is over. Out!"

"Where are they?" asked Monsieur Lemay, who had recovered his self-control.

"Any business of yours?"

"Yes. I know these poor people. I met them two years ago in their homeland. They had a canoe, and children. I can testify to it. I have photographs."

"So what?"

"I shall file a complaint. I have connections. These poor folk will be handed over to people who care. I shall find a steamer sailing for Chile. They will return to their home."

The man cackled.

"By what right? I am a fairground entertainer. These people are my employees. I have papers in good order to prove it."

"You are lying!"

"Well, anyway, your friends aren't about to prove it!" the man said with a threatening laugh. "As for you — out! We'll help you to the door. Courvalec!"

Courvalec was the ticket seller, the ruffian with the enormous seaman's hands. He could have felled an ox with his fist. He grabbed the special correspondent of *Le Temps* by the scruff of his neck.

"What good will this do you?" Monsieur Lemay asked heroically. "I shall be back with the police. You would be wise to act reasonably!"

"Introduce me, Maurice," said the brute.

"My associate, Captain Courvalec, deep-sea fishing captain, retired."

With an effortless toss, Courvalec sent Monsieur Lemay sailing toward the exit.

"Reasonable?" he growled in a voice ravaged by tobacco and alcohol. "Nothing to be reasonable about. I registered these four savages on my ship's manifest with the port authority at Punta Arenas; they were only too happy to get rid of these beauties once and for all and get an honest tip into the bargain! These Alacalufs of yours are lucky not to be Onas or Tehuelches. Everywhere else in Patagonia they pay bounties to Indian hunters. But look at me: I spoil them; I feed them; I heap them with affection; I look after them in ways you couldn't begin to imagine; I'm even teaching them a trade!"

"A trade?" Monsieur Lemay asked doubtfully, knocking the dents out of his top hat.

"Fairground entertainers!" the bully roared in triumph. "Hired for the duration of the Universal Exposition, then off on a tour of France and Europe. Want to see their travel pass from the St.-Malo harbor police? The permit from the director of the sideshow section of the Universal Exposition? Will that do?"

"For the moment," Monsieur Lemay answered cautiously, reflecting that if he was to have any chance of saving his charges it would be better to remain intact.

Reaching the exit, where he was out of range, he turned and said:

"You have not heard the last of this, you scoundrels! I will be back!"

★　★　★

He moved heaven and earth, the perfect knight Gaston Lemay, shattering his lance on hearts of stone and his sword on the stupidity of regulations, floundering perilously over the secretions of easy consciences, secretions as black and foul-smelling as the ink of a threatened octopus.

First of all, Monsieur Poivre de la Mirmande, member of the Institute, President of the Geographic Society, the first man to whom Monsieur Lemay turned for advice, certain that at the call

of such a substantial personage all Science would rise and march
in unison on the Champ-de-Mars to free the Holy Sepul-
cher . . . Monsieur Poivre de la Mirmande, ensconced in the
armchair of the great Dumont d'Urville, heard him out punc-
tiliously, masking his irritation by toying with his paper knife.
Then he slowly nodded; finally he spoke.

"A most dramatic affair. I quite understand that it should move
a man of feeling such as yourself, Monsieur Lemay. I myself am
overcome. But it is also a thorny matter in which we must move
with infinite caution, for you are also a man of science, a member
of our Society. Was it not you, my dear colleague — in that
remarkable book we were rash enough to give the seal of our
public approval — who first drew public attention to the survival
of this cannibal population in the Strait of Magellan? In pondered, precise language, to be sure, but with a want of rigor
perhaps more suited to popularization than to scientific anal-
ysis . . . which is always a pitfall. So much so, indeed, that you
yourself may suffer repercussions if you stir up public opinion.
People will start to ask questions. And they will not be entirely
wrong! You yourself will be compromised, and the other members of our Society along with you. You believe yourself to be
acting generously. You will be perceived as grotesque. I cannot
allow you to do this, at least not in this way. Act if you must — but
in your name only. I shall not demand your resignation, for you
have as yet done nothing wrong. But I will ask you to sign it for
me. Later, if you decide to be discreet, we shall tear it up together.
But in your place I should think twice before descending into
such a squalid arena. The members of our Society, my dear sir,
may explore the Strait of Magellan, but the Champ-de-Mars —
that would be ridiculous!"

At the offices of Le Temps, on the Boulevard des Italiens, came
the same reply in different terms. Of course they had appreciated
Monsieur Lemay's excellent series, well-documented, incisive,
crisply written, on his voyage. They also liked the short articles he
sent in from Carpentras. But in the case of this Parisian matter,
Monsieur Lemay could scarcely expect to take the place of a
Parisian · reporter. They would send someone — the gossip-

columnist covering the Exposition, for example, although of course you had to think of the scandal . . . The reputation of the Exposition, in the very heart of the capital of the Rights of Man (if by any chance any of this happened to be true) . . . Could Monsieur Lemay swear that Monsieur Maurice's lodgers were being held against their will? The cage — well, that was just for the show. Fairground folk were not like other people. No, decidedly, *Le Temps* was not interested . . .

Monsieur Lemay kicked his heels at the Chilean Legation for two hours before standing in front of an insolent young bureaucrat who said that if indeed there existed a few vestigial savage groups in the Strait of Magellan, they could in no way be considered Chilean citizens, even though Monsieur Lemay seemed to believe — like all Frenchmen — that Chile was a backward country. The matter therefore did not concern the Legation. The matter was closed. Monsieur Lemay would not be admitted again.

At central police headquarters he was sent from office to office and warned: "Your allegation does not stand up. If it did, the special Exposition squad would have acted on it long before now. In any case, you are not entitled to file a complaint. Only the families of the alleged victims or the diplomatic representatives of their countries may exercise this right, if they so wish. Write to the families, my dear sir, go and see the Chilean Legation . . ."

Write to the families!

Monsieur Gaston Lemay crisscrossed the whole city — even, despairing of the legal authorities, asking help from the Church. At the shelter of the Little Sisters of the Poor on Rue Notre-Dame-des-Champs, amid an odor of soup and straw mattresses, they explained to him that as long as the number of beds permitted, they accepted anyone who knocked of their own free will at the door of the shelter. But in this particular case, the Little Sisters of the Poor would need police permission to shelter them before they could go to the sideshow section of the Exposition and claim the poor savages. "Go to the police, dear sir!" Then, seeing Monsieur Lemay's distressed reaction, the nun added:

"Try the priests of the Foreign Missions, Rue du Bac. They have a lot of influence . . ."

At the Rue du Bac, Monsieur Lemay realized that he was really going around in circles. The floorboards in the mission parlor smelled of beeswax polish, and birds sang amid the shrubs in the garden. A crucified Christ observed the interview, but doubtless He had other plans. They told Monsieur Lemay that had it been a question of Chinese, or of Negroes from Madagascar, the thing might well have been feasible, given France's political and religious spheres of influence. But the Strait of Magellan, Tierra del Fuego, and Patagonia came under the wing of Don Bosco's Italian Salesians, who had just established missions there. He must write to their mother house in Rome . . .

Write to Rome!

Monsieur Lemay was starting to lose hope. He had so few contacts in Paris that he soon made the rounds of them all. His former traveling companions deserted him. He wrote to them all, receiving only pious encouragements in reply. He bored everyone. No one believed him any more. When he showed people the photographs taken aboard the *Junon,* they said, "All these savages look alike. And in any case, they're fairground entertainers now. They don't need your help. Your kind heart is leading you astray . . ." They came close to hinting that he was a dupe. Finally he himself began to doubt. Monsieur Poivre de la Mirmande refused to receive him. He did not see the "dancer" and her unhappy companions again. Every day he joined the line outside the ticket window, hoping to lose himself in the crowd, but each time the awful Courvalec was waiting, laughing nastily and blocking the entrance with his hulking form. At night the sideshow section was closed off to the public. To get in you would have had to climb a high fence, and Monsieur Lemay was no longer young or strong enough. There was no way of approaching the wagons, which gave off cooking smells and the joyful sounds of supper as fairground folk and freaks alike happily replenished themselves. Standing outside in the dark, Monsieur Lemay strained his ears for sounds of distress to pierce the laughter; but nothing of the kind happened, and he felt ridiculous standing there with heart pounding like a lovesick swain. Sadly, he returned to his hotel. Before retiring, he would contemplate for the hundredth time the five tickets he had bought (creating a serious hole in his finances) at the Paris offices of the Messageries Maritimes Havraises steamship company for passage aboard the steamer *La Seine,* sailing in ten days' time for Valparaiso via Punta Arenas . . . *La Seine* would leave without him, he knew. Yet he had imagined himself aboard with these poor savages, delivered from Courvalec's clutches and returning to their families at the meeting place of the canoes off the Charles Islands . . .

One slender hope remained, in the person of a young police inspector attached to the force specially formed for the Universal Exposition. This man, whose name was Flérac, had heard him out thoughtfully instead of showing him the door, had taken notes, and had promised to look into the matter, assuring Monsieur Lemay that he would let him know if he saw any possibility of acting. A fortnight went by with no further news from Flérac.

On the fifteenth morning a gentleman called at the hotel. It was Flérac.

"I wanted to talk to you here rather than at the station," he said. "There is no official investigation and I have no warrant. Let us go somewhere quiet."

The hotel reading room was empty at that hour. They sat down.

"Well?" Monsieur Lemay asked impatiently.

"Well . . . I believe you were telling me the truth, but we have no proof beyond my own conviction and my confidence in you. Obviously from my superiors' point of view we have nothing that would warrant any attempt at legal action. The file is closed."

"Then is all lost?"

"In a sense, yes," replied the young inspector. "Courvalec's work and residence permits are in order, as he told you. Moreover, to avoid unnecessary headaches we have always turned a blind eye on the activities of some fairground people, such as those who exhibit freaks or other oddities. The fact is, experience has taught us that the ones who seem persecuted, exploited, exhibited in conditions that would disgust a normal man, are in fact consenting, and make a good living out of their physiological misfortunes and their deformities. It's a closed world, and it sticks together. We disturb it only if it disturbs public order. That is not the case here."

"But you know my poor savages do not belong to that world!" exclaimed Monsieur Lemay.

"I know it, but once again there is nothing to prove it. I have twice visited these rascals in their marquee. The first time anonymously, the second giving them my name and showing them my police badge. The second performance was no different from the first, like a play in which everyone knows his part down to the smallest detail, including the horse-meat meal at the end, which raised the roof each time. Even with a policeman in the audience, Monsieur Maurice did not change his act one iota. That proves he is sure of himself and thinks he has nothing to fear from the law. Afterward he willingly took me to the wagon just behind the tent where your savages are living. It was acceptable, not all that dirty, the usual kind of thing with these gypsies. Mattresses on the floor, blankets, a lamp, plates and dishes, an outhouse nearby . . . all the usual wagon amenities. That's how fairground people live. You can't ask for more, and there's no law that says you can. Your four poor devils were in there, wearing old clothes — which suggests to me that their primitive nudity is just a showman's stunt, not their natural state any more. I looked at their lunch pails. There was rice, dried vegetables, some pieces of fish, and a pot of tea that was still warm. They didn't look unhappy, at least not physically. Just absent, and that's what made me think of you: How could I get them to understand me? So I opened the wagon door wide and said 'Come!', beckoning them into the free air outside and sweeping my arms up and down like a bird trying to fly away. The partners gave themselves away when they protested. 'You have no right to try to woo them away! They've signed a contract!' They showed me this contract. It was a document marked with four crosses, legally acceptable as the signatures of illiterates, and certified by a Punta Arenas attorney, probably with a well-greased palm. I repeated the word 'Come!'

several times, pointing to the open door and miming the flight of
a bird leaving its cage. I honestly did all I could. Not one of your
charges stirred. The old one was eating greedily from his lunch
pail. The couple looked at me with a mixture of slyness and
stupidity, as if they saw no difference between the two rascals and
me. It was Madame Third's eyes that aroused my suspicions. It
was as if she were asking me a question. Her eyes were soft and
very sad. That was what decided me. I am offering you a chance,
Monsieur Lemay. I shall take responsibility. This evening we will
go to Courvalec's together after the last show. They do not know I
lack the authority, and we'll be able to bluff them for twenty
minutes or so. I shall keep the wagon door open. If your charges
recognize you, perhaps they will follow you. After that, it's your
business."

★   ★   ★

Two wagons stood side by side behind the marquee. One
brightly lit, the other in darkness. The first had windows with
curtains. The second looked more like a cattle wagon, with a
barred slit for a window and a chained and bolted door. Inspector
Flérac knocked at the door of the lighted wagon. They heard
voices and the sound of glasses and dying male laughter, as well
as a low cry. Someone asked, "Who's there?"

"Inspector Flérac, police department. Open in the name of
the law!"

"It's after dark, Inspector. A little late for the law," replied
Courvalec's slurred voice.

"Routine check," said the inspector. "But if you'd rather be
turned out of here at the crack of dawn, that's fine! You have
thirty seconds to decide."

This time they heard hurried footsteps inside the wagon, as if
its surprised occupants were quickly trying to straighten things
up. A muffled voice said, "Get them dressed, for Christ's sake!"

The door opened. Captain Courvalec had obviously been
drinking. He wore a dirty singlet, and his suspenders trailed
down from his pants. Monsieur Maurice stood swaying behind

him. Through bloodshot eyes, the Breton seaman peered at Monsieur Lemay, standing behind the inspector.

"I might have known," he growled. "I should have bashed his brains in."

"Should we call out the lads?" asked the "tamer."

This was a classic fairground workers' tactic for frustrating the police, who would find themselves mobbed by hideous grimacing monsters suddenly boiling out of every wagon. The inspector rapidly weighed the risks. Since he was acting on his own initiative, he could not hope for reinforcements. He had but a little time to bluff.

"I am investigating a report of unlawful detention," he declared. "This gentleman is the complainant. I have a warrant to check. It won't take long."

Screwing his eyes up, the ruffian bellowed with laughter.

"Detention? My my my!"

He looked back into the wagon.

"Over here, ladies. Come and show the inspector how happy you are to be here!"

The two "ladies" dragged themselves rather than walked. Wearing old gypsy dresses, bosoms bare, caked with makeup, paper flowers in their hair, they leaned against one another for support, hiccuping.

"They are drunk!" exclaimed Monsieur Lemay.

"You can say that again!" said the brute with savage joy. "You might call it their little weakness. Well, ladies, so long as you don't want to get up and leave, you might as well go back to bed. Uncle Courvalec will be right with you."

"Madame Fourth" went back. Her eyes expressed nothing beyond gloomy animal drunkenness, stabbing Monsieur Lemay's heart. She held on to the furniture as she walked, then collapsed onto a cot at the back of the wagon. Soon they heard her snores. "Madame Third" did not move. Swaying on widespread legs, her dress open over her thighs, she seemed to be singing something, chanting in a barely audible monotone broken by hiccups.

"Back to your kennel!" roared the Breton, raising his hand.

Then, collecting himself, he gave a grimace intended to be an appeasing smile.

"She'll go of her own free will, you'll see. Detention, for these two little birds? How could anyone say such a thing?"

"What about the others?" asked the inspector. "Why do you keep them locked up?"

He pointed to the chain on the door of the second wagon, from which no sound had emerged.

"Those two? They're drunk as lords — but that's part of the contract: three meals a day and all the wine they can drink. And can they drink! I do them a favor by locking them in at night. If they woke up and left they'd wander off as helplessly as kids; they'd get lost, they'd break their necks in a manhole, they'd fall into the Seine, get robbed in Les Halles . . ."

"Open up!" ordered the inspector.

Rolled up in blankets, "Mister First" and "Mister Second" were sleeping dreamlessly, like logs, mouths wide open. The wagon stank of spilled red wine, cold food, tobacco.

"It's not the Ritz, I'll grant you," said the giant, sensing that he had won the day. "But they have all they need. Want me to wake them?"

The inspector shrugged and Courvalec, pressing his advantage, thrust out a hand.

"And what about that warrant, Inspector? You wouldn't be here without a warrant, would you?"

In the port of Rouen a steamship was soon to leave for the Strait of Magellan. Five berths were reserved in the name of Monsieur Gaston Lemay and family. Fog was slowly closing over the Cape of the Virgins, over Cape Froward, over the Charles Islands, all receding into the nothingness of the irretrievable, and Monsieur Lemay reflected sadly that he had lost the game . . .

"Listen!" Inspector Flérac said to him.

"Madame Third's" chant . . . A single note that suddenly swelled and burst from her throat in a dramatic crescendo. Now they could pick out words, guttural intonations. Her voice was no longer hesitant but absolutely strident. *Akwal,* many, many suns and many moons, *akwal aswal yerfalay,* the song of the world

of the Kaweskar, the great song of lamentation, the song of terror
in the face of life, the song of the People, persecuted since the
dawn of time, who had no word to express happiness but only to
say *akwal,* many, too many suns and moons, when would it
finally come to an end? Yerfa the younger sang as she had sung
on the deck of the white men's ship as it bore her far away from
Lafko . . .

"Shut your mouth!" bellowed Courvalec.

He seemed worried. It was the first time he had heard this.
Not a man of feelings, he had no way of guessing at its meaning.
He sniffed like a dog baffled by a strange smell.

"We have one small chance left," blurted the inspector. "It's up
to you!"

Inspiration, a burst of feeling, a rush of pity . . . Monsieur
Lemay stretched out a hand, then two, and grasped "Madame
Third's" hands. She leaned forward to jump, for the wagon steps
had been pulled up.

"No you don't!" yelled Courvalec.

"You —" the inspector ordered.

He did not finish, but launched a hard uppercut that briefly
removed the former whale hunter from the land of the living.

"Now run!"

They ran hand in hand with the woman, one on either side of
her. She seemed weightless, she did not stumble, she ran as fast
as they did, more lightly even on her bare feet. Their cab was
waiting at the entrance to the sideshow park. They tumbled into
it. Sarcastically eying this wild-haired, half-dressed gypsy, the
driver asked:

"And where might the gentlemen be headed now?"

"Keep your comments to yourself!" snapped the inspector.
"Police!"

"Fine," said the driver. "But where to?"

The inspector looked at Yerfa — and that is what we shall
henceforth call her, even though no one knew her name beyond
the stretch of the Strait of Magellan bounded by Cape Froward
and Cape Tamar. Her lips were daubed a heavy red that made
them seem thicker still, her lids were coated to the temples with

blue cream, the rouge on her cheeks accentuated her prominent
Mongolian cheekbones — they had had her to rights, those two
vermin! She looked like a streetwalker, the kind that sold themselves for twenty sous in the moats of the fortifications on the
outskirts of the city, the antechamber to death for the prostitutes
of Paris.

"Who will take her in?" said the inspector. "The night shelters
turn away prostitutes — and that's what she looks like, alas! The
only ones I can think of are the Little Sisters of the Poor, as long
as the police request it. Perhaps I can arrange that."

Monsieur Lemay had taken out a handkerchief and was wiping the poor woman's face; she just sat there, motionless on her
seat. All fear had left her eyes. The result was pathetic. She looked
like a woman who had been crying, her tears washing the
makeup in rivulets down her face.

"Not the Little Sisters of the Poor," said Monsieur Lemay.
"What would she think of them, since we would not be able to
tell her? That we are abandoning her yet again, alone in the
company of unknown people in a huge gloomy dormitory? I
shall take her to my hotel. I shall sleep in an armchair. Tomorrow
there will be time to think things over."

He leaned out and hailed the driver:

"Hotel de Suède, Rue des Saints-Pères."

Fortunately the hotel lobby was empty, but the night clerk
almost dropped in his tracks.

"Ma . . . Ma . . . Madame cannot accompany you upstairs,
Monsieur," he stammered. "This is not a *maison de rendezvous*."

What could they possibly tell him? Yerfa had no notion of
modesty, and Courvalec most assuredly had not taken the trouble to inculcate it in her! One of her breasts had fallen out of the
front of her ragged dress, and she did not even attempt to hide it.

"It's out of the question, sir, out of the question," the night
clerk repeated desperately, returning Monsieur Lemay's key to its
pigeonhole.

"And with this, still out of the question?" Inspector Flérac
cut in.

He flipped out his police badge. The clerk still hesitated, unable to believe this horrible scene, his eyes glued on Yerfa.

"Just for tonight, if you sign the register yourself, Inspector. I shall make my report tomorrow, and the management will decide."

"Where are you going next?" Flérac asked Monsieur Lemay.

"To Rouen. Then to the Strait of Magellan aboard the steamship *La Seine.* I shall return her to her home and then come back."

"You are a good man, sir. May I shake your hand?"

Under Yerfa the younger's gentle gaze, they exchanged a warm, long look.

Once in his room with the door locked, Monsieur Lemay began to clean Yerfa's face with a damp towel. His heart heavy as lead, he felt he was wiping away the spittle of the crowd, of the night clerk, of Courvalec, of Darwin, of Monsieur Maurice and his audience, of Monsieur Poivre de la Mirmande, and of a certain special correspondent of *Le Temps,* author of a flippant travel report. Then, indicating the bed, he said: "Now lie down and sleep," averting his gaze out of modesty although he and his traveling companions had laughed without a second thought at the sight of this poor creature naked. Finally he turned out the light and settled himself in an armchair, a blanket over his knees. Light from a gaslamp in the street outside dimly illuminated the room through gaps in the curtain. The soft gaze was still on him. Monsieur Lemay did not know it, but God knew: This was the first and last time that two human hearts had made contact across the hundred-century-abyss separating the Kaweskar from other men.

★ ★ ★

They knocked very early next morning. The management had decided that Monsieur Lemay must leave the hotel. Since he had some shopping to do—doubtless to clothe "Madame"—they gave him until noon. For the good name of the hotel, it was requested that they leave by the service entrance.

They immediately took the train for Rouen. At a small hotel in the port, under the half-mocking, half-alarmed gaze of an uninquisitive hotelkeeper, Monsieur Lemay took two adjoining rooms. How could he explain that his companion could not bear solitude, that she clung to him like a drowning person, screamed with terror in her sleep unless she felt Monsieur Lemay's presence close by, and that there was no other reason? The spittle bounced off his serene soul.

Yerfa allowed herself to be led like a big retarded child. She showed no curiosity. Throughout the train ride to Rouen she scarcely glanced out of the window. She merely started when the locomotive whistled, then fell back into her stupor. From time to time she raised her eyes to make sure Monsieur Lemay was still sitting opposite her, and once reassured seemed to thank him with her eyes. She did not speak. Monsieur Lemay tried to teach her a few words of French, which she repeated with a flawless accent, clearly connecting the words with the objects he pointed out. But he had to give up. His pupil — beyond a doubt gifted — refused to go on. Yerfa the younger had retreated into a sealed world that admitted only herself and this gray-haired stranger with his gentle, helping hands, who had entered that world and allowed himself to be shut in with her. Beyond that, she understood nothing and did not try to understand.

In restaurants, Monsieur Lemay picked tables away from other customers and seated Yerfa with her back to other tables, or else ordered meals in their rooms, for Yerfa ate with her fingers. She also drank a lot, and when the wine carafe was empty she looked so sad that Monsieur Lemay always yielded, stopping only when she approached the degrading stages of drunkenness. She dressed herself more or less unaided, but every morning Monsieur Lemay had to check her appearance, the lacing of her boots, the buttoning of her dress (she always missed one button out of two by inverting the buttonholes). Only her hair received her full attention: It was long and black and, now that it had made the acquaintance of soap, responsive to the comb. Irresistibly drawn to mirrors, she combed her hair long and lovingly in public. In restaurants diners were flabbergasted whenever she turned around in her chair at the sight of this unclassifiable creature's moonlike, yellow, animal visage. The battery of looks subsequently trained on Monsieur Lemay—who did not leave her side for a second—clearly held both envy and disgust. More spittle . . . Monsieur Lemay was no longer concerned. He no longer returned the looks. He knew very well what people thought, and how nasty their thoughts were, and how far their thoughts were from the truth. At night he stroked Yerfa's forehead and hair, or sat by her bed for long hours, holding her hand. Then, when she was asleep, he went to his own bed, leaving the connecting door open, and reflected in the dark on the mystery of fate; while Yerfa, who was not asleep although her eyes were closed on her closed world, patiently waited for the stranger to come and rewaken the life that had sought sanctuary in her belly. Finally, though, she too fell asleep.

On the morning *La Seine* was due to sail, with Monsieur Lemay's trunks already on board, Yerfa the younger stepped down from the cab onto the quayside and saw the big ship with her crew milling about in preparation for casting off. She began to tremble. Her eyes questioned Monsieur Lemay, who saw in them not her usual gentleness but an intense fear. "What is it, my child?" he asked her. Despairing of ever knowing her true name—if she actually had one—this was how he now addressed her. How could he possibly understand that she was no longer anything but a kind of lost meteorite, forever unmoored from her own distant universe? How could he know that to survive that first crossing, that intergalactic trajectory between two eternally separated worlds, to confront the inconceivable, she had exhausted all her moral strength, so that the idea of a second crossing absolutely terrified her? Intuitively, Yerfa the younger possessed a kind of awareness of the relativity of time. Where she was at this moment, she was not. Where she had come from was now so far away in her mind that the only ones she could ever hope to meet there again would be the long-forgotten dead. Life? It was no longer anything beyond this gray-haired stranger who, having taken her by the arm, was now for some reason taking her to a world where she would lose him. Without a cry, without a word, she broke free and ran to take refuge in the cab, whose door had remained open while the driver carried the last pieces of luggage to the gangway. There, huddled in upon herself, she refused to budge.

Monsieur Lemay had his trunks removed from the ship; the cab driver loaded them back onto his cab and drove them to the railroad station. Yerfa was back in her closed world again. The clip-clop of the horse's hoofs and the rocking of the carriage soothed her. She responded with her brown, soft eyes to Monsieur Lemay's smile.

★   ★   ★

Carpentras was not a tolerant town. The facades of its houses maintained a close and malevolent watch upon one another across its narrow streets. Monsieur Lemay's housekeeper, Madame Louise, suffered the tortures of the damned. She considered giving her week's notice. She became the butt of whispered comments in the shops, of endless long-winded roundabout insinuations, all meant to goad her into admitting that Monsieur Gaston Lemay was living with a young cannibal of frightening ugliness and unsurpassed vice; that he was so besotted that he had taken her into his home and locked his door on the world in order to gloat privately over his prey.

It was true Monsieur Lemay no longer went out. It was no longer possible for him to do so, because the distress in the young woman's eyes whenever he prepared to take his leave intensified with each passing day. Yet if he stayed by her side her calm, gentle expression returned, and at such moments he, Monsieur Gaston Lemay, was inexplicably happy. The days went by, empty of activity. Yerfa would sit on the ground in the garden, surrounded by unfamiliar flowers she did not even glance at. She had given up wearing shoes, but endlessly combed her hair. She still ate with her fingers. Madame Louise refused to serve her, and Monsieur Lemay shared his meals with her in the second-floor bedroom, carrying the tray upstairs himself. It was in a sense a second isolation, echoing the first confinement represented by the permanently closed front door and the high garden walls.

In truth Monsieur Gaston Lemay, almost undone by grief and happiness, was watching Yerfa slowly die. She spat blood. Her coughing broke his heart. Shaken with fever, her body ran with sweat while her eyes spoke of her acceptance of her fate. It had started in Rouen, and grown steadily worse. She had the lost look of an animal that felt itself going, but did not know why it was suffering or what death was made of. She was also losing her reason, but slowly, gently, without violence. A local physician, Doctor Bontemps, came round. He hugged the walls as he approached the house; then, confronted with this patient from beyond his world, he was seized with a sort of respect. He examined her and spoke of galloping tuberculosis, but also of schizophrenia and of a general physical debility—her liver in particular was severely damaged—all pointing to a fairly rapid decline punctuated by brief remissions.

Remissions . . . They lay in Yerfa's brown, gentle gaze. She could no longer sleep alone. At night Ayayema howled, just as lost as Yerfa the younger and seeking revenge for this terrible isolation. Every night Monsieur Gaston Lemay took Yerfa the younger into his bed, while the chimes of St.-Siffren obtusely tolled off hours that no longer meant anything in this world below. And he, Monsieur Gaston Lemay, the stranger, opening Yerfa the younger's thighs, never knew that in discovering happiness he was also giving it. The ultimate failure of communication.

Over the grave of the savage female, buried in Carpentras cemetery amid a desert of betrayed friendships—an officiating priest, Doctor Bontemps, and nobody else—where it can still be seen today, Monsieur Lemay had a marble plaque engraved with these words:

HERE LIES AN UNKNOWN
UNIDENTIFIED YOUNG ALACALUF WOMAN
1879
ETERNAL REGRETS

Right down to the regrets, it was exactly the same epitaph the seamen of the Chilean ship *Almirante Hohenlo* hastily burned onto the wooden crosses marking the graves of the unhappy women abandoned by *loberos* on the shores of the great Strait . . . Monsieur Gaston Lemay never recovered. No one in town ever greeted him any more, but since he never greeted anyone anyway — particularly his former friends — he did not care. He began to hate eminent persons. He confirmed his resignation from the Geographic Society to Monsieur Poivre de la Mirmande in an immoderately couched letter. He too was leaving this world. He stopped sending articles about Carpentras to *Le Temps*. What more could he say of a town whose most vindictive acts would be blown away in a second by the storm winds of the Strait of Magellan? He waited.

He did not wait long.

A letter from police headquarters in Paris:

My dear Monsieur Lemay,

Out of respect for the truth as we know it, I have done my best to hush this terrible business up. Monsieur Maurice and Captain Courvalec were found horribly murdered in their wagon near Sedan where they were putting on their show. They were not a pretty sight. Cut into pieces. Surrounded by their own bones, on which half-eaten shreds of flesh were still hanging. Vengeance was terrifying.

I should not write this to you, but in this particular case I must declare myself in favor of cannibalism. They found your three charges hiding in the forest. The old man was dead, probably of fatigue. The gendarmes shot the other two, the man and woman, who rushed them like wildcats. They were right to do it. What charges could have been brought against these unhappy savages? And what crime would they have been expiating by putting their necks under the guillotine? Or, trailing from prison to prison, what could they have understood of their destiny?

Your devoted
Flérac
Inspector of Police

Tsefayok, Yannoek, Kostora, pitched into the common grave in Sedan cemetery after nightfall . . .

In his turn Monsieur Lemay lost his reason. He dreamed that he was holding a naked, hirsute, cannibal woman in his arms; she had Yerfa the younger's face and was gorging herself on her own flesh.

Cannibal! Had he not said so himself?

★　★　★

Monsieur Lemay left Carpentras. Shutters barred. No explanations. He shipped on a three-master out of Bordes, the *Marie-Anne,* bound for Chile. He was never seen again, nor were the *Marie-Anne* or any of her twenty-seven crew. Captain Louis Lacroix, unforgettable historian of the age of sail, who died in the nineteen-fifties, listed the name of supercargo passenger Gaston Lemay among the victims of the disaster. Captain Lacroix added no comment.

CHAPTER ELEVEN

THE
DEAD-DEAD
MAN

Harris Bay, 1910.

Lâlat-Lâlat, the Dead-Dead Man, was particularly fond of Dawson Island. Sixty years after Reverend Watkin's tragic end he returned there in force. From wherever you stood you could see him on his tall cross on a hill overlooking Harris Bay. There, in 1895, the Catholic Salesian missionaries of Monsignor Fagnano, apostolic commissioner for Patagonia, had founded a prosperous and lavishly supplied settlement.

Harris Bay lay on the eastern shore of Dawson Island, across from Cape Anxious of doleful memory, where the hopes of the ministers of the Patagonian Missionary Society had foundered. Across the bay, some ten miles beyond wind-lashed Whiteside Channel, lay the rain-sodden mass of Tierra del Fuego and the glaciers of Nose Peak, as well as the mouth of a broad gulf biting deeply into the big island. Lieutenant Montaner of the Chilean Navy christened it Useless Bay, in imitation of earlier cartographers and geographers who translated the melancholy of the landscape into pessimistic place-names.

But Lieutenant Montaner was wrong. Useless Bay was not useless at all. Ringed by moist meadowland where grass grew in fair abundance, it turned out to be ideal country for large-scale sheep-raising. Deep inside the bay sprawled the *estancia* El Plantano, where a Chilean millionaire's bailiff held sway over 300,000 sheep and a score of fierce half-breeds with orders to clear the shore of any trace of Indian nomads. An Alacaluf head fetched one Chilean gold pound. There was killing. The same thing was happening along the whole shoreline of the big island and on the coast of the Brunswick Peninsula, where Cape Froward stood. Matters became so bad that the Chilean government—which had turned a blind eye to the killing and only realized the extent of the slaughter after an attempt by the missionaries themselves to count heads—decided to turn Dawson Island into an Indian sanctuary, entrusting it to the Salesians, who had been established at Punta Arenas for fifteen years. Trapped between the *loberos* in the north and the sheepherders in the south, tired of begging for skimpy donations by risking their last healthy young women aboard ships sailing through the great Strait, hunted down by the Chilean Navy, which paid the Salesians the bounty price—one gold pound—for every Alacaluf handed over to them, the clans converged on Harris Bay. At the same time, from waterways much further north, from the Messier Channel and from Wellington Island, the last of the clans to escape the *loberos* limped in to the missions awaiting them in distant Chiloé.

The Strait of Magellan was now empty of its first inhabitants. One after another, the wigwam ribs rotted and collapsed on the old campsites. The canoes were pulled high and dry at Harris Bay. The Dead-Dead Man could at last count all those who had come to him, including the children.

★   ★   ★

By the measure of this empty land, the Harris Bay mission was a city. First a church vast enough to house the Salesians and their female helpers, the nuns of the order of Mary Auxiliary: The Alacalufs in an unexpected flash of humor nicknamed them "penguins" for their black-and-white habits. A further complex of buildings housed the civilian helpers, woodworkers, foremen, skilled laborers, all Italian or Chilean; a sawmill; a machine-driven carpenter shop; stables; a spinning and weaving work-shop; a cheese factory; a slaughterhouse; a school for children and adults; an infirmary (but no doctor); and a shelter for the dying; this, along with the cemetery, was soon the mission's most crowded area. There were also wharves, warehouses, and a jetty regularly visited by a two-hundred-ton schooner that supplied the mission's needs, the *Maria Auxiliadora,* owned by the Sales-ians. And finally, lined up along real streets transformed for two-thirds of the year into quagmires, there were several dozen identical little houses, each equipped with a stove and simple furniture, where the clans had been settled—but properly, any promiscuity incompatible with Christian morality being forbid-den: couple by couple, living only with their own children, for there was no longer any question of tolerating those warm heaps of grease-smeared bodies haphazardly intertwined under the sealskin covers. The Salesians had shot nine out of ten of their dogs—domesticating the Alacaluf packs had been beyond them—and permitted only one dog per family. Thus organized, sedentarized, fed, housed, heated, baptized, provided with an official identity, the Alacalufs were finally civilized. In the rec-ords of the Salesians—who spoke not a word of Alacaluf—they were registered under the names of the archipelago's explorers: Ladrillero, Sarmiento, Gamboa; or, even more frequently, as geographical names: Messier, Wellington, Canales, Eden, Froward . . . They no longer fished, or very little. It was forbid-den, lest the nomad bug bite them all over again. The women no longer dived naked for cholgas: It was forbidden in the name of decency. These nomads of the sea had become a kind of sub-sidized peasantry, voluntary half-prisoners, increasingly rootless, whose supervisors tried to occupy their time in the stables or the workshops in the hope that a taste for work and acquaintance with new techniques would lead to their assimilation.

Nor were they permitted to go on covering their bodies with seal blubber to combat the damp and the cold. The men wore coats and pants, and the women shawls and dresses: These arrived aboard the *Maria Auxiliadora* by the baleful, the fruit of old-clothes collection drives by the mother house in Rome. It was no good their laying on layer after layer of clothing — which they neglected to keep dry — they merely enclosed themselves inside heavy, saturated casings. Thus bundled to the eyeballs, these people who had once scaled cliffs and leaped from rock to rock now shuffled about clumsily, losing all mobility and even the *taste* for mobility. They huddled around their stoves for hours, eyes staring at the ground. They ate their fill — and sought nothing more. The Harris Bay mission, with its 250,000 acres of forest, 75,000 acres of pasture, 7,000 sheep, 700 head of cattle, was prosperous, and was run like a commercial enterprise. Into the plates of the Alacaluf (no longer permitted to eat with their fingers) dropped a generous daily gaucho-style meat ration with dried vegetables and preserves — the meat too fresh, the dairy products fermented. This dietary imbalance, in a people that had lived exclusively from the sea (and had been kept alive only by the daily need to find enough to eat), caused many health problems, particularly among the young, without anyone at the mission ever beginning to speculate about a possible chain of cause and effect. This combination of physical inactivity, of inadequate clothing, of brutal departure from their traditional way of life exposed the Alacalufs to every epidemic, moral as well as physiological. What we would now call *stress* (a pathological disposition that had always dogged this tiny unhappy race in its desolate corner of the earth) wrought havoc among clans fragmented and compartmentalized into little wooden row houses under the gaze of the Dead-Dead Man of Harris Bay. Syphilis too. They had forgotten to vaccinate them. Not that they had the means to do so. Despite the regular link with Punta Arenas, the infirmary lacked the most rudimentary medicines. The Christian charity of the Salesians was not in question. But their level of intelligence — or rather, their level of stupidity — was. So was their crass inability to anticipate and forestall the looming disaster. And we are also bound to condemn their lack of real love, for it is beyond comprehension that their hearts failed to speak after their medical skill proved wanting. A cold afflicting Father Antonio, the Harris Bay superior, an influenza afflicting his deputy Father

Gregorio — and the Alacalufs began to die of tuberculosis. *Akwal,* many, far too many suns and far too many moons had gone by . . .

The Harris Bay mission, which ten years earlier had sheltered almost 600 "canoe Indians," almost the total population of the clans, numbered no more than a hundred by Christmas Eve, 1910. At the foot of the hill where the Crucified One stood, the long shadows of more than 500 crosses stretched across the earth in a twilight glow that would endure until daybreak on this, the shortest night of the year. The battle had been lost before it began; they had been ignorant of its very existence; they had been weaponless; they had known neither its rules nor what was at stake. Yet on that battlefield had perished Pedro Ladrillero, whose real name was Tchakwal; Carmen and Cristobal Wellington, that is Aksa and her husband Yatse; Tereskat who had come from the Skyring Sea and Kyewaytçaloes from the Otway Sea, although what you saw stenciled on their crosses were the names of Jesus Eden and Juan Froward; Conchita Froward who had been called Waka; Petayem who had abandoned his Mount Sarmiento campsite to die six months later under the name of Julio Messier. And so many others had perished, so many children, small children, lying in smaller graves and under lower mounds scarcely marking even the memory of a life; the life of Taw, for example, son of Lafko, son of Taw, buried under the name of Francisco-Alberto Gamboa, dead a month after he was born at almost the same time as his mother Wauda, now resting in peace under the verbal disguise of Evita-Maria Gamboa, which meant nothing to Lafko and which was simply the Christian version of the only fitting truth: unidentified young Alacaluf woman.

It was Christmas. Fear was abroad in the little houses, dimly lit by candles, where the last survivors of the clans prepared for Midnight Mass. In the huge church, busy with religious auxiliaries pink with excitement and joy, the Baby Jesus' straw crib lay empty between the ox and the ass of the Nativity Scene. The little doll representing the Christ Child would not be laid there until midnight, when it would be escorted in by the women and children singing psalms and bearing small gifts. This time last year the joy of the good auxiliary sisters had been a little dimmed by the death of a newborn child the day after Christmas. In childlike Spanish, adapted from pidgin, Father Antonio tried to explain to the Indians that the Lord in His goodness had chosen this blessed day to take away little Luis-Maria — for this was the "name" of the son of Kyewa, Tonko's wife — to play with Him and His angels in Heaven until, fully grown, he might welcome his parents in their turn. The homily had moved the auxiliary sisters to tears and smiles of ecstasy. The Indians, still excellent mimics, had reacted in exactly the same way although they were convinced, behind the smooth masks of their faces, that the *Dead-Dead Man* had demanded a life so that he could be reborn again this night in the straw crib of the Nativity scene.

It was Christmas. Fear was abroad. Another Taw, son of Taw, son of Lafko, born of Kala the younger, wife of Taw, had fallen seriously ill a short moon earlier. He refused his mother's breast. He was breathing with difficulty and his yellow skin had turned gray. His staring eyes rolled as if he could see Ayayema inside his head.

★   ★   ★

Lafko thought.

He thrust logs into the stove. It was too hot in his house. A damp, overpowering heat, not the fierce violence of fire. There was no flicker of flames on naked skin, for the flames were invisible, and they were all clothed. Their bodies might be warm, but not their hearts. They missed the dancing red glow that was one of the mysteries of life. They also missed all those who were dead. The church bells rang out joyously. It was time for Mass.

How old was he? He was an old man, but still vigorous. He had lived many lives. After Yerfa the younger's capture by the crew of a stranger ship when they were both twenty years old, he had once again retreated northward into the great Strait. He had set up his wigwams on the Charles Islands with the survivors of his clan, Kanstay, Tonko, and Taw, his son, Kala the elder and

Tsefayok, who was the son of Tsefayok the elder who had also
been kidnapped and was never seen again, and Kostora, daughter
of Yannoek and of Kostora the elder; Lafko had taken her as his
wife, and she had given birth to several daughters who had one
after another climbed aboard the strangers' ships; and who had
finally been taken away one after another by the big gray ship of
the Chilean Navy, sick, eaten away, disfigured, to die in a quaran-
tine hospital in Punta Arenas or Puerto Natales, staring at the
ceiling, alongside the lowest of the prostitutes of those two
towns. The big gray Chilean ship numbered the living and the
dead. With its two stacks belching black smoke, she was their
black-winged guardian angel. One day her captain had told him:
"You should go to Dawson Island. You will be protected there.
You cannot go on living here . . ." And Lafko had obeyed, like
Tchakwal before him, like Petayem, Yuras, Kyasto, Tereskat,
Yatse, like Kyewaytçaloes all the way from the Otway Sea. Many of
these names were no longer in use, for there were not enough of
them left alive to carry on the names of the clans whose canoes
rotted beside the warehouses on the Harris Bay jetty.

But not Lafko's canoe.

Lafko had never given up fishing and hunting seal and cormorant. He periodically put to sea in the company of his son
Taw and two or three women of his clan, Kala the younger, Yerfa
the child, who dived naked among the rocks far from the
disapproving gaze of the "penguins." They were brief escapades,
lasting only twenty-four hours, for fishing was forbidden; but
they meant at least one night on bare ground inside the wigwam,
watching the seal fat crackle and bubble over a small fire while
Yerfa the child, far from the "penguins'" hearing, sang the song
of *Lahaltel* the otter, who lolloped along on splayed feet calling
out *aw, aw, aw* . . . It was thus that Yerfa the child, having
smeared her body with fat (carefully rubbed off before the return
to the mission next day), had warmed Lafko's old heart by
opening her thighs under the sealskins.

When they returned Father Antonio would say, "So, Felipe,
you run off all the time! Lucky it be you, you good worker, good
Christian, good husband. But you maybe go for get drowned one

time! Me need you here!" To which Lafko would reply, "Me no
want make *padre* sorry. Me want blessing *de usted*." And he would
bow his head, as he had been taught, in feigned contrition.

For Lafko spoke the mission's pidgin Spanish. He could even
trace a few letters he had learned at the sisters' school where, in
twenty years of instruction, only three adults and half a dozen
children had been taught to read. He had a gift for woodwork
and was good with hammer and nails and plane. It was he who
made the coffins, and since he had mastered counting he now
knew what *akwal*, many, many dead meant in the language of the
white men. He led the processions. He sang hymns. He knew
several psalms by heart. In public he was all attentiveness to his
wife Kostora (who was old and whom he no longer touched
except to beat her), which earned him the "penguins'" praise. He
washed his hands and the tip of his nose every morning, removed
his cap when addressed, religiously took Communion every
Sunday, sticking out a thick tongue stained brown with tobacco
juice; and apart from the disorder in his house and the mound of
refuse on his doorstep (the fathers had long despaired of finding
a remedy, so the Harris Bay native quarter resembled a public
dump), he behaved like a civilized man. With this single reserva-
tion — that he did so only under the name of Felipe-Maria
Gamboa, a name which meant nothing to him, and which
committed Lafko to nothing.

Felipe-Maria Gamboa was a robot. So were the hundred other
survivors in the mission, the Wellingtons, the Frowards,
Ladrilleros, Messiers, Canales, Edens, all meekly preparing to
attend Midnight Mass, mechanically brushing their clothes. As
they had done last year, the sisters distributed cookies, candy,
jam, simple toys for the children, who pretended to be interested
in them, tobacco, a few bottles of wine — eliciting some genuine
smiles — black shawls for widows and blue ones for the younger
women. A season of joy. Around their stoves they mimed joy. But
none of them felt joyful; and in all their hearts there lurked a
small, fierce, clawed animal sent by Ayayema, which was quite
simply apprehension. *Akwal*, many, many dead. They understood nothing of this god who was born every year although he

was quite dead dead and motionless on his cross. They had been assured that he was a good god. Good perhaps for the white men but not for the Kaweskar, who had no word for *goodness*.

Before going up to the church, Father Antonio made the rounds with Father Gregorio. He lingered a while in every house, patting the little ones' cheeks, turning a blind eye to the mess, congratulating young mothers on their children's healthy appearance. The mortality rate had shot up during this year 1910. All these deaths in succession distressed him; but he attributed them to the exhaustion of a people who had lived too long, who were too few in numbers, who were weakened by inbreeding and by millennia of hardship and suffering. At least he had come along in time to help the strongest to survive and adapt, and the others to die a Christian death and enter life eternal. It was God's will. He asked no more.

"Felipe," said Father Antonio, "you go for fish tomorrow? Me see you near canoe. No fish tomorrow! Tomorrow big feast day!"

Lafko's canoe was all ready. He had gone to it in the half-night when everyone was asleep. With his own hands he had fashioned the clay container for the fire. He had cut and shaped a new oar. Under an old tarpaulin he had concealed axes stolen from the workshop, knives, otter pelts, and other essential articles he had pilfered here and there over the past several moons. On a beach unknown to the "penguins," the body of a big seal awaited him by the ribs of a wigwam; by now it would be in just the right condition to yield blubber in abundance, as well as meat and a new skin. Felipe the robot replied:

"Me want what *Padre* want."

"You good man," said the monk paternally. "And how papoose?"

"Papoose" was Taw, son of Kala the younger and of Taw, son of Lafko, the child Ayayema held by the feet because the Dead-Dead Man demanded a life that night in order to be reborn in the crib. That was what Lafko thought, while Felipe-Maria Gamboa grinned from ear to ear.

"Eat plenty, do real good."

"That good," said the monk with relief. "Well, it's time. No be late for church!"

The second chimes were ringing for Mass. The wind had risen too, foretelling a night of storms. Hardly was the door closed than a wordless activity galvanized all the occupants of the house. Their faces were solemn, but their eyes glittered. They rolled blankets up like sausages. From the shelves they took tobacco, wine, biscuits, twine, a rusty can filled with needles and hooks; they ignored the clothing strewn in disorder on the floor and the wooden cross nailed to the door. Tonko the child, second of that name, raked the red embers from the stove and carefully covered them with ashes. Finally Lafko reached under his straw mattress, where he had been hiding it from prying "penguin" eyes, and pulled out the little seal-gut bag containing the sacred treasure: red mud mixed with grease, which he daubed on his cheeks and forehead; the white down band, which he knotted round his forehead; the carved stone spearhead with the drawing of a little man scratched on it, a crown of four dots in diamond formation framing his head. The stone was warm, warmer even than his own hand, warmer than yesterday or the day before yesterday. It had started to grow warm the night Lafko was awakened by a dream in which he saw himself carrying the newborn child away through rain and storm gusts. That same night the child had fallen ill.

Lafko thought. He looked at his family. He also looked at his dog, waiting with wildly wagging tail. The bells pealed out a third time. Mass must have started.

"*Arka!*" he said, up, while far above the clouds a voice he did not hear called to witness angels, cherubim, seraphim, thrones, principalities, and powers: "This is my beloved son Lafko, in whom I am well pleased . . ."

The Harris Bay settlement was deserted. Midnight Mass had emptied it. Metal roof-sheets clattered noisily under the furious onslaught of the wind. Clouds raced overhead, low and swift-moving, glowing stark black in the crepuscular light of a sun that had only just set and would soon be rising again. From one or two of the neighboring houses other forms were stealing, also with dogs at their heels. Doors banged in the wind. No one thought of closing them. This was a departure with no return. All trotted in silence, barefoot, toward the canoe. Kala the younger hugged the baby to her under her otter-skin cape. Only Lafko lingered for a moment, making a detour to the hill where he stuck four red wands in the ground like a fence around the cross. Hurling handfuls of stones at it, he yelled, *"Lâlat-Lâlat!* Leave us in peace!" Then he hurried off to join the group, already struggling to launch the canoe, bodies half-immersed in the breakers.

Arka! Away! The nomads were returning to the sea. They were reversing the course of time by fleeing back to their origins. How many were they? A dozen. Taw the younger and Taw the child; Kala the younger and Kostora; Yerfa the child who had had her first blood and would soon give Lafko a son who would be called Lafko the child; Yannoek and Tsefayok the younger; Tonko the child and old Kanstay, all of whose family had perished at the Harris Bay mission, with the exception of his daughter Kyewa and his granddaughter Wauda; and finally another baby that had neither mother nor father and was named Waka the child . . . Four strong men to work the long oars, Tonko keeping the fire, and Yerfa handling the rudder, standing upright, her young moonlike yellow face lashed by an icy rain that shut the mission roofs from sight — the hill with its cross and the Harris Bay church where the robots were singing without regaining consciousness, their souls numb, their minds empty.

They fought all night long, numb with cold, drenched, the women bailing without letup. Twenty times the canoe came close to capsizing. Not once did they think of giving up. At daybreak they had to take cover, hastily putting out the skimpy fire round which they had been trying to warm themselves. The *Maria Auxiliadora* was out looking for them, beating the shallows on the other side of the rocky bank that concealed them. When the schooner's masts disappeared over the horizon that night they set off again; it was not until the second night that they found the wigwam, the seal carcass, and the dry wood Lafko had stored under a tarpaulin. They lit a huge fire and took all their clothes off. They melted down seal blubber and covered themselves with it as soon as it began to heat up and give off a pleasant stench. Packed into the wigwam with the dogs, biting into seal-crackling, tearing strips off the meat that hung in sweating chunks from the wigwam ribs, they had found themselves once more. They even welcomed into their circle, with something approaching relief, their three persecuting spirits: Ayayema the malevolent, Kawtcho the burrowing giant, and Mwono who launched the fury of the elements down his mountainsides. At least they would dream in a familiar land.

The sick child suckled its mother. Its breathing grew less labored. It slept.

Time had stopped.

★   ★   ★

Smallpox, tuberculosis, syphilis, fatal influenza, or simply a waning will to live . . . eighty graves were added during the year 1911 to the 500 already neatly laid out in the Harris Bay cemetery, and two more canoes had escaped. There were no more Christmases. In September the *Maria Auxiliadora* took Father Gregorio, Father Antonio, the auxiliary sisters, the "penguins" of both sexes — hearts full of sorrow but still uncomprehending — back to Punta Arenas. The sheep ran wild, the cattle died for want of care, the sea demolished the jetty, and the vast process of decomposition peculiar to these southern latitudes swallowed up the last memory of all these illusions.

Only four or five canoes still wandered the great Strait, Lafko's, Kyasto's, Yuras's . . . After a few months of solitude, their wandering life led them back to the shipping lanes around the Charles Islands and Cape Tamar. They were now so few it was easy to lose heart . . . They learned to beg all over again, to drink liquor, to prostitute their women — by now an increasingly rare currency on these male seaways. At least they were no longer dying at the frightening rate of Harris Bay. On the other hand, almost no babies were born. Every dying human community is obliged by destiny to renounce its own biological perpetuation. Discouragement engendered sterility.

Every so often they disappeared into the maze of inner water-ways, lured back by the hunting instinct, by memories of the whale feasts, and above all by that peculiar mental disposition that had always impelled them to flee, to seek refuge within themselves. But these remissions were infrequent and of short duration. Soon they would be back again on the *carrera,* the Strait of Magellan, which they had once called *tchas* but which was now marked out with buoys and beacons; they were beggars rather than nomads of the sea; they tied their canoes to the buoys so that they could wait for passing ships without having to battle the current.

Then, abruptly, the landscape changed.

In 1913 President Wilson opened the Panama Canal, at one stroke canceling the need for the vast navigational detour around Cape Horn or through the Strait of Magellan. Punta Arenas died as if struck by lightning, its coaling station deserted, its wharves empty. The two keepers of the Evangelists lighthouse, the west-ern sentinel of the Strait, logged only five ship movements for the whole of the year 1914. War slowed this rate still further. Then in 1920, eight ships. In 1925, four; in 1930, two; and so on. The small three-monthly steamer between Punta Arenas no longer even stopped at the Charles Islands. Too lice-ridden, too filthy, too dejected, too abject, sorrowful, their eyes expression-less, the Alacalufs no longer inspired pity. They were the wreckage of another world, and they were a nuisance. The whaling ships also disappeared, replaced by factory ships work-ing much farther out to sea. The only sympathetic caller was the gray vessel of the Chilean Navy on permanent station in the Strait of Magellan. Her name would be, successively, *Ultima Esperanza, Micalvi, Cruz del Sur, Almirante Pikkendorf;* her com-manders young officers who treated these wretched people with the compassion of the seafarer. Their reports finally struck a chord of alarm in a few of the more human souls inhabiting higher officialdom.

What to do?

They made a law. A *Law for the Protection of the Indians,* adopted in 1940 by the Chilean government.

It was too late. Apart from the handful of Alacalufs in Punta Arenas — who no longer counted, since they were completely absorbed into the town's lowest sub-proletariat — those of Puerto Natales — who were in no better condition — and those who had disappeared in Chiloé during *lobero* raids, a grand total of thirty-five *canoe Indians* were left.

Including Lafko.

CHAPTER TWELVE

PORT PARADISE

It was now only a matter of years, of a very few years. Time had stopped for the Alacalufs; life had frozen; yet it all happened very quickly.

The stage had shifted. Leaving the great empty Strait behind them, the clans wandered north into the Messier Channel where Chilotan *loberos* still hunted. We have already noted the morbid, almost masochistic fascination these seal-hunters exercised over the Alacalufs. Whenever they camped in the proximity of these brutes, who sometimes beat them, sometimes killed them, and always exploited them, sleeping with their women and girls and small boys, reducing their children to slavery, doling out wine and liquor as generously as they transmitted their loathesome diseases, the Alacalufs at least had the feeling that they were alive. The few who managed to break free did so not by retreating into their maze of waterways but by throwing themselves on the mercies of the Chilean military authorities — two air force sergeants consumed by boredom and depression — at the Puerto Eden weather station in the Messier Channel. Soon they were living there permanently.

The spot, bearing the Hebrew name for Paradise — a few stilt huts, a rickety landing, a radio mast — was one of the gloomiest places on earth. It rained so hard and so often that the Alacalufs drank fresh water that accumulated on the surface of the sea in preference to water from the mountains, which was full of the bacteria of vegetable decomposition. You almost never saw the nearby mountains, just the black granite walls of the Messier Channel closing you in, and the channels feeding into it. At 150 feet, the cloud cover was so low that you felt shut into an empty corridor in some immense abode of giants.

The law for the protection of the Indians? It was working. Five prefabricated huts, their paint never refurbished, oozing damp, housed what remained of the last five clans; on the beach behind them was a huddle of five wigwams covered not with sealskin but tarpaulin, where the Alacalufs liked to go and sleep with their dogs in atavistic renewal on a floor of insalubrious refuse piling higher each year around a fire that gave off more smoke than heat — for they could no longer even differentiate between wood that was dry at the core and waterlogged wood. The only more or less warm spot in Puerto Eden was the kitchen-recreation-room of the weather station. Depending on their mood and disposition, the two sergeants — one a radio operator, the other a meteorologist — sometimes invited in the least grimy of their charges, particularly the children, who would watch them playing cards or leafing listlessly through out-of-date magazines. Porridge with condensed milk was their one dietary innovation. They made it often for the children. But these young air force technicians, simple noncommissioned officers with no particular instructions or training relative to the protection of the Indians, were left entirely to themselves. Sometimes one of them would offer advice. To the girls, for instance, warning them to be careful of the *loberos* in the area — although they had no authority to police such matters. To the mothers about washing the children's clothes, for there was no lack of soap. From time to time a woman would acquiesce, and start scrubbing away at some rags in a bucket, then drape them over a bush to dry. Since it rained practically every day, the garments would never dry, but would be put on again damp or wringing wet. There was also a small medical cabinet well stocked with costly specialized drugs whose use nobody understood, but no aspirin or teats for nursing bottles or any other elementary products of this kind. The sympathetic gray ship called twice a year, her arrival greeted by the last half-dozen Alacaluf children clustered on the radio mast. She stayed for a day or two, dropping the ship's doctor who administered shots and carried out examinations and prescribed treatments that would at once be forgotten in the lethargic drift of life on shore. The ship would also land a handful of exhausted scarecrows picked up at the bend of some channel. They had abandoned their canoes without a backward glance to join — neither in obvious joy nor in obvious sadness — those of their kind who had capitulated before them.

The big event, the only event, was the free distribution of food: rice, noodles, powdered milk, sugar, lard, canned meat, dried vegetables. At first it took place once a week. Clan by clan, they immediately tossed the lot, along with a little water, into iron pots that were black with soot and never scoured. Gravely, the whole family would watch the cooking, each member stirring the mixture from time to time with a stick. Then, pulling the pot off the fire, they all dipped in together with spoons or cholga shells, digging happily into the mash. They devoured everything at one go, just as they had done at the time of the whale orgies. This was the only way they had ever fed themselves — gluttonously, without a thought for the morrow. For the next six days they ate only mussels collected off the rocks. Even these were a rare commodity since the women had stopped diving. They held them carelessly in the general vicinity of the flames, skewered on a stick as in the old days. These upheavals in their dietary rhythm had so many troublesome effects that the gray ship's doctor recommended daily ration distribution. Now everything was eaten first thing in the morning, and once the thick mush had been gulped down the rest of the day was spent in listless inactivity. The women wove small baskets or carved clumsy bone harpoons, too ill-made ever to accomplish their purpose — hasty, botched work, carried out in boredom and for the sole purpose of being bartered for drink in the unlikely event that a ship came by. Others laboriously painted their bodies whenever the children on the radio mast announced the approach of a *lobero* boat. Even the oldest and most repulsive of them, like Margarita Canales with her suppurating blind eye, would tie a ribbon in their hair and meet the arrivals.

If he was in a good mood, the radio operator held classes for the Alacalufs in the post kitchen; but there was nothing to make him do this except his kindness and his conscience, both of which generally faltered when confronted with the inanity of the endeavor. One by one, the cemetery took away the most gifted of his pupils. The others, the dunces, brutalized, stupid, the ones who tore off their clothes to climb on the rocks; who splashed about naked in the icy water; who accepted the radio operator's porridge but ran away immediately afterward; who bridled if you ruffled their hair, withdrew into themselves if you smiled, and unconsciously refused to become what might be called the two sergeants' "teacher's pets" — those were the ones who survived.

An absurd life in which neither time, nor effort, nor striving, nor even sadness, had any more meaning. The days flowed into one another with dreary sameness, without surprises, without celebrations, without song, with the one daily break of the ration distribution. The Alacaluf understood nothing of it all. He was content to await death. That was his only activity.

★   ★   ★

Carlitos had been very sick. The new radio operator, Sergeant Peralta, was a fine young man, very fond of Carlitos — a friendly, smiling child who spent most of his time with the two white men. Uncertain how to nurse him through his illness, Peralta gave the sick boy a room at the station, with a bed and white sheets. The meteorologist, Sergeant Gimenez, and Peralta took turns nursing him through the worst of the fever. They could not bear the idea that this child, the most gifted of the six children who represented the entire youth of this people, should be carried off in his turn. For weeks they fed him, washed him, and kept him warm. They even took advantage of a routine call by the *Almirante Pikkendorf,* the gray ship that had been making the supply run since the mid-seventies, to outfit him like any small Chilean boy with shirts, sweaters, shorts, real school textbooks, notebooks, and a pen. Carlitos adapted well. Without any apparent difficulty, the dirty, ragged little savage became just like any other young Chilean despite his Mongolian features, his yellow skin, his short bowlegs, his thick lips, the shock of black hair that pulled teeth from combs, and his reluctance to wear shoes for any length of time.

When he had recovered, Carlitos stayed on as the weather station's guest. From the bed in his room overlooking the vast sweep of Eden Bay he could see the wigwams (there were now only three of them), the huts (two were permanently closed, while the cemetery boasted a few fresh graves), and five little companions, his playmates, rolling about in the wet grass. He had meekly let himself be separated from them. He was beginning to speak Spanish almost fluently. He had also learned how to help his adopted fathers in their household tasks. He swept and dusted and set the table for meals. He asked questions and took an interest in his schoolbooks and in the illustrated magazines; they opened up a new world for him, and he daydreamed for hours of new things, of human beings, of unknown landscapes. He was always clean, and liked to wash his hands, working the soap up into thick suds. He loved to stroke furniture and cloth, discovering new sensations through touch. Seeing him spruced up and shining in his new clothes, the two sergeants exclaimed proudly, *"Es un verdadero nino de la ciudad!"*

But every now and then, particularly in the evenings, Carlitos slipped away from the station. Barefoot in the rain, he ran to the wigwams, slipped under the wet canvas of the entrance and resumed his place in the family circle, wolfing down roasted cholgas with their whiff of high tide. Inside the wigwam was his father Taw, a proud, muscular little man who refused to set foot in the station and insisted on paying for his daily rations with the pelts of the otter he trapped. Yerfa, his wife, was a sad and taciturn woman who saw her son, her only surviving child, inexorably distancing himself from her. In an effort to hold on to him she hugged him and clumsily kissed him, miming the kind of affection she had seen white people show one another. It was for her son that she dived, the only one among all the women of the clans still to do so, bringing up beautiful fat clumps of cholgas from the bottom. There were also three children from the other wigwams to profit from this bounty, Wauda and her brother Yannoek, and little Kyewa. Then there was his one-eyed grandmother Kala, known to the *loberos* as Margarita Canales *la puta*. He, the little boy, was Lafko. Carlos Canales, Carlitos, was his name only for the white men, the name listed at the station, first chosen by the meteorological sergeant of the day some thirty years earlier when Lafko, father of Taw, had come to Puerto Eden, abandoning the nomad life without even remembering that old Lafko, his grandfather, had been called Felipe-Maria Gamboa before he had been obliged to escape Dawson Island. Official names were white men's business. But they themselves were still of the clan of the otter, *Lahaltel,* as they had been since the dawn of creation.

Lafko never stayed very long. The atmosphere in the wigwam was gloomy. There were frequent quarrels. Taw beat his mother, Margarita *la puta,* berating her for her escapades aboard the *lobero* boats. But on other nights he beat her because her dissolute activities had not procured them enough wine — and he, Taw, was very thirsty. The clan of the otter was often drunk. Then Lafko would slip outside and become Carlitos again. He would run back to the pretty blue-painted station with its Chilean flag and its snug, clean kitchen where the two sergeants were playing checkers and listening to Radio Fuegia, *La Voz del Sur,* relayed from Puerto Natales.

"You stink of smoke and dead fish," said Gimenez, the weather man. "Go wash and change your shirt."

"And I'll fix you pancakes with sugar and some nice hot chocolate," said Peralta the radio man, giving the child a friendly wink.

Back in the kitchen, washed and clean, Carlitos sat quietly looking at the photos in *Vea* and *Nuevo Zigzag,* where beautiful girls laughed with flashing white teeth and flaunted their lustrous hair and beautiful golden skin.

★   ★   ★

A year went by in this way. It would soon be time for their replacements to arrive, but Peralta and Gimenez hoped they would not be leaving alone. The air force was studying the file on Carlos Canales, the promising young Alacaluf. Whenever headquarters came through on the radio Peralta listened anxiously for a decision. An affirmative answer would be their best possible reward, the vindication of all their efforts.

The Chilean Air Force, which ran Puerto Eden and which found itself the unexpected and inexperienced custodian of the last Fuegian Indians, had been seeking vainly for two decades for a young school-age Alacaluf more advanced than his fellows to send to noncommissioned-officers' school in Santiago. There was nothing new in the idea: They merely wanted to train a leader able to haul his people onto the paths of civilization. Now, it seemed, that rare bird had been found. Carlitos was thirteen. He spoke fluent Spanish, read and wrote flawlessly, and had mastered elementary schoolwork. His memory was quick and retentive and he was eager to learn. He might not make a brilliant student, but he would at least be normally gifted. Moreover, he had risen both morally and physically above his squalid origins. For nearly a year now he had been living like a white boy, sleeping in a bed, eating properly, keeping himself clean. The answer they were waiting for came: It was yes! That night they broke open a bottle of Rancagua champagne. Peralta unfolded a white cloth to cover the oilcloth tabletop and set out four pretty blue candles, giving the table a festive look. Gimenez dug out old photos of himself in noncom's uniform, surrounded by his classmates. He showed them to Carlitos.

"Look! That's how you'll be soon."

The child looked and smiled. He liked the idea. He had only the vaguest understanding of what it all meant, but the two sergeants' enthusiasm quickly won him over. He attempted a military salute. They all laughed.

Nobody laughed in the wigwam of the Canales family. The mood was one of deepest gloom. With a battery of kicks, Taw dispatched his old one-eyed mother to "buy" drink from the *loberos*. He did not look once at his son. By the time the boy was due to sail, the father was dead drunk and unable to recognize him. Since military regulations insisted on parental consent, it was Yerfa who signed the form with a cross. She tried to embrace her son, but he quickly wriggled out of her grasp, fearful that he would go aboard stinking "of smoke and dead fish."

The *Almirante Pikkendorf,* which carried him away to the world of the white men, brought him back again six years later.

★   ★   ★

Too short for the military — the admissions board had agreed to bend the rules in his case — but set sturdily on his small bowlegs, with a powerful torso filling out his impeccably buttoned tunic, his silver-braided cap pulled down over his low forehead, the nape of his neck clean shaven, white-gloved as if on parade, Sergeant Carlos Canales of the Chilean Air Force jumped down from the boat to the Puerto Eden jetty so radically transformed that the dogs hurled themselves at him with bared fangs, ready to bite. At least they did not confuse him with the miserable drove of thirty or so brutish, filth-encrusted people watching the new radio operator, one of their own kind, disembark. The new meteorologist was a white man, and it was the white man who now came toward them with a friendly greeting. The other did not even glance at them. Kicking out with his boots, he silenced the dogs and sent them cringing away in terror.

In six years things had gotten even worse. There was no lack of money for medicine, food, or repairs to the huts which Indian apathy, even more than the wind, had reduced to tottering hovels. But very few of the noncommissioned officers who did their tour of duty at Puerto Eden possessed the human qualities of a Gimenez or a Peralta. Most served out their time in idleness and gloom; they awaited their replacements and showed not the slightest interest in the last of the Alacalufs, who were now filthier and more brutalized than ever, walled in on themselves for good. They had buried one of them only yesterday in the overgrown cemetery. Nobody bothered to keep it up any more, and it was thick with ferns and bracken. Too much of a chore. And since Gimenez and Peralta, nobody even took the trouble to write names on the crosses.

Carlos settled into his childhood bedroom. He plastered the walls with photos of himself in uniform or on a beach with a white woman — his wife, a nurse (left behind in Santiago even though she might have been more useful here, but regulations forbade it). And there were many magazine photos of naked women with blonde heads and blonde pubic hair. From his window overlooking the bay he stared disgustedly at the three wigwams standing in their sea of filth, and at the three last huts whose poverty seeped out through cracked planking and flaking paint.

He immediately laid down rules. No *Indios* in the station. None of these lice-ridden monkeys in the kitchen. The days of porridge and condensed milk were over: They could make do with what they were given and be thankful. And anyway you didn't dare touch them with a ten-foot pole — they were all riddled with pox. Whenever his path crossed theirs he pretended not to understand if they addressed him in Alacaluf, answering only in Spanish. His grandmother, *la puta,* was dead. He did not even visit her grave. His mother and father were treated no better. When his mother was bold enough to come and reproach him one day he threw her out, screaming, "Just look at yourself, you old bag of shit! How could you be my mother?" There were three he particularly hated, a youth and two girls of about his own age, his childhood playmates Yannoek, Kyewa, and Wauda. He bolted and barred his memory. Nothing capable of touching him could break out; for it was quite *impossible* that he, Sergeant Carlos Canales, radio technician, owner in Santiago of a white wife and a small car, could ever have had anything whatsoever in common with these filthy *Indios,* particularly the girls: They

hung around the station smiling hideously and showing off their
big backsides, their yellow tits sloppily tucked into horrible dirty
dresses, their nigger lips clumsily smeared with greasy
lipstick . . . God, who did they think he was! Even the children
disgusted him. Yet there were not many of them and they were so
subdued you hardly ever heard them. When the weatherman—
Sergeant Galdos—suggested he show a little heart he would
reply: "Heart! You really think they have a heart? Let me tell
you—the answer is no!"

On the other hand, he was a fanatic for order. He started out
by having the men and boys assemble at eight every morning
under the flagstaff, no matter what the weather, spades on their
shoulders. And, he put them through military drill, even insisting that they wear shoes so that their heels gave the requisite
audible click. "Atten-SHUN! At ease! Present ARMS! At ease!
Atten-SHUN . . .!" He bellowed out the orders with sadistic
pleasure and doled out savage punishments: No rations for the
families of those absent without permission. His mother had to
start diving again in the icy sea, for Taw, his father, stubbornly
refused to be present. Then he launched his ragtag army into the
offensive against the garbage heaps "which are the shame of
Puerto Eden." Burning them raised such a stench—he osten-
tatiously held his nose—that he decided to bury them. This was
a never-ending task. In this rain-saturated soil the holes immediately filled up with water. Carlos yelled, stamped his feet,
mercilessly chivvied his poor charges. He would have beaten
them if he had not known that the vigilant Sergeant Galdos
disapproved of such methods.

He also concerned himself with the state of the huts, insisting
on daily ventilation as in the barracks back in Santiago. This
instantly chilled everything the Alacalufs had taken so much
trouble to get warm. He instituted spot inspections, testing for
dirt in cooking pots with a disgusted forefinger, ordering women
and children to undress and rubbing a small section of their
skin—never the same one—with a damp white rag. If the rag was
soiled—punishment. Many were punished. And he snickered
nastily at seeing them all lined up in front of him naked. Back at

the station kitchen, he washed his hands over and over, raising huge amounts of lather, and grumbling, "What pigs!" When Galdos pointed out that this was not a prison camp he shouted furiously: "Prisoners? What do you think they are, then? They're prisoners of their own dirt and stupidity! Maybe once they're civilized we can set them free!"

He allowed himself just one exception to the web of regulations he had spun: Every evening he invited one *Indio* to the station. It did not matter to him whether it was a man, a woman, or a child, so long as all of them appeared in rotation. He did not offer hot chocolate, or wine, scarcely even a cup of black coffee — for he was miserly on top of everything else. It was not from the goodness of his heart that he invited them in, but simply so that every one of them could see him play his nightly game of checkers with Galdos in the majestic condition of a civilized man initiated into the mysteries of the white men.

Curiously, he spared the three wigwams and the last canoe (his father's, high and dry but still seaworthy) his persnickety inspections. He explained to Galdos that it would truly be beyond him to enter the wigwams because of the stink of shit, of rancid smoke and dead fish. In fact, though, it was probably a kind of invisible frontier he felt unable to cross without instantly disintegrating.

★   ★   ★

But two months later he crossed it.

Almost from the day of his arrival, he had begun to drink more and more *vino tinto,* then rum, and finally *raide,* the grain alcohol of the *loberos.* It took him at nightfall, the hour of terror among the Alacalufs, the hour of Ayayema, of Mwono, of Kawtcho. It was probably also triggered by the extreme tension his new guise and the presence of his blood kin triggered within him. And finally, in all probability, by hereditary alcoholism. When Galdos mentioned it to him, reminding him of his career, his responsibilities, his wife back in Santiago, the trust of his superior officers, he would reply with drunken pledges: "I'll stop tomorrow, I swear!" And, pouring himself another glass: "This is the last one, I promise!"

One night, very drunk but still conscious, he slipped out while Galdos was asleep. Half-dressed, he ran barefoot through the rain to the wigwam where the two girls slept. This time the dogs did not growl the way they did whenever they were approached by Sergeant Carlos Canales of the Chilean Air Force. Inside the wigwam animals and humans all moved over to give him room between "Big Backside" and "Yellow Tits," thus named from contempt, and now Wauda and Kyewa once more.

Before dawn he returned to the station just in time to put his uniform on, but not to wash, and eat breakfast with the meteorologist in the kitchen. Without thinking, Galdos said, "Funny smell in here, don't you think?" Then, looking at Carlos, he understood.

The next three nights Carlos did not return. On the morning of the fourth the canoe had disappeared, along with Sergeant Canales and five *Indios,* a man, a woman, two girls, and a youth: Taw the elder, Yerfa his wife, Wauda the younger, Kyewa the younger, Yannoek.

"*Arka!* Up!" Lafko had said, the white headband round his forehead.

It was the last escape. This time, he himself would not come back.

At one stroke, the Alacaluf community of Puerto Eden was reduced by a third. The best had gone, the only ones who could have saved the group, or at least delayed its demise. Those who remained were wrecks who had lost the will to live, and knew it. In the night following this departure, Kala and Kostora sang in the two last inhabited wigwams. *Akwal,* many, many suns and many moons had shone down on the sufferings of the People . . . The song of the world of the Kaweskar, the great song of lamentation . . . A long plaint, sung on a single strident note that faded slowly. At dawn it died away for good.

No one would ever hear it again, unless he parted the ferns covering the little cemetery and listened, if God permitted it, with his heart . . .

*   *   *

Lafko headed south, then turned east up the great Strait, rowing as far as the Charles Islands at the opening of the somber Barbara Channel. Time had swept the beaches clean of the only material remains his people had ever left on this earth: the ribs of abandoned wigwams and heaps of empty mussel shells.

Before they vanished into the frozen labyrinth with Yannoek and Kyewa, Yerfa, Wauda and old Taw, the last vision they carried within them of this world, like a final—and equally mysterious—reenactment of Magellan's arrival, was a huge, slowly moving, brilliantly lit liner, her name spelled out in enormous glowing letters written by hundreds of electric light bulbs strung between her stacks: *France.** Aboard, they were being discussed. In the first-class smoking room bald gentlemen in dinner jackets, glasses in hand, and ladies with daring décolletés listened to *An Evening at the End of the Earth,* a masterly predinner lecture on the voyages of Bougainville, of Cook, of Darwin—even of Monsieur Gaston Lemay, whose book *Aboard the Junon* was in the ship's library—and their encounters with hideously ugly savages, naked, stinking, cannibalistic, who had now utterly vanished from the face of the earth.

No doubt about it, there was a brief tremor of emotion, one of those imperceptible flutters of the soul when it is miraculously unveiled somewhere between the vintage champagne and the caviar. Then someone raised his glass to the health of the vanished race.

Arka, farewell!

---

* This was the *France*'s last round-the-world cruise. She would shortly meet her own death in the scrapyards of Le Havre.

CHAPTER THIRTEEN

LAFKO

Destiny had been served. The circle was closed. Once again we find Lafko where we left him at the beginning of this story. He is alone.

His wanderings lasted about ten years. Deaths, drownings, kidnappings, defections to the compassionate gray ship, everyone in his canoe had finally left him: Taw the elder, Yerfa the elder, Wauda his wife, who was life, Yannoek and Kyewa, even the two sons born to him, and now reclaimed by Ayayema, Taw the child last of all.

Lafko no longer dreamed of all these dead. His nights were peaceful. He even saw the sun shine. It was as if the snow and wind brawling furiously all around had spared the tiny beach where he had set up his wigwam. Cholgas were plentiful, and he killed a small seal, which left him with a full belly every night. What did he remember? Nothing. He had lived twenty thousand years and it had been but a moment. Now he waited.

At night he saw portents in the heavens. The Southern Cross was unusually bright and flashes of light darted about among the stars. He saw the corpses of Pektchévés ferried past in ever-increasing numbers by currents that swelled and raced faster every day. Sometimes the earth shook, and each night the voice of the great ocean grew louder as if it was drawing near. He removed the little carved stone spearhead from his seal-gut bag and waited. The stone was now so hot he could barely hold it in his hand.

God created man in His own image, but Lafko did not know this. God had always kept it hidden from him. The small stick figure crudely engraved on this stone by the first of all the Lafkos at the beginning of the long journey was the sign inspired by God, the sign vouchsafed to Lafko alone, chosen from among the billions of human beings who people the surface of the earth, but Lafko had never decoded the message. He had simply trusted in something he did not know and could not imagine.

The heavens shattered in an apocalyptic thunder and a torrent of stars. The glaciers melted. The mountains split. Huddled safe on his beach, on the last remaining strip of dry land, Lafko watched mighty waves roar past, bearing the carcasses of ships, as if some terrible storm had torn all the wrecks of ancient times from the bottoms of all the seas. The little carved stone glowed red, like an incandescent brand. Lafko seized it in his hand, burning himself to the bone, and screamed.

Now all was calm. Lafko walked on the clouds, surrounded by white forms escorting him and peopling the whole sky. At last a voice said to him:

"Here you are. Be welcome in your own house, Lafko. It is true that you are small and ugly, that your intelligence is limited, that you smell bad, that you are dirty.

"But look: You are just like me!"

First Narrow

Second Narrow

Skyring Sea

CAPE
TAMAR

Providence I.

Otway Sea

Isabel I.

TIERRA

Punta
Arenas

Desolation I.

Desolation I.

Brunswick
Peninsula

Useless Bay

Santa Inés I.

Charles Is.

Port Famine

CAPE
FROWARD

STRAIT • OF • MAGELLAN

*Harris
Bay*

▲
Nose Peak
2,730 ft.

Dawson I.

CAPE
ANXIOUS

Whiteside Chan.

Clarence I.

Barbara Channel

Cockburn Chain

Magdalen Ch.

▲
Mt. Sarmiento
7,540 ft.

CORDILLERA

Western Furies •
Eastern Furies •

P A C I F I C

O C E A N

TIERRA DEL FUEGO

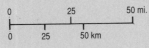